OUT OF SPITE, OUT OF MIND

SCOTT MEYER

ROCKET HAT INDUSTRIES

Published by Rocket Hat Industries

ISBN-13: 978-1-950056-00-2
ISBN-10: 1-950056-00-7

Cover design by Eric Constantino

Magic 2.0: A Partial Explanation

One night, while exploring a server he probably shouldn't have been, Martin Banks discovered a file that proved his reality was computer generated. By editing the file, he found that he could perform feats that seemed like magic—things such as flight, teleportation, and time travel. He knew that his newfound power could drastically improve his life, but he'd have to be careful, and avoid drawing attention to himself.

He did neither of those things. Instead, he immediately messed things up very badly and attracted the attention of government agents.

Martin fled to Medieval England, a time and place where people believed in magic, and wizards were revered. He reasoned that he could be the most powerful being in the world and live a life of ease and luxury if he showed some restraint, and used his power wisely.

Once again, he did neither of those things. He immediately messed up very badly, which attracted the attention of several other people who had found the same file, had developed even better powers, and had migrated back in time to live as wizards long before Martin got the idea.

Among Martin's new acquaintances were Gwen, the woman he grew to love; Phillip, who became his best friend; and Brit, a woman who had tangled her own timeline so thoroughly that her past self and her future self now uneasily coexisted in Atlantis, a city that her future self had built in the past, and her past self would one day build in her future, which was also the past. One thing all of these wizards shared in common was that they wanted nothing more than to enjoy their lives and not bother anyone.

They do neither of those things. Instead, they all tend to mess up on a regular basis, and attract the attention of pretty much everybody.

1.

Brit the Elder's house exuded the sort of serenity that's only possible in a home when nobody's there to enjoy it. A small amount of light from the outside filtered in through the blinds, partially illuminating an interior that contained just enough furniture, mementos, and objects d'art to qualify as deliberately austere, rather than just empty.

In the midst of all of this stillness and silence, Brit the Elder materialized. Other magic users would simply pop into existence, or appear after an animation and sound effect intended to impress any witnesses, but which usually just resembled the beaming-in special effect from *Star Trek*. Brit the Elder had spent a great deal of time perfecting her own materialization macro to be subtle, yet noticeable. The result was that she appeared to slip elegantly into existence, like a silver spoon rising to the surface of a bone-china bowl full of vichyssoise.

She appeared standing straight and tall, as was her habit. She glanced around to verify that she was alone, following which her entire skeleton seemed to sag, and she said one word.

"Shit."

She said the word slowly, as if it had seven syllables, or she was trying to communicate the concept of shit to someone who spoke a different language.

Without bothering to turn on any lights, she staggered two steps to a nearby chaise lounge. It was meant to be gracefully lain upon, preferably while reading a design magazine. Instead, Brit the Elder planted her rear end directly in the chaise's middle and slumped forward as if she were sitting on a park bench holding a plastic bottle of vodka wrapped in a paper bag.

She often returned from her visits with Brit the Younger feeling a bit wrung out. She disliked confrontations to begin with, and Brit the Younger was almost always angry with her. Brit the Elder found it all particularly upsetting because she had *been* Brit the Younger, long ago, and watching her younger self lose her temper made Brit the Elder remember those emotions from when *she* lived them, and *she* was angry with Brit the Elder, whom she had disliked intensely at the time, and whom she herself now was. The experience usually left her feeling a unique combination of self-directed anger, remorse, confusion, and more self-directed anger coming from the opposite direction.

It was always bad, but this time it was much worse.

What's happening? she thought. *What am I going to do?*

Just having those thoughts was enough to make Brit the Elder panic, but she fought it down, forcing herself to breathe slowly and think logically. She fidgeted with her right foot, pressing the tips of her toes against the floor.

Okay, she thought. *Calm down. Think it through. I remember clearly, back when I was Brit the Younger, the wizards in Leadchurch made Kludge an offer that would help his gang work together with them. I remember Kludge turning down the deal Phillip offered him, but Brit the Younger says he took the deal, and she's Brit the Younger right now, so you'd think the memory's a lot fresher for her.*

Where does that leave me? For the first time I can recall, something has happened differently from how I remember it happening. How is this possible?

She could see three options. The two most appealing possibilities were that she had misremembered, or that Brit the Younger was wrong.

Either of those options amounted to a mistake on her part; the only difference was when she messed up: when she was Brit the Younger or when she was Brit the Elder. She hated making mistakes, but it was far preferable to the implications of the third possibility: that there was some error in the code.

The error could be in her code, which might lead to her death. Or, the error could be in the code that generated the entire known universe, which might lead to the destruction of everything. She figured an error was bad news for her either way.

A fourth option occurred to her, but she liked it even less. It was possible that her memories were not tied to Brit the Younger's experiences. All of the beliefs that had governed her every action for the last several decades of her life might have been completely misguided, causing her to be a hateful monster to Brit the Younger for no real reason at all.

Of those options, the easiest to verify was that she had misremembered, so she decided to start with that.

Brit the Elder rose from the chair and walked from her sleek and modern great room, down a tasteful hall, and into her minimal, functional office and workshop, where a walnut desk supported her computer: an original one-piece Macintosh.

The computer's plastic case had long ago faded from its original stylish gray tones to a dingy yellow, not dissimilar to the color of a dehydrated man's urine. It was a common problem with the plastics used in the cases of the early Macintosh computers. Once, Brit had been amazed that Steve Jobs would allow a product to ship with such an obvious aesthetic flaw, but in time, she realized that Steve Jobs didn't consider anything that would cause a customer to want to buy a newer computer a flaw.

Brit the Elder sat down in front of the computer, absentmindedly rubbing the toes of her shoes together as she wiggled the mouse back and forth to rid the screen of flying toasters. She navigated through the file structure, to the folder that held her journals.

Her many, many journals.

She had started keeping a daily record of her thoughts, hopes, dreams, and actions when she was a teenager, back when that meant trying to keep track of which member of her current favorite boy band was dreamiest. She found that keeping the journals helped her make sense of a day's events and organize her thoughts and ideas, so she kept it up, switching later to the computer from the paper notebooks.

The journals were a daily catalog of her irritating interactions with her future self, but they also held the day-to-day account of every other time traveler she'd met, every major event she'd witnessed, and her feelings about all of them. There was a weird stretch of nearly a decade when the notes got spotty, but she wasn't quite to that bit yet. Some of the entries contained notes so detailed that they described people's actual physical movements and timing information down to the second. It was an invaluable record, and Brit the Elder used it to appear nearly omniscient.

Reading the labels on the grid of file folders, Brit scanned all the major events of her life: her discovery of the file; her notes from her experiments where she learned how to fly, teleport, time travel, stop the aging process, and do any number of other things that others thought of as magic; her account of when she decided to travel back in time to find Atlantis, or, if Atlantis didn't exist, build it herself; and the angry screed she wrote when she traveled back, found Atlantis waiting for her, and discovered that the city hadn't existed until a future version of herself went even farther back in time, built the whole place herself, then waited around for her younger self to arrive.

She poked through the scores of folders that documented the years she spent as Brit the Younger, living in Atlantis, in the shadow of her future self, who the whole city looked to as a leader simply because she'd gotten there first, even if she had done it much later.

She'd stopped writing the journals when she became Brit the Elder. She didn't want Brit the Much Elder reading her thoughts, and was certain that she would, because that's exactly what she herself was doing to Brit the Younger.

Of course, she told Brit the Younger that she hadn't looked at the journals in years. That was the only reason Brit the Younger still kept them. In retrospect, she was more than a little embarrassed that she had believed such an obvious lie when Brit the Elder told it to her, all those decades ago.

Brit searched through the folder for the current decade, then the year, then the month, and pulled up the MacWrite file for the current day.

She waited as the antique computer churned through the daunting task of opening a single-page text file.

Of course, I just misremembered it, she thought. *I got caught up helping tend to the wounded from the dragon attack, so I didn't bother to read the journal this morning. It figures that this'd be one of those rare times when I misremember something. I'll just double-check; the journal will confirm what Brit the Younger said, and I'll laugh this off.*

The screen filled with menu headings, a ruler, and Brit's recollections from this very day, when she'd lived it the first time, more than a hundred years earlier.

Brit leaned in close to the screen, silently absorbing the words, clicking intermittently to scroll downward. She blinked, rubbed her eyes, and leaned in closer.

Phillip explained the offer to Kludge. He was resistant. Phillip explained that Kludge and his gang wouldn't be harmed in any way, but that we would want them to try their hardest to kill us, but Kludge wanted no part of it. We even described the fake, rideable dragons they'd get to use, but his distrust just runs too deep. Maybe someday we'll win him over, but it won't be any time soon.

Brit the Elder leaned back in her chair, staring at the computer's tiny built-in monitor. She kicked her shoes off as she continued reading, hoping to find something about Kludge changing his mind.

Just a few minutes ago, the journal continued, *Brit the Elder came over. I told her that Kludge had declined the offer. She said she already knew that, that he would come around eventually, and congratulated me on how well my friends and I had handled the situation. She was trying to be nice, but I wish she wouldn't bother if she doesn't really mean it.*

Brit the Elder shook her head. *Even when I'm nice to her, she assumes it's insincere, the little snot.*

Her memories matched the historical record, but did not match the events that had actually happened. Back when she was Brit the Younger, she had experienced the event of Kludge refusing Phillip's offer. She then wrote about Kludge refusing Phillip's offer in her journal, which proved that it happened the way she remembered it. Except that it appeared that the opposite was true: Kludge accepted the offer, which was not possible. Events had not unfolded in the way that the events had unfolded, which was, of course, a paradox. She could only conclude that either there was something wrong with the program of the universe, or the last hundred years of the journals perfectly matching observed events had been a long series of coincidences. She found one of those answers a lot more likely than the other.

A glitch is the simplest answer. Of course, glitches can cause further glitches, then cascade failures, then system crashes. Occam's razor may have just slit the world's throat.

Brit the Elder sat frowning, for over a minute, before coming to the decision that this was a problem she couldn't frown away. She couldn't rely on her memories, or her notes about what would happen tomorrow. For the first time in a very, very long time, she didn't know what was about to happen.

I'm completely in the dark. I don't know what to do. Well, that's not true. I have a good idea what the logical next move is; it's just that being in the dark might be preferable.

She sat in silence for a moment, trying to puzzle out some simple solution that didn't involve doing anything she loathed. Bracing herself against the floor with one foot, she drew the other one up into her lap and absentmindedly scratched at her toes. *This all seems bad, but what is it so far? One anomaly that only I noticed. It's probably just some little hiccup. I have no reason to believe anything else is wrong. What is going on with my feet? They don't itch, exactly, but still . . .*

She looked down at her foot, illuminated by the gray light from the monitor, and let out a small, strangled shriek. She lifted up her right foot to get a better look. At first it looked perfectly normal, but then, without warning, it changed to a crude approximation of a human foot constructed entirely out of triangles the color of her skin. Her foot remained in this unnatural condition for a couple of seconds, then changed back to her ordinary, regular foot.

She stared at it for a long time, watching it transform back and forth at random between flesh and bone and living polygons. She only looked away when she realized that the toes of her other foot felt odd as well. She lowered her right foot, and lifted and stared at her left foot, seeing that it was doing the same bizarre thing. She slouched down in the chair, gripped the seat base for support, and put both feet up on her desk. She stared at them for a moment, then very slowly, as if the word had fourteen syllables, said, "Shit."

2.

Almost twenty-four hours later, evening was falling over Atlantis like a freshly laundered bedsheet, descending over a bare mattress just before getting its hospital corners tucked in. The citizens walked home after their day's activities. Merchants either packed up their goods or shouted to anyone who would listen that they were selling them at a loss to keep from having to carry them away.

The light from the sunset reflected off the silver sequins of Martin's robe and wizard hat, and the silver bust of Santo on the head of his staff, projecting a million pinpricks of light that danced and bobbed on the walls, the ground, and Gwen, who walked beside him. Her robe and hat were made of a subdued tan material, but caught the eye just as much as Martin's as they were expertly tailored and draped to Gwen's petite frame.

"Why are we walking again?" Martin asked.

Gwen said, "You know why. We discussed it, and agreed that it was a terrible idea to ever teleport to Gary's."

"We agreed it's a terrible idea to teleport to Gary's if he knows we're coming," Martin corrected her. "We might as well ask him to set up a nasty surprise for us. And I know that we're flying from Brit and Phillip's to Gary's place. I just don't understand why you wanted to walk from your place to Brit's."

"Oh. That. For fun."

"Fun? We can fly and teleport, and walking across town is your idea of fun?"

Gwen laughed and took Martin's arm. "Look around you! What's the point of living somewhere beautiful if you always teleport past it, or fly through too quickly to enjoy it?"

Martin looked at his surroundings and admitted she had a point. One of the advantages to the fact that Atlantis was built inside an immense bowl floating rim-deep in the Mediterranean was that when one looked out, across the bowl, almost the entire city was visible from any one spot. The narrow streets formed concentric rings, growing both larger and higher as they radiated outward, built on the roofs of the buildings along the streets below, like terraces cut into a hillside. This encouraged the sorceresses in charge to make sure that any proposed new building, garden, or pathway met certain aesthetic standards. Martin saw a vista of minimalist glass buildings, beautifully manicured green spaces, and palm trees rustling gently in the Mediterranean breeze, all tinted pink by the distant sunset.

"Okay, I see your point. But why don't you ever want to walk anywhere when we're at my place?"

"Because your place is in Medieval London. The streets are paved with mud, and people poop out their windows."

"The second of those statements sort of contradicts the first. I guess that means you'll want to live in Atlantis, then."

"I live in Atlantis now."

"I mean later, when we live together."

"We've talked about this, Martin. I'm not interested in living together out of wedlock."

"I know that, Gwen. That's not what I'm saying."

Gwen stopped walking and stared at him. "Martin Banks, are you asking me to marry you?"

"Oh, Lord, no!"

Gwen said nothing.

Martin said, "Let me rephrase that."

Gwen's eyes narrowed. "Please do."

"What I mean is, I wouldn't propose like this, just casually dropping it in conversation. I'd make a much bigger deal out of it."

"Good."

"Yeah. And I don't know that we're ready for that quite yet, but I do think I'd like to be married to you eventually."

Again, Gwen said, "Good."

Martin took a step closer to Gwen, and lowered his voice a bit. "What do you think?"

"I think it's good to know where you stand."

"And where do you stand, Gwen? Do you think you'd like to be married to me eventually?"

Gwen resumed walking, at a brisk pace. "I'd rather not discuss it."

"Just tell me how you feel. Your gut instinct."

"My gut instinct is that that would be discussing it, which I've already told you, I'd rather not do."

"You don't want to marry me!"

"I didn't say that. Maybe I think I might want to marry you, but I worry I could change my mind later, and I don't want to commit myself right now."

"Is that any better?"

"I'm not saying it is. I'm not even saying that's how I feel. I'm just saying that it's a different reason."

Martin chewed on this for a moment, following Gwen as she double-timed it through Atlantis. Brit the Younger's apartment was in sight now, and it seemed Gwen couldn't get there soon enough.

Finally, he said, "So, either you think you might want to marry me, but you fear that you'll change your mind, or you don't want to marry me, but you want to keep the option open in case you decide you can't do better. I'm gonna be bummed either way, aren't I?"

Gwen remained silent.

"Which, I'm sure, is why you didn't want to discuss it."

Gwen stopped at the door to Brit the Younger's apartment and rang the bell. She glanced over at Martin. "A smart woman keeps her options open."

Martin said, "All I've done is told you how I feel. My options are just as open as yours, and I'm just as likely to change my mind as you are."

Brit the Younger opened the door. She pushed her glasses higher up on her nose and smiled. "Gwen, Martin, I'm so glad you stopped by."

Martin and Gwen stopped looking at each other and instead focused on Brit, attempting unsuccessfully to hide the emotions their conversation had just dredged up.

Brit said, "I *think* I'm glad you stopped by. Come in."

Brit the Younger's front door entered directly into the main room of her apartment: a large, high-ceilinged space, one whole wall of which was a curved window that looked out into the dark blue depths beneath the surface of the ocean. Along the back wall there was a table and chairs, as well as a large kitchen where her domestic servant and close friend Nik was puttering away on some unidentifiable project. The other wall featured two incongruously rustic wooden doors.

Gwen entered first and made a beeline for the long, low couch. She sat at one end and pressed herself into the armrest, giving the impression that no matter where on the couch Martin chose to sit, she wanted to be as far from him as possible.

Martin didn't make any effort to sit down, either on the couch or any of the other chairs. Instead he walked steadily toward the two wooden doors set into the wall.

"Thanks for having us," he muttered as he walked past Brit. "Where's Phillip?"

Brit said, "In his rec room. Would you like anything? I could have Nik—"

Martin mumbled, "No, I'm good," and went through the door on the left.

He emerged from the door thousands of miles and thousands of years away. Physically, the door should have led into Brit's bedroom closet, but both of the wooden doors were enchanted, programmed to act as portals from Brit's home in the bronze-age Mediterranean to Phillip's two properties in Leadchurch, a town in Medieval England. The door Martin chose led to the attic above Phillip's office and workspace.

Phillip had filled this attic with all of his favorite things from his original time. Being a product of the mid–nineteen eighties, that meant a lot of white leather and neon lights. At the far end of the room, Phillip's pristine, white Pontiac Fiero occupied a place of honor. Through speakers the size of large tombstones, Sting advised that if Martin loved somebody, he should set them free.

Martin walked to the bar, where an iPod he'd given Phillip as a gift was wired into Phillip's high-end 1985 rack-mounted stereo system through an old-school cassette adapter. One of the advantages of having a friend who was from a time thirty years prior to his own was that Martin could give him wildly outdated technology, then laugh inwardly when it blew Phillip's mind.

Without asking permission, Martin pressed the cassette player's stop button, ending the song with a resounding kachunk.

Phillip stood with his back to the room wearing no shoes, his sky-blue robe hanging open like a dressing gown, and his wizard hat crammed half into one of the pockets. He hunched over his vintage arcade game, a full-sized cabinet labeled *GORF*. His staff leaned against the wall next to the cabinet.

Martin stood beside Phillip, his body canted at a slight angle, looking down at the screen as he had since his early adolescence whenever a friend was playing an arcade video game. A ship maneuvered around the bottom of the screen, shooting up through a curved shield at an orderly formation of spacecraft, which drizzled down return fire.

Martin shook his head. "Isn't this just a rip-off of *Space Invaders*?"

Phillip said, "No. The beauty of *GORF* is that it isn't just one game. It's made up of several different games. It's a rip-off of *Space Invaders*, followed by a rip-off of *Galaxian*, followed by a rip-off of *Tempest*, topped off with a second, slightly different *Space Invaders* rip off."

"Ah. I see. I didn't know that. I've never made it past the first level."

"Too difficult?" Phillip asked.

"Too boring."

They heard a rapid knocking at the door, forceful enough that it was not so much a request for permission to enter as a warning that entry was imminent. The door back to Brit's apartment creaked open, and Nik leaned in.

"Can I offer you a cold drink? Maybe a quick bite to eat?"

Martin shook his head. "Nothing for me, thanks."

Phillip kept his eyes glued to the game and his hands on the controls, but said, "Yes, it's kind of you to offer, but we'll all be leaving pretty soon, I should think."

"I suspected as much, but if you change your minds, the offer stands."

"You take awfully good care of us, Nik," Phillip said, most of his brain still preoccupied with shooting fictional invaders from what might be called space.

"That's my job."

"You do it well. If there's anything I can ever do to make your job easier for you, I hope you'll tell me."

Nik said, "Thank you Phillip. I will," and withdrew back into Brit's apartment and closed the door behind him.

Phillip said, "That man is a treasure. I'd be lost without him."

Martin smiled. "Not lost. Just hungry and living in squalor."

Phillip's eyes darted up to Martin for a second, then back to the game. "I don't think that's quite accurate."

"I knew you before Nik came into the picture. It's accurate."

Phillip continued slamming the joystick back and forth and pounding on the fire button. "You're in a mood. What's wrong?"

Martin groaned.

"You and Gwen are fighting."

"Again."

"And you said something stupid."

"I sort of accidentally proposed."

Phillip laughed. "So that's a yes. I take it her response was less than enthusiastic?"

"She didn't answer."

"She said nothing?"

"No, she said that she wasn't going to answer."

"Ouch." Phillip let go of the joystick, allowing his final spacecraft to be destroyed. Martin watched the animation, and heard the burst of static from the speaker that signified the spacecraft exploding and its entire crew perishing in the vacuum of space.

Phillip stroked his short brown beard as he turned to face Martin. "Look at it this way. You and Gwen are meant to be . . ."

Martin smiled.

"Or," Phillip continued, "you're not. If you're not, there's nothing you can do to change that."

Martin scowled at Phillip. "That doesn't make me feel any better."

"It wasn't meant to. You're fighting with the woman you love. You're going to feel awful. For me to try to change that would be counterproductive."

"Phillip, have I ever told you what a good friend you are?"

"No, I don't believe you have."

Martin said, "Yeah, that's not by accident. We can't all be as happy as you, with your drama-free relationship. You're lucky."

"I am very happy, and lucky, but Brit and I both put a lot of work into avoiding drama. She's the most important person in my life.

Keeping her happy is well worth all the effort I put in, and more. If I keep her happy, she'll stick around, and that will keep me happy."

"That's fine for you. But what if you were in a relationship with someone who wasn't putting in the effort?"

"Martin, you're my best friend and one of my favorite people, but if you think being in a relationship with you hasn't required effort on Gwen's part, you haven't been paying attention."

Martin opened his mouth to respond, but stopped when both men heard a distant knocking from downstairs.

"You expecting anyone?" Martin asked.

"No. I'd better see who it is." Phillip started down the stairs, then stopped, bent down, and picked up a pair of canvas high-tops decorated with Union Jacks before continuing on his way, sliding a bit in his socks. Martin followed close behind. Phillip would have been more inclined to just let an unexpected visitor knock, or shout at them to come back during business hours, but the last time someone came calling unexpectedly at his office door, it had been to announce that the town was under attack by dragons. He was disinclined to ignore the knocking now.

Martin followed as he walked down the stairs and through the séance room, where a small table and a crystal ball disguised Phillip's Commodore 64 computer. They passed through a beaded curtain into the front room, where walls full of small, dusty shelves held countless small, dusty bottles containing old, dusty specimens, or powders— which in many cases was just old dust.

Phillip opened the front door, but nobody was waiting outside. He and Martin looked out on one of Leadchurch's many dirt roads, lined with buildings made of grayish-beige stones, wooden beams, off-white plaster, and thatched roofs. It had often occurred to Martin that here, in Medieval England, before the invention of advanced paints and dyes, everything was essentially dirt colored. This was lucky as it helped hide the dirt, with which everything was covered, because advanced detergents hadn't been invented either.

Phillip shrugged and started to close the door, but Martin stopped him, leaning outside. He looked to the right and saw nothing of interest—just Leadchurch at dusk. He looked to the left and saw a group of kids, one of whom was carrying away a rectangular package about the size of a hardbound book, carefully wrapped in shiny red paper. The kids were giggling quietly, as if trying to contain their amusement. One of them looked back furtively at Phillip's door, and when he saw Martin, quickly looked away, shushing his giggling friends.

"Hey," Martin shouted. "Did you see anybody knock on this door?"

The boy carrying the package said, "No, sir." Then he and his friends darted around a corner and out of sight.

"Those kids just totally ripped you off," Martin said.

"You think?" Phillip leaned against his counter and pulled one of the canvas Union Jack high-tops onto his foot. "More likely they just knocked on my door as they walked by as a laugh."

"I'd bet anything that whatever was in that package was for you."

"Oh, well. Whatever it was, I'm sure they need it more."

"What if it was something nasty? Some kind of practical joke or something."

"Then it would serve them right for stealing. Even if it was for me, I'm not going to go chasing them down for it, whatever it was. Bad for the image."

Martin cast one last rueful look in the direction the boys had fled, and started to pull the door closed. His gaze swept across the street and caught a glimpse of a shadowy figure across the way, lurking in the gap between a timber-and-plaster building and a thatched hut.

The lurker was adult sized, and seemed to be built like a fairly husky male, but it was hard to tell anything beyond that, as he wore a rough, brown, full-length cloak with a large hood pulled over his head. He seemed to be looking in the same direction Martin had been, the direction in which the roving gang of untrustworthy youths had gone. The hood's subtle movement gave Martin the impression that the person inside was shaking his head. The hood twisted around, and while Martin couldn't see the person's eyes, or any of their face, the way it stopped moving abruptly while pointed directly at Phillip's door left Martin with the distinct impression that the robe's owner had noticed Martin noticing them.

"Hey," Martin shouted. "What's your deal?"

The figure jolted, having either been startled or suffering a full-body spasm, then darted around behind the building, out of Martin's sight.

Phillip finished tying his shoes and stood, testing his weight on each foot to judge if he had tied them tightly enough. "Martin, you're far too young to enter the yelling at young punks phase of your adulthood."

"What? No, I'm not yelling at the punks. They're long gone. No, there was someone else."

"Where?"

Martin pointed to a gap between two buildings across the street. "He took off, too, whoever he was."

Phillip looked where the person had been, as if the size of the empty space they'd left would help Phillip identify him. "What did he look like?"

"I don't know," Martin said. "He was wearing a big, heavy cloak with a hood. All I saw inside the hood was darkness."

"So, a Jawa. You saw a Jawa."

"No, it wasn't a Jawa."

"Are you sure? Were they trying to sell any used droids? Always check the motivator—"

"It wasn't a Jawa! Jawas don't exist, and if they did they wouldn't be in Medieval England. Wrong . . . I dunno, what do you call it? The wrong surroundings? The wrong context?"

"Milieu," Phillip said.

Martin scowled. "Yeah, that. The wrong that. Besides, Jawas were little, and had glowing eyes. This guy was . . . guy sized, and I didn't see any glowing eyes."

"Then maybe it was Orko. He'd be a better fit for a medieval setting. You know, Orko, from *He-Man*?"

"Yes, I am familiar with Orko," Martin said, more than a little indignant. "And, again, Orko was small, and had glowing eyes, and he flew. He didn't even wear a hood. Orko had a pointy hat."

"Oh, yeah." Phillip pulled his wizard hat from his pocket and placed it on his head. "He was a silly-looking little git."

Both Martin and Phillip heard the beaded curtain behind them rustle. They turned to see Brit the Younger and Gwen.

Brit the Younger handed Phillip his wizard staff, a long, knurled branch of wood with a small glass vial full of red liquid fastened to its head. "What's going on?"

"Nothing," Martin replied.

Phillip said, "Martin thinks he saw a Jawa."

Brit and Gwen both asked, "Where?"

Martin said, "It wasn't a Jawa, just someone dressed like one, and it doesn't matter. Whoever it was, they're gone now. We should go."

Phillip pointed across the street. "Over there, between those two buildings."

Brit and Gwen stepped outside and looked across the street.

Brit said, "I don't see anybody."

"Me neither," Gwen agreed.

"Of course not," Martin said, following the ladies outside. "Like I said, they're gone now."

Gwen squinted at him. "Then why did you want us to look for them?"

"I didn't."

Brit rolled her eyes. "Then why did you bring it up?"

Martin could see what was going on. Gwen was irritated with him, and Brit was Gwen's best friend, so now they were a unified front against him. Martin turned and looked at Phillip.

Phillip looked at Martin, *his* best friend, then at Brit the Younger, the woman in his life, then at Gwen, the best friend of the woman in his life. Phillip did some quick mental calculations, then stepped slightly closer to Brit and Gwen and frowned at Martin.

Martin sighed. "Can we just go?"

Gwen said, "After you."

Martin pointed his staff upward and lifted into the air, followed by Phillip, Brit the Younger, and, finally, Gwen.

3.

Agent Miller sat with his left elbow hanging out of the car window, right fingers drumming on the steering wheel. His eyes shifted focus at regular intervals between the building across the street he was assigned to watch and the car's rearview mirror, which he'd decided to also keep an eye on.

The car had been backed into a diagonal parking space. This had seemed like a lucky break at first, as it gave the agents an inconspicuous place to park with a clear view of their subject. Miller now realized that it left the rear of their car vulnerable to anyone walking down the sidewalk as he and his partner concentrated on their assignment, watching the Luxurious Rothschild Building.

Agent Murphy sat in the passenger seat, poking at the trackpad of his laptop. "You wanna roll that window up? It's freezing."

Miller growled, "I'd love to close the window, but if I do, the windshield fogs up. Not that you'd know it, staring at your computer while I watch the subject."

"The file's out there somewhere, Miller. We just have to find it again. And at least the laptop's generating a little bit of heat. You can roll the window up a little. Then the window wouldn't fog all the way up, and we'd still be able to see the Luxurious Rothschild Building."

"Yes, Murph, but just rolling the window part of the way up won't make it any warmer in here, will it? And you don't have to call it *luxurious* every time you mention it."

"That's the name of the building, Miller. The Luxurious Rothschild Building. That's what it says on the sign. That's what it says on Google Maps. That's what the building's called."

"Yeah, well, you can just say *the Rothschild Building*. I'll know what you mean. Who puts luxurious in the name of a building anyway? What the hell even *is* that?"

Murphy shrugged. "I dunno. It makes sure you know the building's luxurious. It's probably good marketing. Or maybe the guy the building was named after was called Luxurious Rothschild."

"Sounds like a pimp."

"We're in Reno. I'm sure a lot of the buildings are owned by pimps."

Miller glanced at the side mirror. He saw a smattering of tourists on the sidewalk for a moment before it was all eclipsed by the midsection of a young man in jeans, a denim jacket, and a plaid flannel shirt approaching with a thick stack of flyers in his hands. Miller groaned and pulled his arm back inside.

The young man stooped down to greet Miller eye to eye. When he exhaled, the plume of his condensed breath extended into the car. He smiled and pushed one of his flyers into Miller's open window. "Hey, sir! If you and your friend are looking for something to do later, why not—"

Miller stared into the young man's eyes but said nothing as he cranked the window shut. The young man stopped talking, but kept the flyer extended so that it got caught in the window. As the glass extended into its slot at the top of the frame, the flyer bent and flapped downward as the young man stood up and walked back to the sidewalk behind the car.

Miller mumbled, "How they found a rental car with crank windows in this day and age, I'll never know."

Agent Murphy asked, "What's the flyer say?"

Miller squinted at the tiny print. "It invites us to Follow the Treasure Trail."

Murphy shuddered. "Jeez, is it for a casino or a brothel?"

"A casino. Declan's, on the strip, about a block down from the Arch. They have this stupid path of gold coins printed on the carpet. You follow it all the way to the back, through a gauntlet of slot machines, and you get a free spin on a giant slot machine. Then you have to walk out through the gauntlet of slot machines. That's how they get you."

"What do you mean, *that's how they get you?*"

"It's obvious, isn't it? They want you to lose all your money on their slot machines, so they make you walk through the whole casino."

"To play a giant slot machine?"

"Yeah. I don't see why this is so hard for you to understand."

"Oh, I understand," Agent Murphy said. "I just don't think that luring you in to play slot machines by promising to let you play a slot machine is as underhanded as you seem to think it is."

Agent Miller flapped his hand dismissively at his partner. "Aw, pipe down. You just don't understand how gambling works."

"Not the same way you do, obviously. You should knock it off anyway. The director's not going to be happy if she finds out you're spending a lot of time at the casinos, Miller."

"What I do on my time is none of her damn business, Murph."

"It'll reflect poorly on the task force."

"This is Reno. It's the biggest little eyesore in the world. The place you go when Vegas is too upmarket. Just being here reflects badly on the task force."

"But the scenery's beautiful."

"Yes. The area around Reno, that isn't actually Reno itself, is lovely."

Murphy said, "It's better than riding a desk. I don't want to go back to the desk, Miller. If we screw up and get yanked from this task force, that's right where we'll be."

"If we're lucky. The Treasury Department probably won't want us back, after both Jimmy Sadler and Todd Douglas escaped. If they boot us from this task force, we're probably out of law enforcement for good."

"Yeah, all the more reason not to screw up, okay?"

Miller nodded. "Yeah, yeah, you're right, Murph. I just get a little . . . Crap! There he is!"

"Where?"

"Coming out of the building!"

"Which building?"

"What?! The Luxurious—shut up! Sadler's on the move!"

Murphy leaned forward. "We'll see."

Across the street, a thin gentleman in his mid-fifties with a neat iron-gray goatee wearing black slacks, a black polo shirt, and a checked sport coat walked out of the front entrance of the Luxurious Rothschild Building, where he lived. Both agents knew he was James Sadler, aka Jimmy, aka Merlin.

Sadler buttoned the top button of his sport coat, as if that would do anything to ward off the chill. He stood on the sidewalk, breathing deeply. After several breaths, he put his arms out wide and spun around twice in a cartoonish show of enjoying his freedom.

"Bastard," Miller snarled. "Why the director won't let us move in and take him, I don't know."

"It's because she figures he'll just escape again."

"Thanks for that, Murph."

"Well, you said you didn't know."

"Yeah, yeah, I get it." Miller jerked his head from side to side, checking the car's blind spots. He brought his hand up to the keys, which were hanging from the ignition.

Murphy said, "You know he's just messing with us, Miller."

"He doesn't know we're here."

"You don't believe that."

"I might."

"Miller. Two hours ago he came down, walked to his car, you tried to start the c—"

Miller gave Murphy a look that stopped him midsentence.

Murphy put up his hands and continued in a softer tone. "We both know what happened. Then he acted like he'd forgotten something and went back inside. An hour later, he came down and got in his car. The same thing happened again, and he got out of his car with some mail he'd left on the passenger seat and went back inside."

"Yeah, and now, he's going to go somewhere. Look, he's getting in his car."

Across the street, Jimmy walked to the parking lot and slid into his glossy black two-door Lexus.

Murphy closed his laptop and started to open his door. "At least let me check the back—"

Miller grabbed Murphy by the arm, stopping him. "No time and no need. I've kept an eye on the rearview, and nobody's snuck up behind us. I'm sure of it."

"Miller, we both know he can—"

"Will you stop talking? He's not onto us, nobody snuck up behind the car, and look, he's started his engine. I told you this time he was on the move."

The black Lexus moved forward and turned to the right, pulling out of its parking space.

Miller said, "Here we go." He turned the key and started the car. The engine rumbled to life, purred for about three seconds, then coughed, sputtered, and died. The fan blew full blast, and a chime sounded from deep inside the dash, but no sound came from the engine.

Miller shouted, "Damn it!"

Across the street, Jimmy put the Lexus in reverse, pulled back into the parking space he had just left, and killed the engine.

Miller again shouted, "Damn it!"

Murphy said, "Just shut the car off, Miller."

Miller gritted his teeth so hard that it felt like his incisors might crack, but he turned the key, silencing the chime and the fan. They heard people laughing behind the car.

Murphy asked, "Shall I go get it?"

Miller turned and looked at him, silently.

"Yeah," Murphy said. "I'll go get it. You, uh . . . you stay here."

Miller continued to stare as his partner got out of the car, then looked back at Jimmy sitting in his Lexus across the street. He heard the laughter continue, and the voice of the young man with the flyers say, "Hey man, it looks like you fell for the banana in the tailpipe!"

The laughter from the tourists grew louder.

"Yeah," Murphy laughed, insincerely. "Looks like it."

Some unseen woman said, "Classic. Banana in the tailpipe. It stops up the exhaust and makes the car stall."

"Yeah," Murphy interrupted. "We all know why. Everyone saw the movie."

A young man said, "I'd heard it doesn't work, though. Saw it on TV where they tried and couldn't get it to work."

Murphy said, "Yeah, well, I suppose this must be some kind of magic banana, then."

Murphy continued to make small talk about bananas, tailpipes, and *Beverly Hills Cop*, but Miller tuned it all out, watching Jimmy get out of his Lexus, looking irritatingly pleased with himself, almost skipping back into the Luxurious Rothschild Building.

Murphy got back in the car, clutching a dirty, soot-smeared banana.

Miller said, "I watched. I watched the rearview mirror. I watched both side-view mirrors. There's no way anyone snuck up behind the car and stuck a banana in our tailpipe without me seeing."

"Miller, it's Jimmy. We've seen him teleport. We know he can make things appear and disappear out of thin air. He clearly used his powers to put the banana in our tailpipe, what, three times now? I mean, it shouldn't even work. That's a dead giveaway."

Across the street, Jimmy continued his stroll away from the

parking lot, exchanged some friendly banter with the doorman, then disappeared into the building, briefly turning his head to let his vision sweep across the street. He cast a surreptitious look at Miller and Murphy, and let them see the smile on his face.

"Why?" Miller asked. "Why would he go to the trouble to keep putting bananas in our tailpipe, when he knows it shouldn't work?"

"It really bugs you, doesn't it?"

"Yeah."

"Well, there's your answer. The end goal is to bother us, and inconvenience us, and we get a chorus of tourists laughing and wanting to talk to us about the banana in the tailpipe, and how it's not actually supposed to work. He knows us . . . let's be honest, he knows you well enough to know that that'll drive you crazy."

"But still, why? If he knows we're watching him, why not just ditch us?"

Murphy shrugged, reopening his laptop. "I figure two reasons. One is that he's not worried about us. And the other is that he's a jerk."

Miller thought for a long moment. "I can't argue with that."

4.

Martin, Phillip, Brit the Younger, and Gwen flew in a lopsided V formation, like a flying checkmark. Even though wind resistance meant little to the wizards in terms of energy expenditure, less wind made for a more pleasant flight, and taking a cue from geese made flying at high speed more fun for everyone, except whoever was flying in the lead; in this case, Martin.

They came in low over the forest canopy, then slowed as they reached a zone of dead trees and scorched earth that thinned into a clearing by the base of a granite cliff.

Martin calibrated his speed and angle of descent in such a way as to drift into a cave, shaped like a screaming skull, about twenty feet up the cliff wall. He decelerated smoothly, landing at the back of the cave at Gary's doorstep—or at least he would have if he hadn't been forced to come to an abrupt stop. In the dim light inside the cave, he saw a person sitting, slumped, with his back to Gary's door. Brit, Gwen, and Phillip nearly crashed into Martin's back, but they all managed to stop with great effort and much muttered cursing.

Martin peered through the dim light at the figure on the doorstep. "Who is that?" he asked. He inhaled tentatively through his nose. "Hubert. What are you doing here?"

"Learning the mystic arts from my master," Hubert, the town of Leadchurch's apprentice dung sifter, said.

From inside the door, Gary shouted, "No you're not."

Gwen asked, "Who's your master?"

Hubert jerked a filthy thumb back over his shoulder toward the door. "The Necromancer. That fearsome mystical warrior known to man and demon alike as Gary."

"No," Gary shouted from inside. "I'm not teaching you squat!"

Phillip crouched down to address Hubert closer to his own eye level, with the hope that the warm, fragrant air coming off of Hubert was rising. "Hubert, what is it you think Gary is teaching you by refusing to let you into his house and insisting that he won't teach you anything?"

"He's teaching me the importance of humility and patience."

"So, things that Gary himself doesn't know," Gwen muttered.

Brit the Younger shouted through the door, "That means he figures you're going to let him inside eventually."

"I'm not," Gary shouted.

Martin asked, "Do you plan to let us in?"

Gary opened the door. Hubert's eyes grew wide with horror and fascination at the sight of him, with his black robe and hat, his skeletal prosthetic leg, and his face hidden by a full gas mask.

Gary pointed down at Hubert. "You, get out of my friends' way."

"Yes, Master!" Hubert scuttled like a crab away from the door, then kneeled, looking up with reverence. Gary kept his eyes on Hubert as he held the door open wide.

Once all of the wizards had entered, Hubert said, "I wait to do your bidding, Master."

Gary snarled, "Good! Then go home."

"Already done, Master. My home is by your side."

Gary slammed the door shut.

"How'd that happen?" Martin asked as they all walked through the ceremonial antechamber where Gary performed magic for any locals who came to him for help. They passed through the circular cave, past the many torches and the stone altar holding an immense, ancient-looking leather-bound book, which concealed a mid-nineties trackball PowerBook.

Gary took off his gas mask and led his guests to the door at the far side of the chamber. "I don't know. He found that old Gene Simmons action figure of mine, and thought it gave him magical powers. I guess he got the bug. Now he wants *more*."

Gary opened the far door, revealing his actual home: a haven of off-white walls and beige carpets. It was clear that he had tried very hard to make his place look nice, but had no idea what nice looked like. It was a home that was quick and easy to tidy up, but would be next to impossible to actually clean.

Gary asked, "So, why'd you fly in? You said you were gonna teleport."

Gwen walked to one of Gary's two giant brown recliners. They'd come as a set with a matching giant brown sectional, and were large enough to hold two well-acquainted people if they each scooched far to the sides. Gwen looked Martin in the eye and planted herself directly in the middle of the seat.

The chairs and the couch faced a faux wood-grain rectangle of pressboard slabs holding multiple electronic devices tethered to a massive Sony Trinitron from the days when having a large flat-screen TV meant owning a huge, heavy box containing a massive glass vacuum tube, the 32-inch front of which was flat. The TV was tethered to a series of dusty black boxes by a series of tangled black cords.

Once settled, Gwen pointed to the corner of the main room where people materialized when they used Gary's preprogrammed teleportation algorithm. In it sat a plastic backyard kiddie pool full of some gray liquid.

"What's that, Gary?"

A guilty smile crept across Gary's face. "Wet concrete. I've enchanted it to harden as soon as any solid object appears in it."

"Any solid object, like our feet."

"That's one example."

"Yeah, well, that's why we didn't teleport in."

"Fair enough. I got Jeff and Roy, anyway. They should be back any minute. Chiseling their feet free shouldn't take long. And Tyler hasn't arrived yet. Should I remove the concrete?"

Martin said, "You know what we're going to say."

"*Of course not?*" Gary asked.

"Of course not," Martin said. He opened the refrigerator, and found it fully stocked—with beverages and condiments. He grabbed a beer, closed the door, twisted off the bottle cap, and threw it into the garbage can, which was full of empty beverage and condiment containers.

A bluish light filled the room. Everyone's attention turned as Jeff and Roy materialized, hovering two feet above the kiddie pool full of concrete. Their shoes had a dirty gray cast about them, and the hems of their robes hung straight down, still weighted by small chunks of concrete stuck to the fabric. On Jeff's wool robe, the gray stains looked incongruous. Roy, on the other hand, wore a trench coat and a modified fedora for his wizard uniform, so the cement stains looked appropriate and gave the impression he'd narrowly escaped angry mobsters.

"Was the concrete hard to get rid of?" Gary asked, obviously hoping the answer was yes.

Jeff said, "It wasn't as unpleasant for us to remove as it will be for you when you find where we put it." He and Roy floated to the edge of the wading pool, dropped to the floor, and walked to empty spots on the sectional, leaving dusty gray footprints.

"Uh, guys, do you think I could get you to take off your shoes and put them by the door?" Gary asked.

Roy growled, "No, I don't. You got a lotta nerve, embedding our shoes in concrete then complaining that we're tracking concrete into your house."

Gwen said, "He's got a point, Gary. Besides, there's not really much anyone can do to mess this place up."

Gary said, "Thank you!"

Jeff shook his head. "Gary, that was an insult."

Gwen said, "No, Gary, I'm sorry. I didn't mean anything by that. Sure, your place is a bit rough around the edges. And through the middle. Really, it's one homogeneous slab of roughness, but it suits you."

"Thank you!" Gary said.

"That was also an insult," Jeff said.

Roy touched down and walked to the dining area, which housed a matching set of chairs and a glass-topped table of the kind meant to grace a retiree's patio, complete with a hole in the table's center designed to accommodate a large umbrella. He nodded to Martin and Phillip but removed his hat to the ladies. "Hello, Gwen. Hello, Brit. It's good to see you again today."

This confused Brit. "I'm sorry?"

Jeff said, "No, Roy, that was Brit the Elder who came over. This is Brit the Younger."

Roy shrugged. "Still. They're the same person, so we have seen her twice today."

Jeff gritted his teeth. "It would kill you to be wrong, wouldn't it?"

"I'll let you know if it ever happens."

"Why did Brit the Elder go see you?" Phillip asked.

"She had some technical questions," Jeff said. "Stuff about the dragons, and what I learned trying to manipulate living things in the shell."

"Mostly, not to do it?" Gwen asked.

"Exactly," Jeff said.

"That answer didn't make her happy," Roy said. "Poor thing. She seemed pretty strung out. Not just tired, but upset, too. I'm thinking maybe I should go over to her place and see if she needs some support."

"What kind of support?" Phillip asked.

Roy shrugged. "You know, comforting."

"I don't know if that's a good idea."

"And I don't know if that's any of your business, Phillip. I mean, you always say that you don't believe she and Brit the Younger here are the same person, so the way I see it, dating Brit the Younger gives you no say in Brit the Elder's affairs."

"It doesn't actually give him any say over my affairs either," Brit the Younger said.

"Right," Roy agreed. "And if you're wrong, and they are the same person, by the time she becomes Brit the Elder, you don't seem to be in the picture anymore."

"But I am," Brit the Younger said, "because I am convinced that we're the same person, and I say leave her alone. If she needs help, let her ask for it. I hate people meddling in my affairs, so when it comes to hers, which are going to be mine eventually, I say we all stay out of it."

Martin asked, "But by making that decision for her, aren't you meddling in her affairs?"

"The affairs are either hers, mine, or both, depending on how you look at it, but none of it's any of your business, so drop it. Okay?"

At that moment, the entire group heard a quiet splash and a loud burst of energetic swearing. They all turned to see Tyler, the last wizard to arrive and the only African American man in Medieval England, standing ankle deep in the kiddie pool full of hardened concrete. He tried to pull his staff free, straining mightily, but it would not budge. He continued swearing, first at the concrete, then at Gary, then at himself for trusting Gary and not anticipating the concrete.

Tyler teleported away, leaving the empty kiddie pool behind. Almost immediately, he rematerialized, minus the large disk of concrete that had been fixed to his feet.

"So he got you," Phillip said. "Don't let it ruin your night."

"I'm mad at myself for not seeing it coming," Tyler said. "But I'm much, much madder at Gary, for being such a turd!"

Tyler turned his attention to Gary. "Okay, we're all here. Three of us are angry. Why don't we just get started?"

Gary stood and held his arms out wide. "Yes, let us begin! Welcome, one and all, to our weekly movie night. As the host, I get to pick the movie. This week's selection is *Blade Runner*!"

Phillip said, "Haven't we all seen that?"

Roy said, "I haven't. What's it about? A guy who runs with scissors?"

"No," Gary said. "And while the rest of you have seen it, which version have you seen? The original, with the narration that the producers made the director put in, or the later version where the director took the narration out?"

"And added a scene to completely change the whole point of the movie," Tyler said. "Or the even later version, when they restored the film so it would look good on DVD?"

"Or the version after that," Martin said. "Where they remastered it again and redid a few of the scenes to look better at high resolution?"

"Or," Jeff asked, "the even later one where the original producers put the narration back in?"

Brit wrinkled her nose like she smelled something bad. "They did that?"

Jeff shrugged. "They do eventually. Ridley Scott released his director's cut to make *Blade Runner* fit his original vision. The producers released their cut to make it fit their original vision, which was for the film to earn them as much profit as possible."

Gary said, "There's no reason we only have to watch one version. I was thinking we could watch all of them as a marathon."

Roy said, "Who'd want to do that? Watch the same movie three times looking for minor differences, like it's a puzzle in *Highlights for*

Children. This sounds worse than when Martin made us sit through that four-hour version of *Dune.*"

"Nothing could be worse than that," Gwen muttered.

Martin laughed. "Gary, remind me, next time it's my turn to host movie night, to get the three-part, basic-cable *Dune* miniseries."

Gary said, "Only if I don't have to attend."

5.

Brit the Elder sat uneasily in a chair made from enough welded square-tube steel to be indestructible, which was covered with just enough foam padding and vinyl upholstery to not quite be comfortable.

She sat in an office that was instantly recognizable as the habitat of an executive-level civil servant. Deluxe imitation wood-grain paneling covered the walls, and a computer and phone that were only ten years out of date sat atop the wood-grain-painted-on-steel desk, right behind a name plate that read *Director Brittany Ryan*.

"No," Brit the Much Elder said into her phone. "I've made my decision. Absolutely not." She winked at Brit the Elder and smiled.

Brit the Elder thought that Brit the Much Elder's voice sounded similar to her own, but slightly higher pitched and more nasal, like an audio recording of her own voice that seemed like a different person when played back. Brit the Much Elder really sounded like Brit the Younger, but less whiny. She looked much the same as Brit the Elder, or Brit the Younger for that matter, with the same face, same build, and same reddish-brown hair. Instead of the retro-hip horn-rimmed glasses the younger two Brits preferred, Brit the Much Elder wore a pair of frameless spectacles. And instead of a light blue wizard robe or a flowing tropical-weight dress, Brit the Much Elder wore a highly structured suit with a knee-length skirt.

Brit the Much Elder said, "I understand all of that, and my decision stands. You are to keep the subject under surveillance but do not move on him under any circumstances. Is that clear?"

She listened for a few seconds to the barely audible squawking noise of the other person talking before cutting him off. "You have your orders, Agent. That will be all. And Agent, try not to fall for the banana in the tailpipe."

She broke into a wide grin, almost laughing as she ended the call and placed her phone on the table. "I transferred those two doofuses to my task force so I could keep an eye on them, since they knew too much, but man, they've been worth it just for the entertainment value."

Brit the Elder was not amused. She knew from the beginning that conferring with Brit the Much Elder was the simplest, most practical, and most logical thing to do. The fact that she tried several other things first demonstrated how unpleasant she found the prospect.

She had also gone to talk to Jeff, as he had experience tampering with the code of living things, but he'd been very careful to leave their memories and other brain functions alone. All she learned from the visit was that Roy was not subtle about it when he took an interest in a woman.

Brit the Much Elder leaned back into her desk chair. She smirked at Brit the Elder and raised her eyebrows playfully. "Sorry I had to be such a hard-ass just then. It goes with all this, I'm afraid." She waved her right hand in the air to signify the office, her title, and the job that gave her both of those things.

Brit the Elder cleared her throat. "I was just asking you if you remember any of this happening from back when you were me."

Brit the Much Elder nodded. "Yeah, that's right. And I don't. It got a lot harder to keep track of our life events after I took off and became Brit the Much Elder. Brit the Younger's only met me once, so her journals are no help. You don't keep a journal at all, and you barely ever see me anyway, so there isn't a pre-written record of what's going to happen to me from day to day. I tried to work from memory for a while, but then I just sort of let it go. It was one of the best things that ever happened to me. I've learned to enjoy surprises again."

"Good for you. And you have no memory of this problem, or of having this conversation before, when you were me?"

Brit the Much Elder leaned back and closed her eyes. "No, I have no memory of this conversation."

"Doesn't that strike you as odd?"

Brit the Much Elder nodded. "Oh yeah, totally, but I'm sure there's an explanation. Maybe Brit the Much Elder made me so mad that I went home and got black-out drunk. I really disliked me when I was you."

"Yeah, and you had—I have my reasons."

"You do. And with the advantage of age, I see now that those reasons are silly. You're holding a grudge against me because of how I treated you when I was Brit the Elder and you were Brit the Younger. But that's how Brit the Elder treated me when I was Brit the Younger, and it's the exact way you're treating Brit the Younger now."

Brit the Elder leaned forward and spoke through gritted teeth. "I'm not mad because of how you treated me. I could take it. I'm mad at you because it means I have to treat Brit the Younger the same way, and I hate myself for it."

"No more than I did. What's done is done; multiple times, in our case. You'll get over it in time. I did. In fact, to make that easier for you, speaking as Brit the Younger, who I was, I forgive you."

Brit the Elder blinked several times as she attempted to process what she'd just heard. "That's very nice, I think. Thank you."

Brit the Much Elder smiled. "Of course. In fact, while I'm at it, I was also you, and on behalf of you, in advance, I forgive myself, who you will one day be."

"Was that supposed to make me feel better?"

"Yes. And it will. By the time you're me you'll be perfectly at peace with all of this crap."

"Fantastic. In the meantime, we have a real problem, and you don't seem to be taking it seriously."

Brit the Much Elder held up her palms, signaling that Brit the Elder should calm down. "Yeah, yeah, I know. I agree, it's weird."

"Weird?! You say it's weird?! We're talking about a logical paradox that casts doubt on every assumption we've ever made about our life, and threatens to corrupt and possibly even crash the computer program that generates our existence. I think it's fair to say that goes beyond just being weird!"

"Okay, it's really weird. I can see that this whole thing has you on edge."

"Yes," Brit the Elder almost shouted. "I'd say it's fair to describe me as on edge. I haven't shown you the best part yet." She kicked off her ballet flats.

For the first time, Brit the Much Elder seemed genuinely alarmed. "What are you doing?"

Brit the Elder said, "Showing you these," and lifted her feet up so that Brit the Much Elder could see them. At first, they looked just like Brit's bare feet, which she'd seen many times before, since they were her own.

Then, they looked different.

Brit the Elder's feet changed from perfectly normal-looking human feet to two crude collections of polygons approximating the basic shape of human feet without any of the details. Her feet remained that way for about a second and a half, then switched back to normal, then cycled to and from the polygon versions several times in the space of a second before changing back to normal feet.

Brit the Much Elder stared. "That's not right!"

"No! No it is not! And you don't remember any of this?"

"Nope. Not at all."

"And your feet . . ."

"No, my feet are fine, and I agree that it's a serious issue."

"And getting more serious. It's spreading. It started with just my toes, now it's the whole feet. And it starts affecting whatever shoes I wear. I've gone through two pairs of flats since I noticed the problem."

"I'll help you in any way that I can."

"Well, good, but I don't understand how you can be so calm about this."

"I'm calm because I'm you in the future, and I still exist. It seems like if this was going to cause some serious problem, it would have by now."

"Don't you see? This is an error, an error in the program that is our universe! The fact that you don't get that but I do is proof that your memories are no longer tied to my actions or thoughts, which means that everything is, on a fundamental level, completely messed up! The fact that you still exist isn't proof that things are fine, it's a symptom of the problem! The universe could crash at any second. It could even be that me coming to you will cause the final logic error, but I didn't know what else to do. And if I'm wrong, then what about the philosophical ramifications of that? What if all these years we've been tormenting each other because we thought we had no choice, but in fact we had a choice all along?"

Brit the Much Elder leaned farther back in her chair. "Eh, I don't know if it's . . . whatchacallit . . . the perspective that comes with age, or if it's that I've seen so much weird stuff at this point that I just don't notice it anymore. Or maybe those are actually the same thing. The point is, I stopped worrying about all of those philosophical issues years ago. When it comes to free will, these days I just figure if I'm meant to have it, I'll have it."

"That attitude must drive Phillip nuts."

"How would I know?"

"Good point."

Brit the Younger was curled up reading in her favorite chair, when Phillip walked out of the bedroom in his full wizard regalia and walked toward the front door.

"Where are you going?" Brit asked, without lifting her eyes from the page.

Phillip stopped dead in his tracks, turned to face her, and said, "Just out for a walk. What are you reading?"

Brit turned the book around to look at the cover, a picture of two shirtless men with long hair, both obscured by motion blur. One appeared to be crouched low and somehow spinning at high speed while the other was suspended midjump, executing a high kick. "It's a book I borrowed from Louisa. It's about this martial art they developed in Brazil called Capoeira. It's a sort of a mix of fighting and dancing."

"Kind of like slam dancing?"

"Well, it's incredibly graceful and athletic, and an efficient fighting style, so no, it is in no way like slam dancing. Where are you going?"

"What?"

"On your walk. Where are you going?"

"Oh, nowhere. Just, you know, out."

"Cool. Enjoy your walk to nowhere."

"Yes. Very good. Quite. I will."

After several seconds of Brit saying nothing further, Phillip again stepped toward the door. He had nearly reached it when Nik called out from the kitchen, "Phillip? Did I hear you say you're stepping out for a moment?"

"Yes."

"Remember, yesterday, how you said to tell you if there was anything you could do to make my job easier?"

"Yes, of course."

Nik leaned to the side to peer around the corner at Phillip. "Well, if you're going out anyway, could you pick up a chicken for tonight's dinner?"

"Of course," Phillip said. "A chicken. How would you like it?"

Nik furrowed his brow and stared at Phillip.

"Just the breast, or the whole thing? Boned? Unboned? With or without skin?"

Nik asked, "What? What are you talking about?"

"Live," Brit said, quietly enough that Phillip would barely hear her, but Nik wouldn't. "In this time period, the only way to buy a chicken is live."

Phillip nodded a quick thanks to Brit. "Never mind, Nik. I was just being silly. One live chicken, coming up."

"Thanks, Phillip. Feel free to wring its neck yourself, if you want."

Phillip cringed and looked at Brit, who was also cringing, but she was smiling at him as she did it.

One of the first lessons any modern person learns when they go to live in the distant past is that everyone, including the domestic servants, are much more hard-core than you will ever be.

Phillip stepped out the door to a sunny Atlantis morning.

Martin materialized on the landing to Brit the Younger's home and watched as Phillip stepped out the door onto the Atlantean street, muttering, "One live chicken."

Phillip closed the door behind him, turned to walk away, and nearly walked straight into Martin.

Martin smiled and said, "Hello."

Phillip let out a tiny high-pitched shriek and jumped a few inches into the air.

"Oh, man, I'm sorry," Martin said, laughing.

"Yes, you sound it. What do you want, Martin?"

"Just to talk."

"Well then, why not just call me?"

"I wanted to talk to you in person, alone. I kinda hoped it would seem like I'd just ran into you, all casual like."

"Well, those hopes have been dashed." Phillip looked at the closed door into Brit the Younger's apartment, then back at Martin. "Still, why just lurk out here? Seems like a waste of time, and I might well have had Brit with me."

Martin smiled. "Oh, I haven't been waiting. I set up an algorithm to watch all of the doors of your and Brit's places and tell me the next time you came out alone so I could teleport over."

"Oh," Phillip said. "That's certainly . . . alarming."

"Don't worry. There's no reason to be alarmed, as long as I only use the algorithm for good."

"Very reassuring." Phillip started walking and Martin followed.

"So where are you headed?" Martin asked.

"Nowhere. Just out for a walk."

"Then you won't mind if I come along."

"I suppose it won't hurt anything if you tag along for a bit."

Immediately upon setting out, Martin saw that there was much more clutter and traffic on the street than usual. The going was slow, as all traffic was squeezed through a narrow channel carved through all of the detritus on either side of the path. The way in front of them was flanked by hastily made scaffolds holding workmen, various tools, and an oblong tin basin. Various wooden planks and other building materials cluttered the ground.

In the distance, near a trough where people let their animals drink, a metal dome-like structure hung high in the air, perched at the top of a metal rail that stuck straight up like a flagpole. The whole assembly looked to Martin like the world's least effective and most dangerous umbrella.

Ahead and to the right, a set of stairs was carved into the wall of a building leading up to the roof level, where the next path up allowed still more people to walk around the circumference of the great bowl of Atlantis. Martin wondered if that path was as crowded as this one today. He considered suggesting that they take it to get out of the crowd, but then he saw a large bucket sitting unattended at the top of the stairs. Farther along the edge, he could see a strange wooden contraption, made up of two big wooden gears and a crank. He took it as a sign that progress would be no less difficult up there.

Martin shielded his eyes, squinting up at the scaffolding. "What is going on here?"

"Looks like some sort of construction," Phillip said.

"Don't the sorceresses do all of the building in Atlantis?"

"Brit the Elder built it to begin with, but I assume the citizens take on the occasional project themselves."

Martin furrowed his brow. "Why wouldn't they just ask a sorceress to do it?"

"I don't know. Is this really what you wanted to discuss, Martin?"

"No. Sorry. It's this Gwen thing."

"Of course it is."

"I think I want to marry her."

"So you say."

"The idea that she doesn't feel the same way, it's just awful."

"I would imagine."

"Phillip, you know, you're not really saying anything useful here."

Martin glanced up at the edge of the path above theirs. They'd drawn closer to the weird mechanical apparatus. Martin saw that it consisted of two large gears, a long shaft, a wooden paddle, and a wooden dowel hanging from a crossbar with a large boot hanging at its end. The boot didn't alarm Martin, even though it appeared to be a modern combat boot. The city was controlled by time travelers; it wasn't unusual to see anachronistic things pop up where they didn't belong. But something about the entire construction bothered Martin, as if he'd seen it before somewhere.

Phillip did not slow his pace. "You haven't asked me any questions, Martin, and you know much more about the situation than I do. Unless there's some specific piece of Gwen-related information I know that you don't, I'm not sure I'm going to be much help. Perhaps if you go think of some specific way I can be of assistance, then come back—"

"Where are you going?"

"What?"

"Where are you going, Phillip? You seem to be in a rush to get somewhere."

Phillip said, "What? No. I'm just out for a walk."

"You're keeping up a heck of a steady pace."

"The whole point of going for a walk is to walk. Otherwise, it wouldn't be walking."

Martin's eyes narrowed. "Uh-huh. And why pick such a congested area for your walk?"

Phillip looked lost for a moment, then said, "Nobody likes to eat in an empty restaurant."

On the path above, the complex wooden machine creaked into motion. Martin didn't see anyone turning the crank, but the two gears rotated, causing the shaft to move, pushing the paddle into the boot, which swung forward and hit the bucket sitting at the top of the stairs.

The bucket fell over, and a large sphere similar to a bowling ball but carved of stone rolled out and started slowly working its way down the stairs.

"Who just leaves a stone ball sitting in a bucket?" Martin asked.

Phillip made only a small grunt to acknowledge Martin's question, which he clearly hadn't really heard, as he continued to work his way through the crowd.

Martin pointed to the stone ball, still torturously working its way one step at a time down the stairs, emitting a low rumble as it rolled, and a percussive bang each time it fell. "And how was a boot heavy enough to knock over a bucket that was holding that thing in the first place?"

The ball reached the bottom of the stairs and rolled along a barely noticeable furrow in the ground. The people near enough to the ball for it to be a tripping hazard all saw, and carefully avoided it, but the bulk of the crowd, including Phillip, remained oblivious.

The ball wended its way along beside the path and finally crashed into the base of one of the scaffolds. The shock worked its way up the supports, magnifying as it went, until the platform, roughly two stories up, rocked violently. Martin watched as the motion dislodged a second stone ball, which rolled along the length of the platform.

Martin slowed to a stop, his eyes glued to the top of the scaffold. "Okay," he muttered, "what is this?"

The second ball fell off the end of the planks, landing in the oblong basin on the platform below, and rolled along its length. When it reached the far end, the floor gave out, leaving a perfectly round hole where the sphere broke through.

The stone ball landed on a pile of loose building materials, hitting the raised end of a thick plank of wood. The ball drove the plank's high end down like a teeter-totter, lifting the far end, which Martin had not seen was under the heels of a statue waiting to be installed.

The statue flew into the air and landed in the water trough, creating a huge splash and nudging the metal pole that held the metal-lattice dome aloft. People scattered as the webbed hemisphere slid down the pole, but not all of the people. Phillip, single-mindedly working his way through the crowd, had not noticed anything odd, and only snapped out of his stupor as the area around him suddenly emptied. He looked up just as the iron dome crashed down over him.

"Well this is just typical, isn't it?" Phillip said.

"Yeah, you never get trapped in a falling metal cage unless you're in a hurry."

"I'm not in a hurry, Martin, I'm just out for a stroll."

"Mm-hmm."

Phillip looked at the metal framework surrounding him. "That said, I think, since I'm going to have to teleport out of here anyway, I'll just go ahead and go all the way to my walk's, uh, natural end point, and walk back."

"Sounds good," Martin said. "Let's go."

"Yeah, Martin, here's the thing; I'd kind of like to continue alone."

"Of course you would. I understand completely."

"Do you?" Phillip looked stricken for an instant, but regained his composure. "Oh, good. Well, see you around Martin."

"See you."

Phillip said, "*Transporto al*," then looked at Martin, and muttered the last part under his breath.

Phillip disappeared.

Martin grasped the steel cage and shook it, feeling its strength. He wondered what it was supposed to do, and why it had been perched at the top of a pole to begin with. He looked at the statue sticking out of the tub of water, the teeter-totter plank, both stone balls, and the boot and bucket at the top of the stairs. It all seemed to be trying to stir a memory in him, but like an urge to sneeze that just fades away, it left Martin unsatisfied, with a squinty expression on his face.

He stood there, concentrating for several seconds before it finally came to him. *Mouse Trap. It's the crazy machine you'd put together in the board game Mouse Trap!*

That one realization triggered a chain reaction of further deductions in Martin's mind. It was too big a coincidence that the mechanism from Mouse Trap would get re-created in its entirety by accident. That meant someone had to deliberately re-create it. That meant that the person who re-created it had to have been from a time when Mouse Trap existed, i.e., the future. That meant that it was created by a time traveler, someone who had found the file. This was too complicated to be Gary's work. Too high-concept, and far too public and risky to be any of their other friends. The cage was only large enough for one person, and was set up in an area that Phillip frequented. It was sort of a fluke that Martin was there, which suggested that the whole ornate ruse had been put together specifically for Phillip, much like the package the night before.

The conclusion hit Martin like a rolled-up towel snapping him in the brain.

It's the Jawa!

Martin spun around, searching the area until he saw the familiar burlap hood peeking over the edge of a roof. The cloaked figure flinched and darted out of sight the instant it became clear that Martin saw him.

The strange thing about teleportation is that it's the fastest, most convenient means of transportation imaginable, once you know where you're going. Selecting and then somehow designating a landing spot close to where you want to be that isn't inside a wall or suspended several feet above the ground, or both, can be a fiddly, time-consuming task, unless you've developed a work-around. Thanks to his dual childhood loves of *X-Men* comics and the game Toss Across,

Martin had. He reached into his pocket, grasped a small beanbag, and threw it, hard and fast, at the spot where the cloaked figure had been. It landed with an audible thump.

Martin said, "*Bamf,*" and teleported, materializing on the upper level where the beanbag had landed. He scooped up the beanbag and hurled it as hard as he could into the fleeing wizard's back. As the beanbag bounced off the running figure's cloak, Martin said "*Bamf,*" again, and materialized directly behind him.

Martin grasped the man's hood, which slid off his head, and quickly pulled tight around his neck, becoming a leash of sorts. Martin's staff fell, clattering to the ground as he pulled back on the hood with both hands.

With his hood pulled down, the Jawa's bald, misshapen head and pointed ears were exposed. He let out a string of strangled curses in a low, guttural voice as he stopped running and turned around, causing the hood and neck of his cloak to twist around to the front of his throat. His emerald-green eyes radiated fury, distracting from his long, pointed nose, his thin, cruel lips, and his mouth full of jagged teeth.

Martin asked, "What are you, some kinda goblin?"

The stranger slapped at Martin's hands. "Maybe! So what? You prejudiced or something? Let go! Let go, damn you," he spat in a deep, unnatural growl as he unleashed a barrage of stinging slaps.

Martin tugged harder at the hood and shouted, "No!"

The two of them stood there, at the center of a growing crowd of Atlanteans, Martin pulling on the hood while the goblin slapped and cursed to no avail. Finally, the goblin grasped his own hood and twisted it, causing Martin's hands to rotate, loosening his grip enough to allow the goblin to break free.

Martin took a hasty step backward to keep from falling down, but tripped over his own staff and landed directly on his tailbone. He sprang to his feet and jumped up and down, hunched over with both hands clasped to the spot where lower back becomes upper butt.

The goblin backed up several steps, watching Martin dance and moan in pain before finally thrusting his finger at him and shouting, "Yeah, serves you right!"

Martin stopped jumping and moaning, but remained hunched over, and left his hands where they were. He looked up at the goblin and shouted, "Who are you, and why are you trying to hurt Phillip?"

"What? I'm not trying to hurt Phillip!"

"Sure. Who are you?"

"I'm nobody you should worry about. Just forget you ever saw me."

"What should I call you?"

"Nothing! You shouldn't call me! Don't talk to me, or about me, or near me. Forget that I exist." He waved his arms around in great, swirling arcs. Ravens flew in from behind every building and around every corner. From any place in Martin's field of vision large enough to conceal even one raven, many appeared, until the air was so full of flying black birds that the bright, cloudless day seemed gray and overcast.

"Listen to me, and listen well, Martin Banks. Do not interfere with me. Forget you ever saw me, or else the consequences will be dire."

Martin asked, "Dire for who?"

The goblin said, "I think you mean dire for whom, and the answer is you, obviously. Dire for you."

Martin said, "I don't think it's that obvious at all." He dove for his staff, slid on his belly as he grasped it, and rolled over. He pointed the staff's head at the other wizard and shouted, "*Malseketa pantalono!*"

The goblin instinctively shielded his head and ghoulish face with his arms. He stood frozen for several seconds, waiting for the spell to manifest itself, then a confused expression came over his face. He scowled, rotated his pelvis a few times, and said, "Okay, what the hell?"

Martin stood up, looking pleased with himself. "I realized a long time ago that it's next to impossible to really hurt a magic user. We're pretty much invulnerable. We can be embarrassed, though. So I started working on the spell I just hit you with. The pants wetter."

The goblin rolled his eyes and whined, "Oh, man, that's just . . . ugh!"

"I know, right? That's kinda the point. You'll be happy to hear it's just water. Of course, it's still a work in progress. The final version will just cause a stain about five inches around. This one completely saturates the pants. It's kinda overkill."

"It's pointless! I'm wearing a robe, you dolt! Nobody can see that my pants are wet!"

"But you know it," Martin said. The goblin stepped forward, then convulsed into a full body cringe. "Aw man, I hate the feeling of wet pants!"

"So you find the discomfort to be a deterrent as well," Martin said. "Noted! Thanks for the feedback."

"Feedback? You want feedback? Here, let me introduce you to my focus group." The goblin swept his arms around and brought them both together, clapping with stiff arms so that his hands pointed directly at Martin. The thousands of ravens that had been swirling around over their heads changed direction as one, converging on Martin.

Martin's brain was certain that the birds were not real. The way they all looked identical, moved in exactly the same repeating pattern, and made the same noise was a dead giveaway that they were part of a man-made macro, and couldn't really hurt him.

His feet didn't want to hear it.

He had turned and run two steps before he realized what he was doing. Of course, before he'd completed his third step, the birds were on him. Martin spun and shouted, and swung his arms wildly, but nothing he did dislodged the flapping, cawing mass of talons, beaks, and feathers. He staggered several steps, blind, caught his balance, and stopped. He continued swinging his arms, but more slowly, and then only a little, feeling to see if it made any difference, which it did not.

Martin stood motionless for a moment, collected his thoughts as well as one could when covered with a chaotic mass of angry, screeching birds, then turned back toward the goblin, or at least in the direction he believed the goblin had been standing, since he only caught the smallest glimpse of light through the mass of birds.

Martin said, "They don't hurt."

The goblin shouted, "What? I can't hear you!"

"It doesn't hurt," Martin repeated as loud as he could. "I'm impervious to cuts and scrapes, so this isn't doing anything."

"Yes it is. It's making you look ridiculous."

"How long are they going to keep doing this?"

"Until I leave, so they'll be quitting in a second."

Martin reached out blindly with his raven-covered hands. "No! Wait! Hold on!" He felt the birds start to let go, and within a few seconds he was completely unencumbered. The birds flocked around the goblin and flew in an ever-tightening spiral, their numbers diminishing until there were only a few birds, then only one, then none, and no goblin either.

Martin looked at the empty space where the goblin had stood. He spun around, and saw the citizens, slowly emerging from their various hiding spots and bits of shelter. He noted that all of the apparatus from the full-sized re-creation of the game Mouse Trap had also disappeared.

All of the evidence was gone.

Not all of the evidence, he thought, looking down at his robe.

Martin was impervious to damage, but his robe was not. The ravens had shredded the outer layer of fabric. The entire surface was in tatters, and every time he moved, sequins dropped to the ground.

Normally, I'd just ask Gwen to repair it, or make me a new one. Right now, I think I'd rather go another round with the birds.

7.

Phillip materialized at the bottom of the city, on the terrace in front of Brit the Elder's home. The great bowl of Atlantis rose on all sides, looming over him and framing the ragged-edged disk of blue sky above.

Phillip looked toward the collection of smooth, opaque glass boxes that made up Brit the Elder's home. A series of sliding glass doors led to the interior, but it was far too dark inside for Phillip to make out any details. Just outside the sliding doors, two Atlantean sentries guarded the entrance. Both stood a full head taller than Phillip and wore the Atlantean Guard's official uniform: shirts of orange netting made with matching, surprisingly short orange kilts.

Phillip waved at the guards and contorted his mouth into the insincere grin he employed to camouflage the displeasure he felt when talking to petty authority figures. "Hello. I'd like to speak to Brit the Elder."

The more senior guard contorted his mouth into the insincere grin he employed to camouflage the pleasure he felt when denying someone something they wanted. "That's not possible, sir."

"I suspect she'd want to see me if she knew I was here."

"I know for a fact we were told not to let anyone disturb her."

The floor-to-ceiling glass doors slid open without warning, emitting a slight hissing sound that drew the attention of Phillip and the guards. Brit the Elder's voice, amplified many times but still reproduced with perfect, ringing clarity, said, "Eh, let him in."

The guard nodded to Phillip, which was as close as Phillip would ever get to an apology. Phillip nodded back, which was as close as he would ever come to saying, "I told you so."

The guard made a point of not watching as Phillip walked across the patio and entered the house.

The place had a genuine sense of disorder about it, but at first Phillip couldn't put his finger on why. The furniture looked exactly as it had when he'd last visited. The carpet was spotless, marred only by a faint wear pattern that a quick vacuuming would erase. A couple of the end tables held empty glasses, and the dining table was strewn with books but, all in all, the place looked much like his own did after he'd tidied up. Yet this was Brit the Elder's home, and Phillip found even the slightest detail being visibly out of place deeply unsettling.

Brit the Elder's voice called out from the deeper recesses of the house, "I'm back here, in the office. Last door on the left."

Phillip found Brit the Elder sitting behind her yellowed Macintosh. The only light in the room was the glow from the tiny CRT screen, shining up on her face from below and reflecting in her glasses, completely hiding her eyes.

Phillip chuckled softly. "Of course, you have the same kind of computer as Brit the Younger."

Brit the Elder sat back in her chair and looked up at Phillip. Even the slightest movement of her head made the shadows shift wildly across her face. "It's not the same kind of computer, Phillip. It's the same computer. I've had this computer since I was in college, as well as when I was Brit the Younger."

"Oh," Phillip said. "Of course."

"But then, you don't really believe that, do you, Phillip? You think I'm some sort of a copy, or a projection of one possible future Brit, but not the literal continuation of the Brit you love, isn't that right?"

"I don't pretend to understand the mechanism behind it, but I do believe that we all, Brit included, have free will. She can make her own decisions, and as such she's not doomed to become anything she doesn't want to be."

"Me, in this case."

"I'm afraid so. Although, I will say that I don't quite understand why she finds the idea of being like you so hateful."

"You're sweet." The unflattering lighting made Brit the Elder's smile look like an eerie grimace. "Have a seat. Sorry the place is such a mess."

Phillip found a chair against the wall and pulled it forward to sit opposite Brit the Elder, just to the side so that the ancient computer didn't block his view of her face.

"I don't see any mess," Phillip said, settling into the chair.

Brit the Elder looked around the room as if she was just seeing it now for the first time. "What? . . . Oh, I see what you mean. It is pretty tidy in here. One of the benefits of the paperless office, I guess. I assure you, my desktop is a mess. So, Phillip, I'm glad you came by. I have a question I've been meaning to ask you."

"Anything."

"Good. When you went to Kludge and asked him and his gang to be sparring partners for your training fights, what did he say?"

"He said yes."

Brit the Elder nodded. "Yeah, so I've heard. What did he say, exactly? Was he ambiguous at all? Was there any room for misinterpretation?"

"At first he was dubious, but when I explained that we wizards would be pulling our punches, but that he and his lads were encouraged to do their best to kill us, he offered to start right then and there."

"Yeah, that's pretty unambiguous."

"Look, I came here because I heard you've been going around asking weird questions, and people said you seemed out of sorts, like you weren't really yourself. Now I'm here, and I see exactly what they meant. What's going on?"

"I don't know what's going on. That's the problem. Phillip, I remember you asking Kludge and the Bastards to be your sparring partners, but the way I remember it, he told you to get stuffed, and it took another year of wooing him to get him to come around."

"So you misremembered something. It happens to everyone."

"Not to me, and I checked, never mind how. I didn't misremember. When I was Brit the Younger, Kludge turned us down. Now he's on board."

Phillip thought for a long moment. "Oh. I see. This . . . this is a big deal."

"Yes, it is."

"The implications!"

"I agree."

"This means that I'm right!"

"I wouldn't say that."

"I've been right all along!"

"I certainly wouldn't say that."

"This is great!"

"No, Phillip, it's a disaster."

"Really? Is it such a problem for me to be right?"

"You're not right, Phillip."

"But, surely, this proves that I am."

"No, you being right is just one possibility that this might suggest. For it to prove you right, it would have to outweigh my entire lifetime of experiences, all of which bolster the position that you're wrong. That's over a hundred years during which every single event I've witnessed, every prediction I've made, every memory I've had, has unfolded exactly as I recalled it. In order for you to be right, all of those experiences would have to have been some sort of coincidence."

"So how do you explain it?"

"Something's gone wrong. An error got introduced into the system somehow. Maybe it was Kludge being agreeable, I don't know. It's hard to say. The point is, there's a logical paradox. From the point where I remember you making your offer onward, I've lived my life as if he said no. But now, from the moment you made your offer on, the rest of the world, including Brit the Younger, has gone on as if he said yes. So far, I'm the only one who has felt any of the consequences, but it's gonna be like ripples in a pond. They'll only get larger, and reach further."

"What do you think will happen if you're right?"

"Eventually, there'll be a logical paradox that the system can't reconcile, followed by a crash."

"A crash? What do you think this crash would look like?"

It wouldn't look like anything. We wouldn't even know it had happened."

"Oh. Good."

"No. Not good. Us, the world, the entire universe, and every living thing in it could freeze and then wink out of existence with absolutely no warning or way to escape."

"But when the program boots back up—"

"There's no guarantee that it would. If it did, there's no reason to believe that the program would generate us again. Even if it did generate another Phillip McCall or Brittany Ryan, they wouldn't be us. They'd be new versions. We would be gone."

"And you think this is likely?" Phillip asked.

"No, not likely," Brit the Elder said.

"Good."

"Inevitable. I'd say that if we don't do something, it's inevitable, and every second that passes it gets closer."

Phillip started to speak, then stopped, and simply sat there with his head hung low and his shoulders slumped.

"I know," Brit the Elder said. "It's terrible."

"I'll say. I've always maintained that you and Brit the Younger are separate, distinct people, and everyone's always laughed at me for it. Now the evidence finally seems to prove me right, and you see it as proof that the universe is fundamentally broken."

"I'm sorry, Phillip, but I'll side with logic, reason, and a lifetime of experience over your opinion and a single anomaly every time. Besides, I have evidence that something's gone wrong with the program." She pointed downward, suggesting that Phillip look under her desk. Phillip looked confused, then smiled uncomfortably, shrugged, and leaned to the side, bending his neck and grasping the corner of the desk for support as he looked beneath it.

It was difficult to see in the dim light, but he made out the hem of Brit the Elder's floral dress, a bit of her exposed shins, and a pair of fur-lined taupe suede pull-on boots that reached clear up to the middle of her calves.

Phillip shrugged. "The boots are odious, obviously, but I don't know that you can blame the program for that."

"One of the sorceresses from the early two thousands gave them to me as a gift. I have to admit, they're comfortable, but I put them on because I didn't care if they got damaged."

"Damaged by what?"

"Watch."

At first, Phillip saw nothing unusual, because nothing was unusual. For three seconds, Brit the Elder's feet looked perfectly normal.

Then they didn't.

The change happened so quickly, Phillip's brain took a moment to register that anything *had* happened. He grabbed his staff and muttered a quick spell, making the staff act as a flashlight.

With the area under the desk fully illuminated, he saw her boots shift from looking like real boots to resembling crude digital representations of boots. Brit the Elder kicked off the boots, exposing her bare feet, to drive her point home. As Phillip watched, her feet shifted from their normal form to the low-polygon version and back several times, seemingly at random.

At that moment, a high-pitched keening noise rang in Phillip's ears. He winced and looked down at his palm, where he saw the sparkling bust of Santo, and heard the eerie organ sting that signified Martin trying to call him. He kept his eyes on Brit the Elder's glitching feet as he took the call.

"Uh, Martin, there's something I need to tell you."

Brit the Elder cleared her throat, and shook her head emphatically.

"There's something I need to tell you, which is that I can't talk now."

"You answered the call to tell me you can't talk?"

"Yes. I didn't want to be rude."

"Whatever. Fine. Don't talk. Just listen. Phillip, someone attacked you."

"You mean someone's going to attack me?"

"No someone already has. That steel cage that fell on you, it wasn't an accident."

"But that didn't hurt me at all."

"It wasn't meant to hurt you. It was part of a big, elaborate plan to get your attention."

"So you're saying that someone is just trying to catch my eye, and they've failed so far."

"Yes."

"That's the least threatening thing I've ever heard."

"Phillip, you have to take this seriously. I don't think he's going to give up. He's tried twice already."

"Twice?"

"That package on your doorstep those kids stole was part of it, too."

"Oh, God, are you on that again? So it's the Jawa who's after me?"

"He's not a Jawa. I never said he was a Jawa. That was you."

"I suppose that's true."

"He's a goblin."

"Martin, I'm sorry, but I have more important problems than your flights of fancy."

"Like what? You told me you weren't going anywhere, and weren't doing anything."

"Yeah, that's right, and it's still more important than your paranoid delusions."

Phillip hung up, then stared at Brit the Elder's feet.

Brit the Elder looked askance at Phillip. "What? Are they doing something new?"

Phillip pointed to the area below the desk. Brit the Elder pushed her chair back and looked at the floor beneath her feet. Every time her feet shifted from one state to the other, the carpet beneath her feet changed as well. A circle a couple of feet across switched from carpet to a perfectly flat smooth surface the same color as the carpet.

Brit the Elder said, "Huh. That's new. Proves that the glitch is spreading to the world beyond me. I suppose it's good to know for sure."

Phillip continued staring at the empty space where her foot had just been. "I, Brit, I . . . Why on earth did you show me this?"

"Because I want your help."

"I don't know how I can possibly help you."

"Neither do I, but together I'm sure we'll think of something."

"But you think I'm wrong about everything."

"Not everything, Phillip. Just one thing. The fundamental mechanism underlying the entire universe. Aside from that, your instincts are usually pretty good. You're a smart man, and a good man, and there's nobody I trust more. Will you please help me?"

"Of course! You don't even have to ask. Of course I'll help you."

"Good. Thank you."

"I think the first thing I should do is tell Brit, bring her in on this."

"No, I'm afraid the first thing you need to do is promise me that you will not tell Brit the Younger anything about any of this until I say it's okay."

"And when will that be?"

"Probably never."

"You can't expect me to keep this a secret from her?!"

"That's exactly what I expect."

"But, she'd want to know!"

"Maybe. Maybe not. I mean sure, we can speculate that she'd probably want to know, but I can tell you for a fact that I don't want you to tell her."

"But you claim to be her! You want me to keep this a secret from you?"

"Yes! That's exactly how you should look at this, Phillip. I am Brit—the older, wiser Brit—and I'm telling you not to tell the younger, more foolish me what's going on. Besides, you can't anyway, because I don't remember you telling me when I was her, so you didn't then, and you can't now."

"But that doesn't matter anymore! Your past and our present have diverged. All bets are off now!"

"NO, the bets are still on, and the stakes are much higher. Think, Phillip! The timeline has split, but both paths are still right here next to each other, and she and I are on the two different paths. Any interaction between the two of us, even if it's just her finding out what's going on with me, could be the thing that crashes reality."

"Then why tell me at all?"

"Because I trust you."

"So does she! I'm the person most likely to tell her."

"And the person most likely to keep my secret, for Brit the Younger's own good and the continued survival of our entire reality. It won't be easy, I know. Especially since you'll have to find a way to keep sneaking away from her to come and help me get to the bottom of this and repair the damage."

"You're asking a lot."

"I'm not, really."

"You don't think sneaking around behind the back of the woman I love is a big deal?"

"I know it is. What I meant is that I'm not asking. I'm not asking you to do something, I'm informing you that you're going to. Logically, you were committed the moment I decided to tell you what was going on."

"You don't remember any of this. How do you know I won't tell her and keep it a secret from you?"

"You're far too smart to betray my trust and risk our continued existence, just to tell Brit the Younger something that's going to make her angry at you anyway. I certainly don't see any upside in that."

"This is a hell of a situation you've put me in."

"Yes, I know, but remember, I'm her. So, if it makes you feel better, in a very real sense, she put you in this situation."

8.

"The subject has started the car," Agent Miller said, leaning forward in his seat and peering through the semi-fogged windshield. He gripped the steering wheel in one hand and put the keys in the ignition with the other.

Agent Murphy continued reading his laptop. "Yeah. Great. Keep me posted."

"He's pulling out of the parking space."

"Fantastic. It's certainly worth getting all excited over. He's definitely not just messing with us this time."

"What's happened to your attitude, Murph? Why am I the positive one all of the sudden?"

"You're not being positive. You smell blood. You're desperate to take Jimmy down, and that's made it easier for him to jerk you around, which only makes you want to take him down even more. It's a vicious cycle, and I'm tired of it."

"Well, the cycle's been broken," Miller said. "He's pulling out of the parking lot."

Miller started the car, which immediately stalled.

Murphy sighed, opening his door. "I'll get the banana."

Miller said, "Hurry. I don't wanna lose him."

Behind the car, people shrieked and laughed. One woman pounded on Miller's side window.

The voice of some unseen pedestrian from the rear of the car rang out, "Ha! You fell for the banana in the tailpipe!"

"Shut up!" Miller shouted, spittle flying from his mouth and hitting the still-rolled-up window. "You shut the hell up!"

Murphy walked to the back of the car, not stopping to answer any of the pedestrian's questions about bananas, tailpipes, *Beverly Hills Cop*, or *MythBusters*.

Across the street, Jimmy's Lexus took a left turn out of the parking lot.

As Murphy got back in the car, Miller started the engine, shifted into first, and mashed the accelerator.

"Hold on," Murphy said. "Hold on. I hadn't even closed my door yet!"

"No time," Miller said. "He's on the move, and I ain't losing him."

As they joined the flow of traffic, Miller leaned far to one side, then the other, muttering, "Where is he? Where is he? There he is! Three cars up. He's signaling a left!"

"Calm down," Murphy said. "You're fogging up the windows."

"Then turn on the defogger. We're gonna get him, Murph. He's gonna slip up, and we're gonna get him."

Murphy fumbled with the climate controls until the vents made a whooshing noise so loud he had to raise his voice to be heard. "No we aren't, Miller. Our orders are to observe."

Miller reached up with his left hand and loosened his collar. "Well, we're gonna observe him slipping up, then we're gonna get him."

"We aren't going to observe anything if this window doesn't clear up."

"Turn the blower up!"

"It's up! The blower is up! It doesn't blow any harder than that."

Both men cranked their windows down. Miller peered through the hazy windshield. "I think he's getting in the turn lane."

"Signaling a turn, then turning. What could that fiend be up to?!"

"If you're gonna be a smart-ass, Murph, at least make yourself useful. Wipe some of this crap off the window so I can see, would you?"

Murphy leaned over, stretched his arm out, and used his bare hand to wipe a small hole in the fog. Cold, condensed water rolled off his hand and fell in fat drops on the dashboard. "The open windows aren't helping."

"Yeah, I can see that." Miller pulled the car into the left turn lane, two cars behind Jimmy's Lexus.

"It's not defogging, Miller. Not at all. It shouldn't be foggy at all, and it's refusing to defog. I mean, look, the spot I rubbed clear is already fogging up again."

"Yeah, so, wipe it again. He's turning! He's turning!"

Murphy wiped a hand-sized clear spot in front of himself and leaned forward to look through it. "Yeah, he's turning all right, Miller. He's taking a U-turn."

"He's trying to lose us!"

The car sputtered and died.

Murphy said, "We should be so lucky." He opened his door and hotfooted it to the rear of the car to remove the banana they both knew was in the exhaust pipe. When he reentered the car, Miller was honking the horn at the two cars in front of them. Finally, both cars executed their left turns.

Murphy adjusted the rearview mirror and said, "Yeah, there was a banana in the tailpipe. We hadn't even shut the car off. We were just stopped, waiting to turn. It doesn't even make sense."

Miller steered their rented sedan through a tight U-turn that made the tires and the power steering system squeal.

"Miller," Murphy continued. "He's messing with us again."

Miller had his head out the window in an attempt to see. He glanced at Murphy and said, "What?" But he was clearly focusing more on the chase than anything his partner had to say.

"He's messing with us! I'm pretty sure he's making the window fog up somehow, and he's leading us around so that the fogging'll be a problem. Miller! Are you listening to me?"

"He's turning again. Right this time."

"You're not listening to me." Murphy leaned over and wiped a large clear patch in front of his partner again.

Miller pulled his head back into the car. "Thanks, partner."

"You're welcome. So he's turning right?"

"Yeah."

"Tell me, are we back near the building he lives in?"

"He's about to pass it. He's . . . he's . . ."

"He's slowing down, isn't he?"

"Maybe it's traffic."

Murphy didn't bother to wipe a spot to look through. He just sat back, watched the scenery roll past his open side window, and listened to his partner shout obscenities as Jimmy pulled back into the parking lot of the Luxurious Rothschild Building, which he'd just left.

When Miller had exhausted himself, Murphy said, "Go up to the next light and pull another U-turn. If nobody beats us to it, maybe we can get our old parking spot back."

9.

Martin materialized without any warning—or entrance music. He hovered in midair, his feet pulled up beneath him to leave as much clearance above the floor as possible. He waved his staff threateningly with his left hand, ready to cast any one of a number of defensive spells he had at the ready. He held his right hand over his eyes, like a child at a scary movie he had mistakenly thought he was old enough to handle, using his semi-spread fingers to filter out anything he didn't really want to see.

Instead of an attacker of any kind, Martin saw only the interior of Gary's home, Skull Gullet Cave. He saw no sign of Gary, nor anybody else, but Martin knew Gary well enough not to take his absence for granted. He hovered, spinning slowly, guarding for an attack that never came. Finally, he removed his hand from his eyes, stretched his legs out, and landed.

"Hey, Gary," Martin shouted. "You home?"

"Back here, in the bedroom," Gary's distant voice replied. "Come on back."

Martin walked past the overbuilt couch and recliners, past the rudimentary kitchen, and down the hallway that led to the bathroom and bedroom. He found the bedroom door slightly ajar and heard hushed voices.

"Is this satisfactory, Master?"

"Yes, but next time, remember to put your gloves on first."

Martin put his hand, fingers slightly spread, back over his eyes, and pushed the door open.

Gary's bedroom was much as Martin remembered it. A very large modern bed, covered with disheveled sheets and a black bedspread, sat in a room devoid of any decorative wall hangings.

At the foot of the bed, Gary stood wearing only a pair of plain briefs. Martin didn't know if he was surprised or relieved to see that they weren't brightly colored and festooned with the logo of some superhero.

A black T-shirt hung limply from Gary's hand. Hubert stood nearby, wearing the jacket and bowtie of a formal tuxedo with tails over his customary filth-colored tunic and britches. He was pulling on a pair of white cotton gloves, making them substantially less white in the process.

"Aw, Gary, please tell me this isn't what it looks like."

Hubert said, "The master is training me to be his buddaler."

"Butler," Gary said. "I'm training him to be my butler."

"Yeah," Martin said. "That's what it looks like."

"The master says that if I can prove my worth and loyalty, he may teach me magic. In the meantime, he's paying me a fine wage."

"And working for me will be a lot more pleasant than his previous job."

"Indeed," Hubert said. "After I'm finished helping the master get dressed, I'm to sort his underwear, culling out any pairs that are too damaged to continue using."

Gary laughed. "Yeah, okay, Hubert. Later on we're going to have a conversation about butler-master confidentiality. Why don't you hand me my robe, then go get to work on breakfast? Martin, would you like Hubert to make you anything?"

"Would I like for Hubert to make food, for me to eat? No. No thank you."

Hubert said, "Very good. And which black robe would the master prefer to wear today?"

Gary said, "You pick one. I trust you."

Hubert reached into the closet and grabbed one from the middle of a cluster of identical black robes, then handed it to Gary. "Is this one to your liking, Sir?"

"Yes. Thanks. That'll be all, Hubert."

Hubert bowed deeply and left the room. Gary sat down on the foot of the bed and started threading a pair of Levis on over his skeletal prosthetic leg.

"You've hired a man to help you dress yourself?" Martin asked. "That's gotta be the laziest thing I've ever heard."

"Not at all. I've gone to the trouble of hiring a man to help me dress. You haven't gotten around to that yet. It looks like you could use the help. What the hell happened to your robe?"

Martin looked down at his shredded, tattered robe, still shedding sequins every time he moved. "I was attacked by birds. We'll discuss that later. Gary, what you're doing to Hubert—it's not right."

"I'm giving him a job! Look, he brought up the idea of learning magic from me. You saw me telling him that it wasn't going to happen. I got to thinking about how desperate he seemed to find a better line of work, and it occurred to me that I couldn't make him a wizard, but I could come up with something better than being a dung sifter. But hey, maybe I'm wrong. If you think he'd be better off in the dung pile, or the dung fields, or the siftery, wherever it is they do the sifting, feel free to go fire him."

"I'm not going to fire him, but this doesn't sit well with me."

Gary pulled on his black robe as he and Martin made their way from the bedroom back to the living room. As they emerged from the hallway and the kitchen came into view, they saw Hubert closing the door to the freezer, holding a frozen breakfast burrito, still in its plastic wrapper. He pulled on the wrapper's flat, heat-sealed end with both hands.

Gary said, "Um, Hubert, don't bother unwrapping it. Just poke a hole in the wrapper, heat it up, and put the whole thing on the plate."

"Yes, Master." Hubert tugged again at the wrapper, straining from the exertion, then lifted the wrapper to his mouth and bit a hole in its end. Martin noticed dark smudges on the wrapper where it had been touched by Hubert's hands and lips.

"So," Gary asked. "What brings you to my home? I don't remember inviting you over."

"I'm calling an emergency meeting."

"Cool. When and where?"

"Here, any second now."

"Convenient. I don't remember agreeing to that."

"You didn't. I'll explain when everyone's here. I wouldn't have pulled a stunt like this if it weren't important." Martin held up his left hand, palm upward.

"*Nomita grupo kvin.*" A glowing orb appeared in Martin's hand. He said, "Okay, Gary's decent and it's safe. Come on over."

In quick succession Tyler, Jeff, and Roy appeared, all floating in midair with their legs pulled up protectively and their wands and staffs outstretched to launch a quick counterattack.

"Relax," Martin said. "He didn't know we were coming."

The wizards descended lightly to the ground and dropped their guards.

Gary looked over the group, took a moment to do some mental math, and reached for his staff: a long, gnarled piece of dark wood with action figures of the members of KISS lashed to its top. "I might still have time to get something ready before Gwen, Phillip, and Brit get here."

Martin held up a hand to stop him. "Phillip and Brit aren't coming. Gwen's deliberately late to make it clear that she's not happy with me right now."

Gwen appeared. She looked around the room. Only after she'd made eye contact and exchanged friendly greetings with every other wizard did she deign to look at Martin.

"Where are Brit and Phillip?"

"I didn't invite them."

"Why not?" Gwen asked.

"We'll get to that."

"Since you're all here," Gary said, "how about some snacks?"

Roy said, "Sure."

Martin said, "None for me, thanks."

Gary clapped twice, in quick succession.

Hubert said, "Yes, Master? What shall I make for your guests?"

All of the wizards turned and looked at Hubert in his tuxedo jacket and mottled white-and-brown cotton gloves.

Tyler asked, "Hubert? What are you doing?"

Hubert puffed his chest out with pride. "The master has agreed to let me be his putler."

"It's butler, Hubert," said Gary.

"Yes, that. Who would like something to eat? It shouldn't take me long to whip something up."

The entire group made immediate, emphatic statements to the effect that they were not hungry.

Gary shook his head. "Okay, Hubert. False alarm. How's my burrito coming?"

"I put it in your demonic heat box as instructed. It should be done soon."

"Good. We have wizard secrets to discuss. You can go outside for a break."

Hubert backed out of the room, exiting to the vestibule that led to the outside world, bowing and closing the door as he left.

Jeff looked utterly disgusted. "He came to you to learn magic, and you're using him as a servant?"

"A properly microwaved burrito is kind of magical. Besides, there's no shame in being a butler."

"He's not a butler," Tyler said. "A butler oversees the household staff. Hubert's your valet. They were also sometimes called a gentleman's gentleman. They tended to a nobleman's personal needs. The butler managed the household staff."

"Oh," Gary said, "I'm still gonna call him my butler. Butlers are just cooler. Like that, what's his name, Jeeves."

Tyler squeezed his eyes shut. "Jeeves was Bertie Wooster's valet, not his butler."

Gwen put a hand on Tyler's shoulder. "You understand that nobody cares, right?"

Martin cleared his throat. "Let's get down to business. I suppose you're all wondering why I called you here."

Roy raised his hand but didn't wait to be called on. "Was it so you'd have a chance to say, *I suppose you're all wondering why I called you here*?"

"I have always wanted to say that. But no."

Gwen said, "I assumed it was because you wanted to apologize."

"I didn't just call you. I called everybody."

"I assumed you wanted to apologize in front of everybody."

"Why?" Gary asked. "What did he do?"

Gwen glared at Martin. "He knows."

Gary smiled and stepped closer to Gwen. "Hey, if you and Martin are on the outs, just let me say that if you decided to give me a whirl, I promise I'd never have any intention of marrying you."

Gwen rolled her eyes. "I'm leaving."

"Wait," Martin said. "This is important. It's not about you and me. It's about Phillip."

Jeff raised his hand and spoke without waiting to be called on. "Is that why you didn't invite him or Brit? So you could talk smack about Phillip behind his back? Because you should know I'm totally going to tell him everything you say."

"No, it's not that, and please don't tell him. In fact, I picked Gary's place for this meeting because I knew it was one place that neither he nor Brit would ever turn up on their own. There's no way either of them would ever come here without a damn good reason."

"Hey," Gary said, "That's hurtful."

"That doesn't mean it's not true. I wanted to talk to you all because I believe Phillip is in danger. He's been attacked twice now, and he won't take it seriously."

Gwen asked, "Why not?"

"He doesn't believe he's been attacked."

"They can't have been very vicious attacks then," Roy said.

"They weren't, but they're escalating. And I know who's behind it."

"Okay," Roy said. "That sounds serious. Tell us exactly what happened."

"Well, okay," Martin said. "The first time, there was a knock on the door. When Phillip opened it, there was nobody there, but some kids were walking away with a package that was meant for him, and I saw someone lurking in the shadows across the street."

Gwen said, "I remember that. That was last night."

"So you can back him up on this?" Roy asked.

"No," Gwen said flatly. "I didn't see any of that stuff. I just remember him arguing with Phillip about it. Wasn't the guy across the street some wearing a *Star Wars* costume?"

"Phillip said he looked like a Jawa, but he didn't even see the guy." Martin flapped his hands away as if shooing off a bee. "Okay, fine.

Yeah. I admit that one's not very convincing. But just now, in Atlantis, I saw the same guy, and he definitely attacked Phillip."

"Okay," Roy said. "What did he do?"

You know the kids' game Mouse Trap? He made a real-life version of that to trap Phillip."

"So, he's captured Phillip?" Gwen asked.

"No."

"So it didn't work."

"No, it worked. The cage came down on him, but he was able to get out really easily. Then I chased the guy. He had a head like a goblin. I'm pretty sure it was a mask. That, or he's just real ugly. Anyway, he sicced a flock of birds on me."

Tyler turned to Gwen. "Man, when you two are fighting he really goes off the rails, doesn't he?"

Gwen said, "Martin, if you really believe that Phillip is in danger, shouldn't you be talking to him?"

"I did. He doesn't believe me. But just say I'm right, and Phillip is being attacked. They're subtle and nonlethal attacks, but he's being attacked, nonetheless, by a magic user. I met him. Look at what he did to my robe."

"Yeah," Gwen said. "I noticed. And I'm not going to fix that for you."

"I didn't ask. Bigger fish to fry. While the attacks haven't been dangerous yet that we know of, do we want to wait around and see if that changes?"

Tyler held up a finger to stop Martin. "Let me see if I understand. You're saying that a shadowy figure has attacked Phillip twice, in ways that are so subtle and indirect that he doesn't recognize them as attacks, even after you pointed them out to him. Is that the gist of it?"

"Yes."

"And what do you want from us?"

Martin looked at the others as if they'd lost their minds. "To help me stop it."

"Stop what?!" Roy asked. "The almost nothing that probably isn't happening? It seems like you should be able to handle that yourself. We're not the ones to help with this anyway. If Phillip's the one in danger, he's the one you should be talking to. And if he won't listen, Brit the Younger would be the next logical choice."

"Yeah, but I already talked to Phillip, and all he did was mock me. If I go to Brit the Younger, what's she going to do? First thing is she'll tell Phillip, then they'll both mock me."

"So you came to us so *we* could mock you?" Gary asked.

"No. I came to you because I hoped, foolishly, that at least one of you might want to help me."

"I'll help you," Gwen said.

"Really?"

"Oh, yeah. I'll give you the best kind of help there is. A suggestion."

"That's the best kind of help?"

"Yes, from my point of view, because it lets me feel like I did something without putting out much effort. Anyway, I suggest that you're a time traveler. Use that to your advantage. Go forward in time and ask some future version of Phillip who was attacking him, and why. If it turns out he was in danger, he'll be happy to tell you so you can come back and save him. If he isn't in danger, future him will get a good laugh out of it. Either way, you'll have helped him."

Martin started to respond, but stopped short when the wizards all heard shouting at the outer door that opened from Gary's antechamber with its large stone altar to the mouth of Skull Gullet Cave.

Gary called out, "Hubert?"

Hubert hustled in from the entrance and bowed deeply. "Master, I am sorry."

"What is it?"

"People to speak to you, Master. I told them to go away, but they refused."

"What do they want?"

"I'd much rather they told you."

Gary crossed through his antechamber, and all of the other wizards followed. Three young men from the village were standing outside the ornately carved stone door. One was a hog mucker, another was a fish gutter, and the third was a hide scraper at the local tannery. Martin didn't know any of their names, but he recognized their smells.

"What can I do for you?" Gary asked.

All three of the young men fell to their knees. The hide scraper pleaded, "Train us, oh Master, like you're training Hubert!"

Gary pinched the bridge of his nose. "Hubert, didn't I order you not to tell anybody about our arrangement?"

"Yes, Master. You did."

"And did you tell anybody?"

"I might have mentioned it to someone, Master."

"And by might have, you mean . . ."

"I definitely did, Master."

"And by someone, you mean . . ."

"Them, Master." Hubert pointed at the three men on their knees, beseeching Gary to train them.

"So you definitely told these three men about our arrangement after I ordered you not to."

"I wouldn't say that, Master."

"But it's true."

"Oh, yes."

10.

Phillip teleported home from Brit the Elder's, his heart heavy with woe, and his brain buzzing with problems. He materialized outside the door of Brit the Younger's apartment. Her living space connected to his despite the tremendous distance and time differentials that separated them, and he thought of her apartment in Atlantis, the building that held his office, and his hut on the outskirts of Leadchurch as one large dwelling.

Phillip reckoned he'd left Brit the Younger's nearly two hours earlier, a long time to be gone for a walk. Brit would definitely ask him where he'd been, and while he fully intended to tell her, he wanted to do it on his terms. He needed to grease the skids, ease into it, then tell Brit the Younger, his Brit, everything. But he had to make it clear that she must keep her distance. She couldn't interact with Brit the Elder until everything was resolved, because it might just cause the entire universe to crash. He had reason to hope she would be fine with that. She didn't like Brit the Elder anyway.

Phillip did some quick mental math and a rough Esperanto translation, then said, "*Reiru unu duonan horon.*"

Phillip seemed to remain stationary, but the sun, the shadows, and the people milling around on the street outside all changed. He took a final quiet moment to prepare himself, then, technically only thirty minutes after he left, Phillip entered the apartment.

He found Brit the Younger exactly where he'd left her, curled up in her favorite reading chair.

She glanced up from her book and smiled. "You weren't gone long."

"Uh, no, I suppose I wasn't. How's the book?"

"Interesting, but Capoeira isn't exactly what I hoped it would be."

Nik leaned out from the kitchen. "Phillip, do you have the chicken?"

Phillip moaned and rolled his eyes at his own stupidity. "I'm sorry, I forgot your chicken. I'll pop out and get you one in just a moment."

Nik said, "Oh, don't worry about it. I need to go get a few other things anyway."

"Oh. Good. Still, sorry about that, Nik."

"I forgive you."

"Thank you," Phillip said, then after a long pause, he turned back to Brit the Younger. "Look, I'd like to talk to you about something."

"Been doing some thinking, eh? Fine." Brit closed her book, placed it on her lap, and looked up at Phillip, still smiling.

Phillip said, "It's about Brit the Elder."

"Oh." Brit's smile withered and died. She picked the book back up, opened it, and returned to reading. "I don't want to talk about her," she said, quietly, almost as if to herself.

Phillip said, "I know she's not your favorite person."

Brit the Younger snorted. "Not my favorite person? When I'm in a great mood, and she's just done something nice for me, she's not my favorite person. Right now she's pretty close to my least favorite. Even when she decides to be helpful, she does it in the least helpful way possible, then acts like she's some kind of saint for it. You know how when we were off fighting the dragons, she helped Louiza with the wounded?"

"Yes. I thought that was quite kind of her. For someone with no medical training to jump in and help Atlantis's only trained doctor deal with the flood of injuries from a dragon attack, I'd say that's commendable."

"That was. What was less commendable is that she refused to tell me how she helped, so when I'm her, I'll have to figure it out for myself. And she talked Louiza into not telling me either. Then she had the gall to come in here, into *my* home, to gloat about the fact that she wasn't going to tell me. And to top it all off, just because she thought it was fun, she decided to mess with me a little bit, pretending to remember something wrong, just to give me a moment of hope that I might not turn into her someday, all so she could have the fun of snatching that hope away."

Phillip stood, looking down at Brit the Younger, stunned into silence by the unexpected ferocity of her response.

"Wait a second," Brit said, rising to her feet and dropping her book to the floor. "Did she contact you?"

"No. She hasn't." Phillip noted that, strictly speaking, this was not a lie.

"Good! Because If I thought, even for one second, that she was somehow interfering in our relationship, I'd have to go track her down and give her a few choice pieces of my mind."

"Uh, do you mean a few choice words? Or a piece of my mind? You sort of combined the two."

"Yeah, because I'm mad enough to do both at the same time. Seriously, Phillip. Tell me if she's bothering you. I'd love an excuse to go over there."

Phillip remembered Brit the Elder's warning that any direct interaction between herself and Brit the Younger could hasten, or, indeed, *cause* the destruction of the entire universe as they knew it.

Phillip put what he desperately hoped was a calming hand on Brit the Younger's shoulder. "No, Brit, there's no need to do that. She hasn't contacted me."

Brit took a moment to calm herself. "Sorry I got so worked up. It's just, Phillip, you're the one thing I have that she doesn't. Our relationship is kind of the only thing that's really mine. If she did something that messed it up for me, I don't know what I'd do."

"I understand."

"Good. So, you wanted to discuss Brit the Elder. What's on your mind?"

"Just that I think it might be for the best if we both avoid her for a while."

Brit the Younger smiled. "Fine by me. What brought that on?"

"Just that . . . while I was on my walk, I realized how much happier you are when you don't have to deal with her."

Brit picked her book up off the floor and returned to her chair. "Good call. I agree to your plan of avoiding my least favorite person. That's a very good idea, Phillip. I find that a nice walk can be a good chance to think."

"Yes," Phillip said. "I suspect I'll be taking a lot more walks in the future."

Martin stood in the séance room of his workspace in Medieval London: a large square room with velvet draped walls, decorated with four large statues in each corner of the room, facing inward. If one of the locals came looking for Martin's wizardly help, he would identify the four statues as "the old gods and the new," but anyone from Martin's time would easily recognize them as Optimus Prime, Boba Fett, Grimace, and The Stig.

Martin opened the small silver box that disguised the Android smartphone he used to run macros and manipulate the file. He picked a time about six months into the future and ran a search. When he found Phillip's location, he initiated travel through both time and space.

Martin got the momentary impression of being in a smallish, darkish room with one other person, but only for a fraction of a second. Before his eyes could even adjust to the new light level, he transported again, this time against his will and with no control over the destination.

He found himself standing alone among rows and rows of theater seats, their wooden bottoms folded upward. Martin looked around the room, but saw nobody else on the main floor. The balcony and luxury boxes above also seemed empty. The stage curtains were drawn shut. Martin appeared to have the theater to himself.

Two powerful spotlights turned on with a mechanical ka-chunk. Brilliant white cones of light shone down from the upper reaches of the theater, illuminating two seemingly random portions of the stage curtain. Martin heard the sound of pulleys turning and ropes stretching. The curtains separated, receding to the sides of the stage with surprising speed, revealing two figures in full tuxedos, complete with top hat, tails, and white-tipped walking sticks.

"Oh, Lord," Martin moaned.

"Yes," one of the gentlemen said, spreading his arms wide. "I am forced to surmise, from your emotional exaltation, that you have come to the stunning realization that you are to be the lone witness to a private performance by those magnificent magicians, those preeminent prestidigitators, those accomplished alliterators, yours truly, the Sensational Sid, and my cooperative counterpart, the Great Gilbert."

Gilbert waved. "Hi, Martin."

Martin said, "Guys, can we just—"

Sid brought the ivory tip of his walking stick down onto the stage floor with a loud bang. "Please, out of respect for the dignity of the performance, we ask that you hold all questions and comments for the end of the show, when I promise they will be disregarded in due course. Now, at long last and at great personal expense, we present to you a special trick, custom designed for the occasion, entitled *Phillip's Personal Message to Martin, on the Occasion of Martin's Leap to the Future to Discuss Possible Danger to Phillip's Well-Being, Posed by What Appears to be an Angry Jawa.*"

Gilbert said, "We spent a lot more time designing the illusion than we did thinking of a snappy name."

"Indeed," Sid said. "And that surplus of effort on the one will show as vibrantly as the lack of effort about the other, I assure you."

Martin glared at the both of them, but folded down a seat and settled in to watch the performance.

From somewhere offstage, Martin heard what sounded like a small, poorly rehearsed band playing "The Final Countdown" by Europe.

Martin shouted, "*Arrested Development.* Very nice."

Gilbert smiled and tipped his top hat.

Two assistants wearing hooded black velvet robes and white porcelain masks to obscure their faces came out on stage. One pushed a large steamer trunk on wheels. The other pulled a fifteen-foot-wide red curtain, hanging from a wheeled frame.

With much unnecessary rhythmic arm waving, one assistant opened the trunk. The other reached into the trunk and produced two more robes, which Gilbert and Sid put on in a needlessly dance-y manner, whipping them around as much as possible in the process. The assistant then handed them two masks, the same as the white ones the assistants wore, except that Sid's was bright red and Gilbert's bright blue. The two magicians threw their hats and canes off into the wings, put up their hoods, and the trick began in earnest.

Gilbert, in the blue mask, stepped into the open trunk and knelt down while Sid, in the red mask, pushed the lid closed, sealing him in. Sid wrapped the trunk with a chain, which he fastened with a cartoonishly large padlock.

One assistant spun the trunk, while the other pulled the rolling curtain in front of it, blocking Martin's view. Sid and the two white-masked assistants pranced rhythmically in a circle around the rolling curtain and the hidden trunk for a few bars.

The two assistants moved the rolling curtain off to the side, then they both sprinted into the wings and out of sight. In the center of the stage, Sid, in his red mask and hooded cloak, waved his hands over the trunk. The lid of the trunk shook, then opened a crack, straining against the chain. A pair of hands worked their way out through the gap, holding two thin metal implements, and began working on picking the lock. Sid ran to the rear of the stage and darted behind the rolling curtain.

As the padlock sprung open and fell to the floor, the curtain also fell, revealing that Sid had vanished. The trunk sprang open and Sid stood up from inside, having somehow transported from behind the screen into the trunk. Sid removed his red mask and hood, held his arms out wide, and turned around, revealing a message embroidered into the back of his robe.

Martin—

You're embarrassing yourself. Just drop it.

—Phillip

From behind him, Martin heard a voice say, "Good bit of advice there, I reckon." Martin turned to see Gilbert sitting in the next row back, looking exaggeratedly relaxed, reclining with his feet kicked up on the back of the seat next to Martin.

"Uh-huh," Martin said, without enthusiasm. "Did you think this whole thing was going to impress me? You realize I can teleport from place to place, too."

"Yeah," Gilbert said. "But the impressive bit is that we didn't. What you just saw was all illusion. No actual magic involved."

"None?"

"None," Sid said. "All misdirection and a trick padlock. We run an honest magic show, using the traditional methods of deception and trickery."

"That's right," Gilbert said. "Instead of cheating the audience by using real magic, like some people we could name." He lightly kicked Martin in the shoulder for emphasis.

"I don't do a magic show."

"Yet," Gilbert said.

"Whatever. So I assume Phillip put you up to all this."

Sid nodded. "Correct."

"And he didn't give you any information, other than that I should drop it?"

"And that you're embarrassing yourself," Gilbert added, "which we could have seen for ourselves."

"Fine. I'll just have to go find Phillip somewhere . . . and some*when* else, and talk to him there." Martin stood up, pulled his ornate silver box out of his pocket, opened it, jabbed his finger angrily at the screen of his smartphone, and disappeared.

Five seconds later, Martin reappeared in the exact spot he'd just left. "Damn it!"

Sid smiled broadly. "Yes! Phillip's set up a macro that will redirect you here if you try to contact him in the future. Now, if you'll just turn your back for a second, we'll reset the trick and do it again."

Martin glared at Sid, poked a few more times at his smartphone, and disappeared.

After fifteen seconds of waiting, Gilbert said, "I think he's gone for good this time."

One of the two assistants walked out onto the stage from the wings. He pulled off his mask, revealing that he was a teenage boy with sandy-brown hair.

The crumpled mass of the rolling curtain shifted seemingly on its own, then slid to the side as a trapdoor hinged open and the other assistant, now wearing a red mask, climbed out. She removed the red mask, the white mask underneath it, and her hood. She looked close to the same age as the boy, and bore an undeniable family resemblance, although she sported a thick mass of wavy jet-black hair.

"So that was him," Sid said. "What did you think?"

"He was so young," the girl said.

"And angry," the boy added. "Really angry."

Sid nodded. "Indeed. I'm sure he's mellowed with age. Most men do."

The boy said, "They get wiser, and stop letting things bother them?"

"No," Gilbert said. "Things bother them more. It's just they don't have the energy to act on it like they used to."

11.

Phillip leaned around the door frame into Brit the Younger's bedroom in a manner he had designed and mentally rehearsed to appear casual and spur of the moment. "Hey, I'm going to go for a walk."

Brit the Younger turned away from her yellowed original Macintosh computer and looked toward Phillip. "Okay."

Phillip's eyes narrowed. "Okay?"

"Yeah," Brit said, turning back to her computer. "Okay. Whatever. Hey, before you go . . ."

"Yes?"

"Can you think of an example of a way that people write down and communicate a series of physical movements so that they can teach them to another person?"

"What, you mean like dance choreography?"

"Yeah, that's the example I came up with. I also thought of drills and square dancing, but those are still kinds of dance. I'm just wondering if there's a better fit. Can you think of another?"

Phillip thought for a moment. "I guess musical notation would fit that description. The musicians have to do the same things at the same time every time."

"Yeah. That's not bad. It's still music based, but interesting. Thanks. Have fun."

"What?"

"On your walk. Have fun."

Phillip shrugged. "Okay."

Phillip walked through the living room, where Nik was doing the dusting.

Phillip said, "I'm just popping out for a quick walk. Need me to grab a chicken for you? I promise, I'll do it this time."

"I told you, don't worry about the chicken, Phillip. It wasn't a problem. If you like, you could get me some butter."

"Butter. Done."

Phillip stepped out the door.

Martin watched as Phillip emerged from Brit the Younger's front door, looking distracted and in a hurry.

Preoccupied as he was, Phillip didn't notice the unusually light foot traffic. He had the entire section of path completely to himself. Phillip also failed to notice the fact that while it was a beautiful cloudless day, there was a dark shadow directly over him, blotting out the sun and growing larger. Had he noticed the shadow, he might have looked up and seen the large black trapezoid streaking down out of the sky directly toward him.

The dark mass fell silently, then came to an instant stop thirty feet above Phillip's head. He remained oblivious, walked down the path, stepped into a blind alley between two buildings, then teleported away.

Martin stood motionless on the roof of a nearby building, his staff outstretched, projecting the force field holding the object in midair. He twirled the staff in tiny circles, causing the object to spin. As it did, Martin saw writing engraved into one side that said *16 TONS*.

Martin looked around and saw only one other person present, lurking in the alley between two buildings across the way. Luckily, it was the person Martin was hoping to find.

"Pants dried out, I trust," Martin said.

The goblin stepped out of the shadows, looked up at Martin, and lowered his hood, revealing his bald head, pointed ears, and inhumanly sharp teeth. "I assume so. I took them off rather than letting them dry on me."

"I hear doing that with jeans makes them fit better."

"I was wearing slacks."

"A goblin in slacks?"

"Eh, dress for the job you want, not the one you have. I see you haven't repaired your robe after my feathered friends used you as a seed bell."

"Yeah, I kind of like it this way," Martin said. "It feels more broken in. So, look, about this sixteen-ton weight you just tried to drop on Phillip. I gotta say, I'm not happy with you about it, although you do score some points for the Monty Python reference."

"Thanks. I considered going with a giant foot, but I found the little fart sound distasteful."

Martin nodded and flicked his staff upward. The sixteen-ton weight flew back up into the sky, disappearing over the city's edge and splashing down in the ocean. "I sort of expected you to stick with the board-game motif. I worried we'd find Phillip dead with a wishbone-shaped hole in his sternum and a glowing, buzzing nose."

"I'm not trying to kill him, Martin. I don't want to kill anybody. That's why I blocked this section of the path off today, so there'd be no bystanders. We both know Phillip's invulnerable. The only danger your friend is in is danger of getting distracted. That's what I'm trying to do, and in the end I'd be doing him a favor."

"If that's true, tell me what you're distracting him from. If you're telling the truth, maybe I can help."

"No, Martin, I have to handle this on my own."

The goblin started waving his arms in the same showy manner he had when he made the ravens attack Martin. "I'm not accomplishing anything standing here arguing with you, so—"

Martin thrust the head of his staff toward the goblin and said, "*Pika pulvoro*," cutting him off midsentence. A sparkling white light radiated from the bust of Santo at the top of Martin's staff, illuminating the goblin. He stopped swinging his arms, stood still for half a second, then let out a high, anguished moan, and started furiously scratching himself. "What did you do?"

Martin smiled. "I learned from our last encounter. I decided to forget embarrassment as a weapon and start using discomfort. You're the first person to experience my new itch ray. Now, tell me what's going on or it's about to get real humid. I'm talkin' Florida-in-July humid."

"You're clever, Martin, but you forgot one thing."

"What?"

"Just because I'm itchy doesn't mean I can't do magic." The goblin whipped his arms around in a series of wide gestures, then went back to furiously scratching himself.

Martin heard a strange noise, more an assortment of noises that combined oddly. There was a base layer of scrabbling, scraping noises, with a counterpoint of squeaking, and a dull undertone of rustling, all of which got louder with each passing second. It was like a combination of the sound of nails on a chalkboard and two pieces of Styrofoam rubbing against each other. It seemed to come from below the building on which he was standing. As it grew louder, Martin couldn't help but step closer to the edge to see what was making the awful noise. He saw nothing on the ground below, but as he looked, a wave of brown and gray lumps poured over the roof's front edge and advanced toward him. His primitive instincts identified what they were well before he got a good look at them. They were rats. Hundreds of rats, surging toward him.

As the rats formed a swirling pool around his feet, Martin fought down the urge to flee and indulged his urge to talk smack.

"You just gonna try swarming me with different animals until something works? Not a great plan."

"I agree," the goblin said. "Luckily, that's not what I'm doing."

"Really? That's what it looks like from here."

"Is it? Then why haven't the rats climbed up your legs yet?"

Martin looked down at the rats, which, as the goblin said, had yet to make any effort to climb onto him. Instead, they remained in a writhing heap, crowded all around his feet, their wiry pink tails stuck in the air as they gnawed on the surface beneath them.

The roof on which Martin was standing gave way, weakened by the chewing and broken by the combined weight of him and the rats. As he fell into the shop beneath, he had only a fraction of a second to register that the Atlanteans inside already stood on any furniture they could as a swirling circle of rodents gnawed at the floor.

Martin landed on the rats, crashed through the floor, and fell to another pool of rats below. He broke through that floor, landed on more rats, crashed through again, landed on more rats, crashed through again, and finally came to a rest where Atlantis's solid diamond outer wall finally curved inward enough for him and the rats to land on it and slide to a stop.

Martin sat, growling for a second, then held his staff out above him and flew straight up, through all of the holes he'd just created, until he erupted back out into the open air, a cloud of rats flying in all directions. He flew through the air in a graceful arc, landing in front of the goblin with enough force to crack the paving stones beneath his feet.

"Oh, you're back," the goblin said. "I probably should have just split, but I kinda wanted to see the look on your face. Anyway, you were gone just long enough for me to call a friend."

Far above the city, up in the sky, Martin heard an eardrum-shattering shriek.

Martin looked up and saw an eagle. At first he thought the eagle was quite close to him, but then he realized it only looked close because it was the size of a small airplane. It almost seemed to flap its wings in slow motion as it descended, still screeching at an ear-splitting volume. As it drew near, it thrust out talons, each the size of a small child wielding kitchen knives, beckoning for a hug.

Martin hunched down, held his staff above him with one arm, and produced a hemispherical force field he hoped would keep him safe. He squeezed his eyes shut and waited for the attack. He heard the screeching and felt the subsonic beating of the giant wings draw closer, sail directly overhead, then recede, as if the bird had merely passed over him. He opened his eyes to follow the immense eagle and watched as it gently plucked the goblin up in its talons before climbing back into the sky.

The goblin smiled broadly and waved at Martin, shouting, "You thought the eagle was here for you? Jeez, self-absorbed much?"

Just seconds before, Martin had been cowering, dreading the giant eagle's attack. Now Martin took off, flying after the eagle, trying to catch up as quickly as possible. As he gained, he kept his eyes on the goblin clinging to the eagle's claws, nothing but blue sky and the sea behind him, looking at Martin with a mixture of amusement and confusion on his face, still scratching the small of his back with his free hand.

As Martin drew within shouting range, the goblin asked, "How long is this itching going to last?"

"An hour or so."

"Why? What do you think it accomplishes? It didn't stop me from doing anything."

"Not yet, but you'll think twice about messing with me again knowing that there's an hour of itching in it for you."

"I wasn't messing with you to begin with!"

"You were messing with Phillip. Anyone who messes with Phillip gets messed with by me."

The goblin laughed.

"I know," Martin said, "passive voice. I'm working off the top of my head here."

The goblin kept laughing. "It's not that. Bad style is the least of what's making you sound stupid right now."

"Whatever. Hey, if you can do magic, and you wanted to get away, why not just teleport out? Why mess around with the whole giant eagle thing?"

"Showmanship is very important. But if it's all wasted on you . . ."

Martin shouted, "No, wait," but it was too late. The goblin teleported away. The giant eagle faded out of existence, leaving Martin flying alone. He slowed to a stop, hovered in empty space above the Mediterranean Sea, then teleported himself back to Atlantis.

12.

Phillip materialized in Brit the Elder's home and found her sitting at the exact same Macintosh he'd left Brit the Younger sitting at before, although now it was an even darker shade of yellow.

"How are your feet?"

"The same, and it's spread up my calves."

"Sorry to hear that. Look, I'm happy to help you," Phillip said, "but I must say, I really don't like lying to Brit about it."

"It's only lying if you tell her something that's not true. I suggest you don't tell her anything at all unless she asks."

"So you want me to act aloof and mysterious?"

"Is it worse than being dishonest?"

"Either way, if she ever finds out that I'm sneaking around behind her back, especially to go meet with you, I'm afraid it'll be the end of my relationship."

Brit the Elder stood up. "I know. I've given that some thought. We need to move our activities somewhere other than Atlantis. Even though we're staying holed up in my home, there's still too much of a chance that we'll slip up and tip our hand. We need to go somewhere there are resources and people who can help us, but where nobody would think to look for us."

"I assume you have a place in mind?"

"Of course. Come along. I'll show you." Brit the Elder put her left hand on Phillip's shoulder, then, with her right, swiped through several menus in a floating interface that only she could see and made a selection.

Brit the Elder's home faded away, replaced by a single unkempt room. Unpainted, unplastered Sheetrock lined the walls, and thin, well-worn carpeting covered what felt like a concrete slab floor with no carpet padding. In one corner, two folding lawn chairs flanked a card table with a bent leg. The opposite corner was filled with a set of bunk beds made from unfinished two-by-fours and sheets of splintery plywood. Phillip inhaled, and instantly regretted it. He reeled as his lungs struggled to separate what usable oxygen they could from the combined aromas of pipe smoke, fish guts, and stale body odor.

"Where are we?" he gasped.

"A hunting shack in Alaska, 1984." She had to speak up to be heard over the wind rushing through the forest outside.

Phillip ran to the window, but all he saw through it were trees and snow. He opened the window, hoping to get some fresh air, which he did. Fresh, freezing cold air. The offensive smell of the cabin flushed out of his nasal cavity, replaced by the searing pain of an instant brain freeze. He tried to slam the window closed, but the ancient and ill-maintained sash jammed in the frame and only came unstuck with great effort.

Brit the Elder said, "I bought the shack and all of the land in a ten-mile radius from two guys who called themselves Pinky and Spud. I put up force fields so that nobody can get anywhere near here, even if they had any reason to want to, which they don't."

Once he'd wrestled the window closed, Phillip inhaled again, grimacing. He looked around the interior of the shack a second time. "When you said we were going somewhere with resources, this isn't what I pictured."

"This isn't our final destination, just a way station. We're going to the year 2018."

"I can't," Phillip said. "I'm from 1986, and we can only travel forward in time as far as the latest point we've already been to."

"Yes. I know. Please come here."

Phillip stepped away from the window toward the middle of the room. "The only way to go any further ahead is to go back to your original time and let history flow forward on its own. That's why we aren't all visiting the future all the time."

Brit the Elder said, "Yes, I know all of that. We all know that. We know it so well that we never bother to question it, or try to think of a way around it."

"A way around it? Like what?"

Brit smiled. "Like this." She placed a hand on Phillip's forehead and swiped her other hand through a floating menu only she could see.

Brit the Elder disappeared before Phillip's eyes, but he barely noticed. The sound of the weather and the forest outside rose sharply in pitch, climbing out of audible range and into a zone on the edge of his perception, where he experienced them as a sort of tickling deep in his ear canals instead of as sounds.

The light coming in through the windows stuttered and strobed, almost like a steady beat, but with flashes of differing intensities and durations. They came so quickly, almost heaping on top of each other in an unpredictable manner, that Phillip feared they might cause some sort of seizure, if he wasn't having one already.

Every inch of Phillip's skin tingled. He felt as if he was burning, or freezing, or both, in rapid succession, over and over again. The feeling would have been overwhelming on its own, blotting out all capacity for thought. When combined with the assaults on his eyes and ears as well, it was a set of sensations that went beyond the mere pleasant or unpleasant. He was incapable of processing the experience. His brain could only note it, and hope to make sense of it at some other time. Later, he would describe it as being like the stargate sequence from *2001: A Space Odyssey*, only much faster and not stupefyingly boring.

The entire ordeal took ten seconds, then it was over. Phillip blinked at the steady stream of grayish light coming in the window. He noted that the wind seemed quieter than it had before. He removed his hands from his ears, and the sound grew a bit louder.

He became aware that he was standing on his left foot with his right leg drawn up toward his chest. Both of his arms were pulled in to his sides, and his shoulders were hunched over in a sort of full-body cringe.

Phillip was most grateful that his skin seemed back to normal. He looked at the backs of his hands and found them obscured by a thick layer of dust, and draped with multiple layers of cobwebs.

Phillip shrieked, jumped, flapped his arms, and hopped around the room, flailing his every extremity in an attempt to shake off as much of the dust and as many of the spiderwebs as possible. After two high-speed laps of the room, he stopped, instead hopping in place and brushing the mess off of his limbs as fast as he could until he finally stood, panting and still filthy, in a cloud of the discarded debris that floated in the still air, much of which just settled back on him anyway.

Brit the Elder appeared in the center of the room, where she'd been before Phillip's brief ordeal. "Welcome to the year 2018. As you may have figured out, I slowed down your perception of time so that thirty-four years passed in what felt to you like ten seconds."

Phillip looked at her with an expression of mingled anger and betrayal, but he could only manage to make a sort of plaintive moan.

Brit the Elder nodded and looked at the floor. "Yes, I know. The experience is surprisingly traumatic, isn't it? I'm sorry about that. I went through the same thing when I had to leap from my time, 1996, to now. Lord knows what all I missed. I can tell you, jumping from 1984 like you did, you missed *Tiny Toons*, *Animaniacs*, and *Freakazoid*."

"Coulda warned me," Phillip grunted.

"Phillip, dear, do you really think anticipating that would have made it any more pleasant?"

"You could have sent me in my sleep."

"And you really believe you would have slept through it? You'd have woken up, terrified. No, this was the best way. And it's over now. You're in the future. We can move on to our actual destination." She reached out to take Phillip's arm, then, looking at the dust and tattered cobwebs covering his sleeve, thought better of it. She touched him gingerly with one finger and initiated another teleport.

The flat, gray light and musty air of the hunting shack gave way to the fluorescent light and overly conditioned air of a public servant's office. Phillip blinked repeatedly as he saw Brit the Elder, still standing beside him, and another Brit standing in front of the desk in a sharp, exquisitely tailored black pants suit.

"Phillip," Brit the Much Elder said. "Hey! Welcome! Good to see you!" She took a moment to look Phillip over from head to toe, then turned to Brit the Elder and said, "Though I wish I were seeing him a little cleaner."

"He was much dirtier than this before," Brit the Elder said. "He was literally standing in a cloud, like Pigpen."

Phillip said, "I'm sorry. I don't think we've been introduced. I mean, I know we've met, in a sense. You're Brit, obviously, but you're not Brit the Elder, and you're not Brit the Younger."

Brit the Much Elder's smile recharged, but she shook her head. "I *am* Brit the Younger. And I'm Brit the Elder. We're all the same, like, you know, the same person, even if you don't want to admit it. But in a way, you're right. I'm not your Brit the Younger. I can't be. She doesn't know anything about any of this. Does she? Phillip, please tell me you haven't told her about any of this!"

"I haven't! I promise. But, I have to say, I wasn't happy about it before, and I'm even less so now that I see you both. I mean, you tell me that I can't tell her because she's another you, and it turns out you already told another you."

Brit the Elder said, "Yes, but that just makes it all the more dangerous for you to tell a third of me."

Phillip shook his head. "I don't like lying to her."

"We know," Brit the Much Elder said. "And we don't like the idea of you lying to her either. We are both her, after all. But, if it's any consolation, we've forgiven you."

"Yes," Brit the Elder said. "Now, I think it'd be a good idea if we showed Phillip to our workspace."

"Yeah, I think so," Brit the Much Elder said. "See you there."

Brit the Elder disappeared.

Brit the Much Elder started for the door, then paused, looking at Phillip. "We're about to go out in front of people from the twenty-first century. The wizard getup might freak them out a bit."

Phillip removed his dusty, cobweb-covered robe and hat, and draped them over the back of a chair. He leaned his staff against the side of the desk as well, and turned to face Brit the Much Elder in what he usually wore under his robe: his Union Jack sneakers, a pair of jeans, and a black T-shirt bearing a picture of a dark red customized hot-rod and the words *ZZ Top, Eliminator*. He looked down at himself and asked, "Will this work?"

Brit the Much Elder smiled. "Sure. Every girl's crazy about a sharp-dressed man. Shall we?" She opened the door and beckoned Phillip to follow her.

The instant they left her office and entered the view of her underlings, Brit the Much Elder's entire demeanor changed. She took on an air of frosty competence, as if she would judge you for the slightest error, and would do a much more professional, efficient job of judging you than anyone else could.

They walked past a desk where a man in his late twenties wearing an inexpensive suit that fit poorly in all the wrong places said, "Director Ryan, you have an appointment in ten minutes. Should I tell them you'll be delayed?"

She didn't bother to look back as she answered. "No, Robbins. I should be back well before then."

They entered a large rectangular room with a small forest of pillars seemingly supporting the low acoustic-tile ceiling and fluorescent lights. Cubicle walls chopped the space up into a grid. The communal sound of people shuffling papers, muttering softly, and generally trying to be quiet filled the air.

"What do you do here?" Phillip asked.

"I run a task force for the Department of Justice. We monitor and investigate all of the various cases that the FBI, the CIA, and various state and local law enforcement agencies deem too inexplicable, unlikely, or just plain stupid for them to sully their hands with. Aliens, Bigfoot sightings," she turned and arched an eyebrow at Phillip, "reports of people with magical powers, claims of time travelers, that sort of thing."

"How'd you get this job?" Phillip asked, trying to hide the genuine interest and enthusiasm in his voice. As the person in charge of investigating magic and time travel, she was in a perfect position to prevent the exposure of people like her.

"I worked my way up, then volunteered for this posting. Most of the other bureaucrats at my level consider this place career suicide. They don't like the idea of having their résumé include several years spent trying to prove the unprovable. I wanted the job, though. I have an affinity for this stuff, as you might imagine. Unfortunately, we've yet to come up with any concrete evidence to prove anything, because, as we know, magic and time travel don't exist." She turned and winked at Phillip.

Before Phillip could respond, a woman in a beige business suit approached and matched speed with Brit the Much Elder. "Director Ryan, thank you for talking to them personally, but my field team still wants to move on their target."

Brit the Much Elder shook her head. "I know they do. I've spoken to them personally about it."

"Sorry, ma'am."

"Not your fault, Saunders. You tell them that we'll contact them if their orders change. Until that happens, they're to hold tight and just observe. I know that the subject played them for fools, and they want payback, but just because they made a mistake before, that doesn't mean they should be hasty and make another mistake now."

"Yes, ma'am. Do you want me to tell them the part about them getting played for fools and making mistakes?"

"If you're talking to Miller, yes. If it's Murphy, be kinder about it. That poor man puts up with enough as it is."

"Yes, ma'am." The woman in the beige suit sped away.

Brit the Much Elder glanced back at Phillip again. "Sorry about that. Business. You understand. Anyway, I've set you up a workspace in a vacant office right over here." She held a door open and directed Phillip to enter.

Inside, Phillip found two desks, two beat-up rolling office chairs, and two equally beat-up office-grade PC workstations.

Brit the Much Elder closed and locked the office door behind herself. A few seconds later Brit the Elder materialized, wearing her UGG boots and the same crisp black suit Brit the Much Elder had on.

"You look very nice," Brit the Much Elder said.

"I'm not surprised you think so," Brit the Elder replied.

"When did you borrow my suit?"

"Yesterday."

"Of course . . . wait, I had it laundered last week. That means . . . Ew! I'm wearing your dirty clothes."

"That's right."

Brit the Much Elder shuddered in revulsion. "I know we're the same person, but still, ew."

Brit the Elder said, "Yeah, I feel the same way."

"Yeah, I know. Okay, I've got a meeting in five, then I'm going home to take a long bath. You two should be fine here. I'm locking the door and I have the only key, so you won't be disturbed. Brit, if someone does get a glimpse of you, just snarl at them until they run for it." With that, Brit the Much Elder disappeared.

"So," Phillip asked. "What are we going to do?"

"Exactly what she said. Research, to start with. The Atlantis Interface keeps a record of any time someone uses it to perform magic. I've downloaded the last twenty years' worth of logs. Millions of lines of it. The task force has access to some advanced search tools. You are going to use those tools to look for anything that might be an anomaly, anything that looks like part of the glitch, or might have caused it."

"Okay. And you?"

Brit the Elder said, "I'll be going through every daily journal entry Brit the Younger has written up until this point, looking for any clues as to what went wrong and when."

Phillip blinked at Brit the Elder. "Brit the Younger keeps a journal?"

"Religiously."

"Is it . . . detailed?"

"Obsessively."

"She never told me."

"Obviously."

"Does she talk about me in them?"

"Extensively."

Well then, if, uh, if there are that many journal entries, maybe it would be faster if we both go through the journals. Then if we don't find anything, we can move on to the logs."

"No, I'll handle the journals. You'll stick to the logs. When you're done with the last twenty years, I'll give you the twenty before."

"But, I just think it'd be better if we both look through the journals. I might see something you don't."

"Maybe," Brit the Elder said, "but you'd see everything that's written in the journals, and none of us want that."

"I do."

"I wasn't talking about you. When I said us, I meant me and the other two Brits."

13.

Miller sat in a different rental car, parked in the same parking spot, glaring sideways at the entrance of the Luxurious Rothschild Building across the street.

The building was directly in front of him. He needed to look at it sideways because he'd resorted to exhaling directly out of the open driver's-side window to keep the windshield from completely fogging over. The plan worked, in that the driver's side of the windshield had only partially fogged over.

The passenger-side door opened, and his partner Murphy slid into the car, shaking his head. He tossed a banana back over his shoulder. It landed on a pile of bananas that covered most of the back seat. Swapping out the rental agency's cheapest, most run-down car for their second cheapest, second most run-down car did nothing to stem the banana tide. Murphy had started checking the exhaust pipe every ten minutes or so, and found a new one there every time he checked. Miller suspected that the bananas replaced themselves a minute or two after one was removed, and told Murphy as much, but Murphy still insisted on checking, trying to see how many bananas he could collect by the end of the day.

Murphy said, "At least we won't be hurting for snacks."

Miller glared at him.

"Seriously, though," Murphy said, picking his laptop up from the car's floor and placing it in his lap. "We should swing by a homeless shelter at some point and donate all these bananas. Some good might as well come of this."

"Really? You think anybody'd want to eat our magic tailpipe bananas?"

"Not if we call them that."

Miller shook his head. "Why won't they let us move in? Sadler's a known fugitive. It's not like we're going to learn anything from watching him. He's obviously onto us. He's not going to show us anything he doesn't want us to see. This is pointless."

"Probably they figure that if we move in, he'll just get away, and then we'll have to track him down again. But if you and I keep watching him, and he keeps messing with us, at least we still know where he is."

"Yeah," Miller said. "That's probably it."

"I think so."

"It's completely unfair to us. And insulting."

"That's why it rings so true."

Miller leaned forward, his eyes wide and his mouth contorted into what an observer might have mistaken for a smile. In fact, he was baring his teeth. "He's on the move."

Murphy squinted through the windshield, but his side was fogged in completely. He gave up, said, "Fine, I'll go get the banana," and again stepped out of the car.

Miller watched, almost salivating, as Jimmy Sadler made small talk with the doorman. Instead of his usual dark sport coat and khakis, Jimmy wore a red nylon windbreaker with an ad for someplace called Sporto's Tavern and Slot Emporium silk-screened on the back. He and the doorman shared a laugh, then Jimmy stepped out onto the sidewalk, and instead of turning left to go to the parking lot, turned right and started walking down the street.

Murphy stepped back into the car. "There wasn't a new one yet. We're good to go, if we must."

"We must," Miller said, starting the car. He turned on the left-turn indicator and started frantically head checking, looking for any opportunity to get across the near lane of traffic and into the far lane, in the same direction as Jimmy.

"What are you doing?" Murphy asked, peering through a clear spot he'd wiped in the condensation on the windshield. "Why the left?"

"He didn't go to his car. I think he's trying to throw us off. That's why he's dressed so weird."

"I see what you mean about the outfit, but we don't know yet if he's going to the car or not."

"What, you think he's going to walk all the way around the block?"

"Miller, what are you talking about? He's walking toward his car."

Miller kept his eyes glued to Jimmy, who was still walking away from the building in the opposite direction from the parking lot. "I'm looking at him right here, and he's not anywhere near his car."

"No," Murphy said, "you're looking at the wrong guy. I've got him, and he's not walking very fast, but he's headed toward the parking lot. Here, look."

Miller whipped his head to the left and the right, looking for holes in the traffic in both directions and trying to keep an eye on Jimmy. "No, Murph, I gotta drive the car and keep track of Sadler. Will you please get with the program? He's almost to the corner."

"No, he's almost to the parking lot, and he's acting weird. I'm not taking my eyes off of him."

Miller thought he saw a hole in the far lane. As he swiveled his head to look at the oncoming traffic, his eyes cast over a figure wearing a denim jacket, flannel shirt, and skinny jeans in a slightly different shade of denim than the jacket. Miller did a double take, but on the second look he couldn't deny it was Jimmy.

He looked back to the first person he'd thought was Jimmy, and saw Jimmy, wearing his tavern jacket and lighting a cigarette as he waited for the light to change. He was sure it was Jimmy. He looked back to the guy in the Canadian tuxedo, and was convinced that it was also Jimmy.

Murphy said, "What the hell? There's uh, there's another Jimmy."

"Yeah," Miller said. "The one I saw."

"No, further down. A third Jimmy."

Jimmy came strutting up the sidewalk wearing a puffy green insulated vest and cargo pants. He and the Jimmy in the denim nodded hello as they passed each other.

Miller gasped. "What the hell?"

The car sputtered and died. Neither of the agents cared.

As the Jimmy in the puffy vest walked past the condo building entrance, the door opened. The doorman stepped out. Despite being several inches shorter and fifty pounds heavier than Jimmy, he had Jimmy's face. He held the door open. A young woman pushing a stroller stepped out. She wore a sweater dress, leggings, and a scarf, and had Jimmy's face, complete with his hair and chin beard. She and the doorman with Jimmy's face smiled broadly as they made small talk, then the woman reached into the stroller and pulled out a baby with Jimmy's face for the doorman with Jimmy's face to coo at.

Miller and Murphy watched this, their faces slack with awe and disgust.

Miller became aware of someone standing just outside his rolled-down driver's-side window. He turned to see a girl, he'd have guessed about twelve years old, in a puffy pink jacket and a T-shirt with a picture of a unicorn on it. Her blonde hair was held in twin ponytails with plastic, rainbow-colored barrettes, and she had Jimmy's face.

"Mister," she said in her little-girl voice. She held up a soot-stained banana. "Looks like you fell for the banana in the tailpipe."

14.

Phillip appeared in the blind alley near Brit the Younger's apartment. He stood motionless for a moment, his shoulders slumped, his staff hanging low, clutched by fingers that barely bothered to support its weight. He put out a hand to steady himself against the nearest wall.

Nine hours, he thought. Hunched over a computer, searching the logs. Ever since I discovered magic, I don't think I've done anything for nine straight hours except sleep.

He pushed off from the wall and slumped his way out into the main thoroughfare until he stopped and used a hand to brace himself against the frame of Brit the Younger's door.

Now remember, to her, only twenty minutes have passed, and you've just been out for a nice, invigorating walk.

Phillip groaned and opened the door. He strode into the apartment, smiling. "Hello Brit! I'm back."

Brit the Younger said, "Hey," without looking up from her book, which appeared to be a textbook with a picture of two ballerinas on the cover.

Phillip settled into a chair opposite her.

"I've been thinking," Brit said. "We should get out of the house today. Go do some sightseeing."

"Yeah? Where do you want to go?"

"Maybe Las Vegas in 1971. See a show. Catch a boxing match. Use magic to cheat at craps. Maybe, if we're lucky, catch a glimpse of Hunter S. Thompson—I know you'd like that."

Phillip said, "Sounds good. If you don't mind, I think I'll go take a quick nap first."

"It's not even eleven yet."

Phillip got up and stepped toward the two rustic wooden doors set, side by side, into the clean, crystalline expanse of Brit's living room wall. "Yeah, I know."

"That must've been some walk."

"Yeah, there was a headwind. Kidding. I didn't sleep well last night. Just a half-hour cat nap, and I'll be ready to go."

Nik breezed into the room, stopping short when he saw Phillip. "Well, look who's back. Did you enjoy your walk?"

"Yes, Nik, I did, thanks."

Nik stared expectantly at Phillip. He glanced down at Phillip's empty hands. He looked around the room, an expression of confusion on his face.

Phillip groaned, "Oh, the butter! Nik, I'm so sorry, I forgot your butter. I'm such a fool! I'll go get it right now; is a pound enough?"

Nik laughed. "Oh, Phillip, don't worry about it. We have enough for tonight. Having some extra would have been nice, but I can make do until I go out tomorrow."

"Oh. Good. Still, I'm sorry, Nik. Again."

"Don't worry about it, Phillip. We all forget things." Nik went back to the kitchen, although less energetically than he'd come out.

Phillip looked at Brit, who smiled. "He understands. Go take your nap. You clearly need it."

Phillip passed through the door and emerged in his hut in the Medieval English town of Leadchurch. He heard the door click shut behind him, then collapsed onto the bed, an eighties-vintage high-end mattress magically disguised to look like a sack filled with straw.

———◈◈———

Phillip awoke after seven hours of not very restful sleep. He remembered a very long dream about sitting at a computer, poring over logs, looking for anything unusual. He knew that he was hardly the only person who sometimes dreamt about the very thing he was sleeping to recuperate from, but he still found it terribly unfair when he woke up.

Phillip traveled back in time six and a half hours. He looked down at the sleeping form of his past self. He felt a pang of envy for a moment, until he remembered that at that very moment the poor bastard was probably dreaming about staring at a computer monitor.

He rejoined Brit, refreshed after his quick catnap. The two of them spent the rest of that day and that night seeing the sights of Nixon-era Las Vegas. As they came home, exhausted, Phillip told Brit that she had now seen the best that the early 1970s had to offer, and Brit said that based on that, she agreed with Phillip's assessment that most of that time period, right up until *Star Wars* was released, had been a waste of time.

They both slept solidly through the night, but Phillip was haunted by dreams of poring over logs on a computer that was set up in the middle of a blackjack table while a game was in progress. His work was slowed by computer crashes, and an argument with a player who split a pair of fours.

The next morning, as the sun crested the rim of Atlantis and foot traffic was just beginning to heat up, Martin stood on the roof of a nearby house and watched as Phillip emerged from the front door of Brit the Younger's apartment.

"Just a quick walk," Phillip almost sang as he backed out onto the street. "You're sure you don't need anything? I'll get it this time, I swear . . . Okay."

As Phillip closed the door, his shoulders and his smile sagged instantly. He walked down the street, his head held low, muttering to himself. "Spent all day in Vegas in the seventies. Ruffles everywhere. Paid good money to have Don Rickles call me a hockey puck. Never understood American humor."

He shuffled along, eyes never rising above the ground five yards in front of him, lost in his own thoughts. He took no notice when a large bucket of honey some thoughtless person had left teetering on the edge of a terrace above tipped and fell over directly above him. The honey and the bucket would have covered him in sticky ooze and possibly left him blinded, with a bucket on his head, if they hadn't hit the force field Martin had created just below the ledge, hanging in midair as if sitting in a transparent bowl.

Phillip shuffled on, oblivious, as only a few steps later, a large pillow-like burlap bag, also left precariously on the edge of the next terrace up, spontaneously ripped along its seam, unleashing a thick, dry clump of downy white feathers. It fell with surprising speed, staying together in one mass with only minimal feather loss until it also hit an invisible force field only a yard above Phillip's bowed head.

The clump of feathers burst on impact, spreading into a swirling cloud contained in a spherical force bubble, like a snow globe.

Still, Phillip did not notice.

"Shrimp cocktail," he muttered. "Canned shrimp and cocktail sauce from a jar. No wonder it only cost fifty cents. Still a total rip-off."

He plodded past a man attempting to move a large barrel. As Phillip passed by, the man lost control of the barrel, which tipped over. The contents, which appeared to be several cubic feet of ball bearings, sloshed forward, but stopped at the barrel's opening as if crashing into a glass lid. The barrel's owner seemed confused by this. Grateful, but confused.

Phillip took no notice of that, either.

"She spent an hour after the floor show talking to that choreographer. Don't know why. That wasn't dancing, walking around topless while wearing giant hats."

Just before Phillip reached the alley he'd taken to using as a covert teleportation spot, he passed a plank of wood leaning against a wall. The plank flopped down, seemingly of its own accord, and a fox sprung out of a hole the plank had concealed.

The fox skidded to a stop directly in front of Phillip, who leapt back in surprise. The fox looked up at Phillip, spun around twice to examine its surroundings, then streaked off down the path and out of sight.

Phillip shrugged and stepped into the alley. A moment later, he'd vanished.

Martin scanned the rooftops and corners, fearing his target had already fled. Something caught Martin's eye, some bit of movement that seemed out of place. He focused in and saw what he was looking for: the goblin who'd been harassing Phillip, standing on a rooftop, head shaking, shoulders hunched, looking directly at Martin. The goblin waved hello.

Martin hurled his beanbag at the goblin with all his might. The goblin slapped it away before it struck his chest. Martin said "*Bamf*" a moment too late, and took the beanbag's place just after it had been batted away. Martin flew backward out of control, tripped, tumbled, and came to a rest on his side. As he wallowed on the ground, trying to get back to his feet, his still badly damaged robe shed hundreds of sequins that fell to the ground in a shower of glittering debris. He cast his eyes around the path and found that the pedestrians had scattered and vanished, as they always seemed to do as soon as there was any sign of trouble between two wizards. He knew they were watching, but from a safe distance, and hidden behind or under any cover they could find.

The goblin pushed back his hood, revealing his unnaturally long nose, pointed ears, and misshapen bald head. "Good work, Martin.

You once again foiled my attempt to distract Phillip. You have no idea what you're doing."

Martin picked himself up. "I know exactly what I'm doing. I'm keeping you from covering my friend with honey and feathers, then tripping him with marbles."

"But you missed the fox."

"Yeah," Martin said. "Good thing it was a dud."

"Well, if you hadn't foiled the honey and the feathers, it would have been a different story. The fox's natural predatory instincts toward chickens was a major component of the plan."

"Huh. I almost wish I hadn't interfered."

"So do I," the goblin said. "Why are you working so hard to keep me from distracting Phillip? I think it's pretty clear that I'm not trying to hurt him."

"You're trying to meddle in his life without him knowing. I can't imagine you're up to any good."

"But Martin, by stopping me, you're meddling in his life without him knowing. Are you up to no good?"

"I tried to get him involved, but he didn't believe me. And I'm trying to protect him."

"That's admirable," the goblin said, "but now the question is, who will protect you?" The goblin threw his arms out wide and bellowed, "*Expecto Patronum!*"

Martin saw a blinding white flash, which gave way to a persistent blinding white light, which weakened and gave way to a blindingly bright glowing white moose.

Martin watched, fascinated, as the moose stepped forward, its great glowing head held high, its shimmering antlers extending proudly, and its glistening tongue licking its sparkling lips, leaving behind a thick film of viscous, twinkling saliva.

Martin said, "You have kind of an animal theme, don't you? You're like Aquaman, only instead of talking to fish, you talk to animals. You're like Landman."

"Dr. Doolittle would be a more apt comparison."

"Yeah, I guess. So, you called up a glow-in-the-dark moose. Great. I like the Harry Potter reference, but what's it going to do, attack me with its moose powers?"

The goblin smiled. "Yes!"

The moose let out a mighty bellow. It sounded hollow, distant, ghostly. The sound gave Martin chills.

The moose galloped up to Martin, stood up on its hind legs, and with its front hooves, started raining blows down on Martin from above. The moose worked its front legs as if it was pedaling a bicycle, but with each stroke, its hooves struck Martin.

He used his arms and staff to repel the blows as best he could, and stepped backward in an attempt to get away. The moose advanced, balancing awkwardly on its rear legs, occasionally touching down with the front legs to regain its balance before rearing up again and continuing its barrage of undignified front kicks, while bellowing in fear and rage.

Martin did his best to evade the angry glowing moose, backing away, blinded by the intensity of the attack, but he found escape impossible. After ten or so seconds of struggle, which felt like a lifetime, Martin said, "Okay, screw this." He tossed his beanbag as far as he could down the path behind the moose, said "*Bamf,*" and disappeared.

From his new position thirty yards away, he used his magic to lift the moose into the air. It hung there, legs and tongue thrashing wildly. Martin pushed the moose out into empty space, over the edge of the terrace, then lowered it to the next level down. Many citizens still crowded the lower level, trying to see what was going on above, but as the moose lowered to their level, they scattered.

He maneuvered the animal under the floating bucket of honey. He released the spell that kept the honey suspended, allowing it, and the now-empty bucket, to fall on the furiously thrashing moose.

Martin pushed the moose forward into the hovering sphere of floating feathers. The beast's churning legs disturbed the air, causing the honey to spread and the feathers to swirl more turbulently. After just a few seconds, Martin lowered the moose, now completely covered with a sickly-looking coating of feathers, to the ground.

The instant the moose's hooves touched a solid surface, it leapt, then ran in a tight circle, then spun in place twice, bellowing, as if asking if anyone wanted a piece of him. No sooner had the moose stopped its thrashing then it started leaping again, as the fox that had failed to attack Phillip streaked into view and started nipping at the moose's heels.

"Huh," Martin said. "It would have worked."

"Of course it would have," the goblin said. "The only flaw in the plan is that you're involved."

Martin flew forward, landing only a few feet in front of the goblin. "Okay. My turn. *Fantomoj de la pasinteco!*"

A thick, dark vapor streamed out of the head of Martin's staff and swirled around him and the goblin, blocking their view of the outside world. Distant voices, unmistakably human and just as unmistakably morose, filled the air, loud enough that one could not ignore the noise, but far too distant and indistinct to make out a single word. It was like the background noise from the world's least enjoyable cocktail party.

The gas swirled faster and more violently. Currents and vortices formed in the rapidly flowing surface, then congealed into the forms of faces that floated above the goblin, looking down, speaking in stern, paternal voices.

"You've never been good enough"

"I can only hide so much disappointment."

"Why can't you be more like your siblings, cousins, or more successful classmates?"

"What is this?" the goblin asked.

Martin smiled viciously. "We established I can embarrass a magic user, and I can make a magic user uncomfortable. Now I'm using emotional warfare to do both!"

The faces grew more numerous, surrounding the goblin. Their voices grew louder and came at an accelerating rate, creating a seemingly infinite chorus of both adults and children.

"Aw, did you wet the bed again? It's okay. You're still little."

"Your team's got last pick, so you're stuck with him."

"Show the note you were passing to the class! Oh, she checked *no*!"

"I expected you'd stop wetting the bed by the seventh grade!"

"Got dumped, eh? She was always too good for you."

"So you didn't get into your first choice of university. We have a fine community college."

"I'm not looking for a relationship right now. Or a casual thing. Or another friend."

"So you didn't get into your first-choice community college. There's still your safety."

"I didn't expect my boyfriend to be wetting the bed when I moved in with him!"

Martin heard a high-pitched shriek that was not part of the spell. He turned and saw the goblin, eyes agape, hands over his ears, mouth wide open, screeching like an air-raid siren. The goblin turned and took off running, cutting through the swirling mist and emerging into the clean air beyond, still screaming incoherently.

Martin followed, the mist dissipating behind him. He held his staff out in front of him and shouted, *"Gluu la ŝuojn."*

The goblin came to an abrupt halt, his scream ending as he fell forward, arms swirling like pinwheels. The soles of his feet remained in contact with the ground as he bent forward at the waist and caught himself with his outstretched arms. His feet seemed rooted in place, so he remained in this position, hands and feet pressed to the ground, his posterior the highest point of his body, for several seconds, grunting and swearing and trying to push off of the ground with his hands hard enough to become upright once again.

Once he finally stood up again, the goblin used his arms to pull on his right calf as hard as he could. His foot didn't budge. He turned his head to look at Martin, his eye full of accusation and dread. "That's really messed up," he said. "You just don't lay a thing like that on a guy! I didn't wet the bed."

"Well, I don't really know that, do I?" Martin said. "But even if you didn't, you were afraid you might."

The goblin said, "Yeah, I'm noticing a urine motif in your work. You should maybe talk to a therapist about that." He tugged on his calf again, then reached down, untied his shoes, and took off running, leaving a now-empty pair of canvas high-top sneakers decorated in the pattern of the United Kingdom's flag.

Martin blinked at the shoes, and looked at the back of the wizard as he ran the inefficient, high-kneed stride of a man with tender feet and no shoes.

"Phillip!" he shouted.

The goblin stopped running, shook his head, and turned, slump shouldered, to face Martin. He brought his hands up to his throat and clenched them as if he were gripping his own skin, then moved both hands up over his face in the same motion one might use to remove a rubber mask. The green skin and fearsome features of the goblin disappeared, replaced by Phillip's familiar face and sky-blue robe.

The two stared at each other for a long moment, then Phillip asked, "Can I have my shoes back?"

Martin released the spell. Phillip walked carefully back to where the sneakers sat. As he drew closer, Martin saw that Phillip's beard was substantially bushier than when Martin had last seen him, with less care taken to shave the neck and cheekbones. His hair also seemed longer and stringier, and there were noticeable bags under his eyes. His robe was wrinkled and marred by numerous stains.

"Geez, Phillip, you look like hell."

Phillip sneered at Martin's tattered robe. "Yeah, we can't all live up to your sartorial standard. It's good to see you, too, by the way."

"You're from the future, aren't you?"

"Oh, well done, Martin." Phillip sat on the ground to put on his shoes. "You got it on the first guess. Of course, you had a fifty-fifty chance. I had to be either Past Phillip or Future Phillip, because if Right Now Phillip wanted to stop himself from doing something right now, all he'd have to do is not do it."

"You haven't gotten any less confusing over time, I see."

"Nothing does."

"That's why you had Gilbert and Sid tell me to drop it. It wasn't because I was embarrassing myself. It was because you're the one who was attacking Phillip all along!"

"Well, yes," Future Phillip said. "I vaguely remembered you mentioning a couple of times that you thought someone was messing with me back when I was . . . him. It was only after I saw that gormless, alarmed look on your face the other night when my package got stolen by those kids that I put two and two together."

"HA! That package was for Phillip! I knew it!"

"Yes, Martin, you knew it. You don't have to tell me that. The fact that you knew it is the whole problem."

"So what was in the package? Was it a bomb?"

Phillip stood up and beat some of the dust out of his much-abused robe, thus getting it on his hands. "What? No! I'm not trying to hurt him. He's me, after all. Why don't you understand that? Deliberately injuring your past self is seldom a good idea, though right now I'd be happy to watch you try it. It was a boxed set of every episode of a TV show I love called *The Prisoner*."

"I know of it. He already has that set."

"No, he has an earlier set that was made while the show's creator was still alive. It has a documentary where all of his costars talk about what a gentleman and a visionary he was. The one I tried to give him was made after the creator dies, and the documentary's full of interviews with the same costars saying he was a bastard who was in over his head and took it out on them."

Martin furrowed his brow in concentration. "So wait, you remember me mentioning that I thought someone was messing with you, so you remember the package and Mouse Trap, but you didn't remember that none of it worked, or that I caught you?"

"Yes, well, I had a lot on my mind at the time, and frankly, some weird events and you talking crazy didn't make that big an impression on me. I put up with both of those things all the time. And as for you catching me, I have no memory of it. Clearly you never tell me about it. Doesn't seem like you're a very trustworthy friend, are you, Martin? Keeping secrets from me like this?"

"But once you remembered that none of this crap worked, why stick with it? Hell, why even try it to begin with? You knew it would fail."

"I knew that it failed the first time. That doesn't mean that it couldn't work this time. If I made it all more inexplicable, and impossible to miss, I thought there was a good chance it might work. Our destinies aren't written in stone. Even though we're time travelers, remembering the past doesn't mean we can predict the future."

"Phillip, we aren't going to have this argument again."

"You can't know that."

Martin started to argue, but looked up at the haggard face of his friend, and instead asked, "What's the deal, Phillip? What are you trying to accomplish?"

"Look, I'm . . . he . . . Current Phillip, the Phillip you just stopped me from tarring, feathering, and foxing . . . is about to make a horrendous mistake. A mistake that leads to something awful happening. I'm trying to prevent that."

"By attacking him with chicken feathers?"

"By distracting him and giving him time to think. Or maybe by just jostling him off of his current path. He's pretty mixed up right now, and is just sort of going from crisis to crisis without thinking about it. If I can just jolt him out of his stupor, I'm sure he'll think better of things. He's a smart man."

"Oh."

"A very smart man."

Martin nodded. "I see."

"Exceedingly practical, and wise beyond his years."

"Really?" Martin asked. "Given the situation, you're going to keep gushing about your own intelligence after all these failed attempts to get your own attention?"

"Yes. Shut up. It isn't his fault, or mine. You keep interfering. He might have gotten to the door faster if you hadn't been talking to him about your girl problems. Or he might have noticed the mouse trap if you hadn't been pestering him about Gwen. And today would have worked if you hadn't been so hell-bent on foiling your imaginary attacker."

"He wasn't imaginary. He was you! Phillip, you sound like a crazy person. What happened to you?"

"I already told you, something terrible that I'm trying to prevent."

"Tell me what it is! Maybe I can help!"

"No, Martin, you're a good friend, and a man of many talents, but averting disaster isn't one of them. You aren't one of the Four Horsemen of the Apocalypse, but you might well be one of their stable boys. The best way you can help would be to stay out of my way."

"I can't do that."

"Look, we both want what's best for Phillip, because you're his friend, and I'm him. We've established that I won't ever do anything to actually hurt him. Wouldn't you agree?"

Martin thought for a moment and said, "Yes."

"Then I have a course of action I'd like to suggest."

"Okay," Martin said. "What is it?"

Future Phillip said, "This," and disappeared.

Martin moaned.

15.

Phillip and Brit the Elder sat in their windowless office, each hunched over their respective Dell econobox computers, poring over digital files.

They worked with the kind of zeal that only comes when you're doing something you find infinitely boring, and want to be done with it as soon as possible. For the last seven and a half hours, neither of them had stirred, except to make quick runs to the bathroom or the fridge (both of which were at Brit the Elder's home, to which they would teleport), nor had they said a word to each other except to ask if the other wanted anything from the fridge, but even that was relatively rare. They were both highly focused on the task at hand, and they knew that stopping to get or enjoy anything from the fridge would only lead to stopping again, and using the restroom, and as such was doubly inefficient.

Their concentration was such that Brit the Much Elder had to clear her throat twice to get them to notice when she arrived.

Phillip turned slowly in his chair and looked up at Brit the Much Elder. She wore her usual neatly pressed suit, an electronic tablet in her hand. He scrunched his eyes shut and rubbed them with the heels of his hands. "Oh. Hi. How are you?"

"Uh, I'm fine," Brit the Much Elder stammered, looking down at Phillip, and at the back of Brit the Elder's head, as she hadn't turned around, craned her neck, or in any way acknowledged that Brit the Much Elder had entered. "I just thought I'd drop in for a progress report."

"We don't work for you," Brit the Elder said, without looking away from her monitor.

Brit the Much Elder asked, "I'm sorry?"

"You should be. We don't work for you. So just popping in and demanding a report isn't cool, okay?"

Brit the Much Elder looked to Phillip for help. Instead, she got a quality demonstration of his blinking and shrugging skills.

Brit the Much Elder took a deep, calming breath and forced a smile onto her face. "You're right, of course. I didn't mean that as a command or anything. I'm just wondering how it's going in here, is all."

Phillip pointed to his computer. "I've only got just a little bit more of the logs left. It's taken two full work days, but it's almost done."

"Any clues?" Brit the Much Elder asked.

"Nothing." He nodded toward Brit the Elder. "She had to scan all of those pages before she could start searching in earnest, but she's also worked later the last two nights. Hey, Brit, how much longer do you figure it'll take?"

She didn't answer.

Phillip said, "I asked her that two hours ago. She said *five hours* then, so I figure it'll take her about three more hours."

Brit the Elder didn't lift her eyes from her screen or alter her body language in the slightest.

Brit the Much Elder looked at Brit the Elder's back and asked, "And have you found anything?"

Phillip said, "Last time I asked that, she said that if she'd found something, she'd have mentioned it, probably quite loudly, while rejoicing that she doesn't have to pore through the journals anymore."

"I see."

"Of course, it would help if we knew what we're actually looking for," Phillip said. "I mean, we're looking for the cause of her glitch, but we don't know what that is. We don't know if something caused her memory problem and that triggered the foot glitch, or if it was the other way around, or if they aren't even connected. The only reason we believe they are is that they both popped up at around the same time."

Brit the Much Elder nodded. "Yeah. I see your problem. And how is the glitching? Still getting worse?"

Brit the Elder kicked her left leg out and pulled up the pant leg of the dark red suit she'd stolen from Brit the Much Elder's closet. Her exposed calf vacillated at random between looking absolutely natural and looking like it was comprised of polygons.

Brit the Much Elder cringed. "That's not good. How far up does it go?"

Brit the Elder sagged visibly.

"Look," Brit the Much Elder said, "I'm not trying to bother you, but this all affects me, too."

Brit the Elder waved a hand dismissively, "Yes, of course it does. I'm not mad. I just want to get this done, you know? The glitching isn't up to my knees yet, but it is climbing. It's also spread to the wastepaper basket I'm using as a footrest. I plan to get rid of it and magic up a new one. Maybe if I keep running through footrests I can keep the glitch from spreading to the floor."

"Okay. Thanks for telling me. And Phillip, how are things with Brit the Younger?"

"Fine, as far as she knows. I, on the other hand, am miserable. I hate lying to her."

Brit the Elder said, "We understand that, Phillip, but I promise you'd hate the result of her learning that you're sneaking out to help me even more."

Brit the Much Elder snorted. "You'd be lucky if you got to explain yourself well enough to tell her you're just helping her. There's a good chance that Brit the Younger might just assume you two are having an affair. I know I probably would have."

Brit the Elder nodded emphatically. "Oh, me too! But would that even count as an affair, technically? I mean, I'm her. Sleeping with me now would just be sleeping with her later on."

"She'd never see it that way," Brit the Much Elder said. "At worst, she sees you as another person who gets on her nerves, and Phillip knows that. At best, she sees you, in a weird way, as Phillip's ex, because you used to date him, albeit in Phillip's present."

"But since we're not together anymore, anything Phillip wants to do should be fine. It wouldn't be cheating, just a post-relationship hookup with her, technically."

Phillip said, "I'll remember that argument, if she accuses me of anything."

Both Brit the Elder and Brit the Much Elder shouted, "No!"

Brit the Much Elder elaborated. "Phillip, if Brit the Younger accuses you of cheating on her, even if you're perfectly innocent, never try to defend yourself using any argument that has the word *technically* in it!"

"I'm not cheating on Brit," Phillip shouted. "I would never cheat on her with either of you, or both of you."

Brit the Much Elder said, "You'd never get the opportunity."

"Damn right," Brit the Elder agreed. "Never, ever."

"I didn't say you would. I didn't even bring the idea up. All I was saying was that I hate lying to her, even for the two of you."

Brit the Elder said, "We know, Phillip, and we appreciate it. Look at it this way, if she does find us out she might not break up with you over it. You know how she feels about me. If she found out you were sneaking off to see me, she'd probably blame me for it anyway."

"Yes, but I also know that the first thing she'd do is track you down and confront you and that, as you pointed out, would probably lead to a glitch that would end the world, so either way, my relationship would be over."

Brit the Much Elder said, "Okay, okay, this is getting a little heavy. Let's just turn back to business, shall we? Neither of you has found anything in the interface logs or in Brit the Younger's journals. What do you want to do next?"

Brit the Elder sighed. "If we don't find anything helpful in the records, and it looks like we won't, the next obvious move is to start looking at my entry in the file. Specifically, we need to find the parts that govern memory."

"I don't like it," Phillip said. "It seems terribly risky. We've never done much research into that part of the file out of fear that even the slightest mistake might irreparably hurt—or even kill—whoever we're looking at."

"Well, we wouldn't just go in and start changing things willy-nilly. We'd do research, plan our moves carefully, talk to other wizards about how to proceed."

Phillip thought for a moment. "We could bring in Louiza. A doctor's input might be helpful."

Brit the Elder said, "No, she tends to be pretty cautious. She'd probably try to talk us out of the whole idea."

"That's what I was hoping," Phillip muttered.

"No, we'd need someone who has experience in this area."

Phillip said, "I'm sorry, but like I said, nobody has any experience in this area. We've never looked at altering memories because it's just way too dangerous. We have too much regard for human life."

Brit the Much Elder smiled. "Phillip, you say *we've* never done much research, but that only means that nobody's ever done it while you were around."

Phillip considered this. "Hmm, no. I'm sorry, but no. I see your point, but none of the magic users I know of would ever be that reckless."

"Nobody?" Brit the Elder asked.

"Nobody."

"Nobody *ever*?"

"Well, I mean, I can only think of two who might fit the bill, and they're both dead, and I don't really like the idea of going back in time and asking that murderous little swine Todd for help."

Brit the Elder shook her head. "I'd never ask Todd for help."

Phillip grimaced. "That leaves the other one, and I don't really want to go back in time to talk to him at all."

Brit the Elder pulled up her electronic tablet and started swiping through files. "That's perfectly understandable. Luckily, we're not going to have to."

Phillip said, "Good."

"Time travel won't be necessary."

Phillip closed his eyes. "No."

"Yes." Brit the Much Elder turned to Brit the Elder. "Phillip doesn't know that Jimmy's still alive?"

Phillip said, "No!"

Brit the Elder said, "I thought it'd be easier to just let you break the news."

Brit the Much Elder said, "Easier for you, you mean."

Brit the Elder said, "Yes, that is what I mean."

Brit the Much Elder made a selection on the tablet. "That's pretty much the definition of shortsightedness. Yes, Phillip: James Sadler, aka Jimmy, aka Merlin, is alive and well."

Phillip shouted, "Noooooooooo!"

Brit the Much Elder said, "Definitely yes. This is a surveillance report by two of our operatives, filed just this morning." She turned her tablet around for Brit the Elder and Phillip. Brit the Elder leaned in to read, smiling.

Phillip leaned back and turned away, averting his gaze as if the tablet were the remains of a dead animal he'd found in his crawlspace.

"Are you sure it's really him?"

Brit the Elder snorted. "Is it typical for an agent to say things like, *the subject is a smug, smarmy bastard* in an official report?"

Phillip moaned. "It's really him."

16.

Martin held up his right hand and said, "*Komuniki kun* Gary."

Floating above Martin's hand, a hazy, bluish, semi-transparent image of a flaming human skull appeared, while he heard the sound of a phone ringing. After three rings there was a click, and Gary's voice said, "Yeah?"

"Hey, Gary. It's Martin. Look, I need to call another emergency meeting, and I need to do it at your place again. Cool?"

"Yeah. Cool."

"Great. Thanks, man."

"When are you gonna do it?"

"Right now. I sent out the notice just before I called you."

"Not cool."

"Yeah, well, you can tell me off when you get here."

"What do you mean, when I get there?"

Martin laughed. "I'm standing in your living room."

"*So* not cool!"

"Yeah. Where are you?"

"I'm uh, I'm out front, tending to some things. I'll be in in a minute or two."

"What's going on?"

Gary said, "Nothing. Don't worry about it. Like I said, I'll be in soon."

"Well, you're right out front. Maybe I can help." Martin opened the door to Gary's antechamber and immediately saw the problem. At the far end of the chamber, beyond the stone altar and laptop-hiding book, he saw Gary standing in front of the open door to the outside. Beside him, Hubert stood in his tuxedo jacket, looking ashamed. Beyond the door, he saw at least ten wretched, desperate-looking young men, all clamoring for Gary's attention.

Martin shouted, "There's more of them, Gary?"

"Word got out," Gary said.

"Yes," Hubert said. "I'm afraid I let slip that he made me his buster."

"Butler. Not buster. Butler, and I don't need any more! I told them they're out of luck, but they know I said the same thing to Hubert, and that he waited me out, so now they won't go away."

Martin nodded. "Yeah, I bet. It reminds me of feeding seagulls. You ever done that?"

"You mean the thing with the Alka-Seltzer? Does that work?"

"Good luck, Gary. I'll be in here. Come in when you can. We have something serious to discuss."

"Yeah, sure. Hubert, go with Martin and tend to the guests."

Martin and Hubert retreated to the inner apartment and closed the door.

Hubert said, "It sounded like the master wasn't happy."

Martin turned to face him. "Don't worry about it. He'll forget all about it when he hears what I have to say."

"Your news will make him that happy?"

"No, it'll make him even more unhappy, but about something other than your friends and my rudeness."

Hubert nodded. "I see. Well, in the meantime, can I bring you anything? Some refreshments, perhaps?"

"No thanks, Hubert. In fact, we're going to be discussing wizard business, so you can probably take the next hour or so off."

"Thank you." Hubert bowed and exited down the hall.

Martin was alone for only a few seconds before Gwen appeared, standing on the floor beside him. She cringed slightly, looking down at her feet, in case she had materialized in or under something nasty.

"Gwen," Martin said, "you can relax. I called the meeting, and I guaranteed there would be no pranks. You can trust me."

Gwen looked at Martin, inhaled through her nose, and said nothing.

"Oh," Martin said. "You're still mad at me? Look, all I said was that when I think about the future, I see the two of us together. Is that such a terrible thing?"

Gwen said, "I'm not mad. I'm uncomfortable. I'm not sure how to act. You told me you plan to marry me, but you didn't actually propose, so now if I stay with you, it's like we're engaged, but we aren't."

"Gwen, I don't know what you're talking about."

"Answer me this, then, Martin. Are we planning on getting married?"

"Yes!"

Gwen stared at him.

"But, uh, not really," Martin stammered. "Not officially. Not yet."

Gwen kept staring.

"But we are. Sort of." Martin deflated.

"See," Gwen said. "It's like you put us in this weird state of pre-marriage where we have all of the responsibility of a married couple without any of the benefits."

Martin said, "I told you what I think. That doesn't mean you're obligated to me. You can leave me if you want to. I'm sure there are plenty of guys rushing to sign up for a lifetime of this."

"Okay, now I *am* mad at you," Gwen said.

Tyler materialized, standing on solid ground with a big smile on his face. "I gotta tell you, it is a lot nicer to teleport when you know you're not going to land in anything unpleasant."

Martin and Gwen took a break from glaring at each other to glare at Tyler, who cringed, but wisely said nothing.

A few excruciating seconds later, Jeff and Roy appeared.

"Okay, kid. What is it?" Roy asked.

Martin said, "Just a second. Gary should be here soon."

"Why?" Roy asked. "Where is he?"

Gary entered through the door to the antechamber. "I'm here. I would have come out sooner, but I was enjoying listening to Gwen and Martin fight. It's a bummer that she doesn't want to marry you, Martin, but I don't blame her. I don't want to marry you either."

Martin clenched his jaw, turned away from Gary, and, slowly, as if each word was having to fight its way out through his teeth, said, "Now that we're all here, I have news. You remember the person I saw attacking Phillip?"

Gary said, "I thought you said he was a goblin."

"The person, who looks like a goblin, you all said I was imagining? I caught him."

Jeff's eyes grew wide. "You did?!"

"Yes."

Tyler raised a finger. "And you're sure you didn't imagine catching him?"

"Yes. Shut up."

Jeff said, "Okay, good. Glad you weren't going crazy, Martin. So, who was it?"

"Phillip."

"No, I mean who was messing with Phillip?"

"Phillip. Phillip was messing with Phillip. I caught someone messing with Phillip, and it was Phillip. Future Phillip."

Gwen shook her head.

Tyler looked both exasperated and sympathetic. "Martin, are you sure Phillip isn't jerking you around?"

"Yes! I mean, technically, he is, because it is Phillip who's been hiding from me, but that's Future Phillip. And he's doing it because he doesn't want me to stop him from messing with Present Phillip."

Jeff muttered, "Wouldn't our Phillip be Past Phillip, because we're in the past?"

Roy said, "Not to us."

Tyler asked, "In your previous job, you didn't run a lot of staff meetings, did you Martin?"

Gwen smirked at Tyler.

Jeff said, "Martin, if, as you say, Phillip from the future is attacking our Phillip, he had to have a reason. Did you ask him?"

"Yes. Of course I asked him."

"And what did he say?"

"He said that he's trying to prevent our Phillip from making some kind of mistake. A mistake that leads to some sort of tragedy or something."

Gary nodded. "Ah, so you've called us all together so we can help him."

"Uh, no. So you can help me stop him."

Gwen let out an amused snort. "Stop him from preventing a tragedy."

"I don't trust him."

"He's Phillip! You don't trust Phillip?"

"Of course I trust Phillip! I'm trying to protect Phillip!"

"From Phillip," Gwen said. "By trying to get all of us to attack Phillip! Why would we do that?"

"For Phillip," Martin offered. "Look, you didn't see Future Phillip. He was a mess, and he was acting squirrelly."

Roy said, "He's been through some sort of tragedy."

"Yeah," Gary said. "And he's got you, arguably his best friend, giving him a hard time."

"I don't like it," Martin said. "He's meddling in Phillip's life."

"And by stopping him, so are you," Tyler said. "Twice. Once from his point of view, and again from our Phillip's point of view."

Jeff said, "Not again, before. Our Phillip's earlier in the time stream, so for him, Martin's meddling is happening before it happens to Future Phillip."

"I'm not meddling!"

"No," Roy said. "You're just changing things about Phillip's life as you see fit."

"Against his will," Tyler said.

"And behind his back," Gary added. "At least, one of his backs."

"Yeah," Roy said. "With the other one you're openly preventing him from doing what he wants."

"Okay," Martin shouted. "So I'm meddling! I'm doing it for his own good. Isn't that what friends do?"

Jeff said, "In theory, absolutely not. In practice, yeah, usually."

"Great, so who's going to help me help Phillip?"

"By stopping Phillip," Tyler added.

"Yes."

After a long and painful silence, Roy said, "This is going to sound like a joke, but it ain't. You should ask Phillip to help."

"Which Phillip?" Gary asked.

"Any Phillip. Martin, if you get some version of Phillip to come in here and tell us that this other Phillip has to be stopped, we might be more inclined to join you."

Tyler asked, "How about it, Martin? Why not go to the future and talk to Phillip about it?"

"I tried that," Martin said.

"And?"

"He told me to drop it."

"He told you that?"

"Not personally. He had the message delivered in a magic act."

Roy shrugged. "Well, there's your answer."

Jeff nodded. "Your confusing, crazy-sounding answer."

Martin stewed for a moment, looking at the faces of his friends. "You all feel this way?"

They all made noises, head movements, or a combination of both that said Yeah, I guess, but we don't feel great about it.

"None of you are going to help me?"

Martin saw another barrage of grumbles and gestures.

"Fine," Martin said. "I'll just have to help Phillip, and stop . . . Phillip myself."

Gwen said, "Martin, don't do anything . . ."

Martin noticed that she'd trailed off. "What? Rash?"

"No," Gwen said. "You're gonna do something rash. We all know that. Just, don't do anything that can't be undone, okay?"

17.

Phillip pushed open the door and stepped from the warm sunlight of the Atlantean street into the relative cool dark of Brit the Younger's apartment. He called out, "Hello, Nik. We're back."

Nik yelled from the kitchen, "You were gone a while. Did you have a nice walk?"

Brit the Younger breezed in after Phillip. "Yes, we did. I'm so glad I decided to go along this time."

"Yes," Phillip said. "I couldn't be happier that you decided to join me at the last minute. Plus, you found so many interesting things to stop and look at."

"There's nothing better than a leisurely stroll. Especially on a day like today, when you don't have anywhere in particular that you need to be."

"Quite," Phillip said.

Nik poked his head out of the kitchen and saw a small parcel in Brit's hands. "Oh, Brit, you got the lamb I asked for!"

Brit held the package up for inspection. "Two pounds, as requested."

Nik took the package. "Thank you, Brit."

Phillip cleared his throat. "We both got you the lamb."

Nik smiled at him. "What? Oh, yes. I suppose you both did."

"Really," Phillip said. "I'm the one who brought it up as we walked past the butcher shop."

"I believe you. Thank you, too, Phillip." Nik winked at Brit as he walked into the kitchen with the lamb.

"I don't think he believed me," Phillip grumbled.

Brit gave him a squeeze. "Oh, Phillip, we just had a wonderful, long, leisurely walk. Don't let Nik's teasing spoil your good mood."

Phillip forced a smile and returned her hug. "You're right, of course. Say, I need to use the restroom."

Brit released her hug and looked at him a bit sideways. "Okay."

"So, I'm going to do that."

"Sounds wise."

"Okay then." Phillip walked toward the bathroom. As he opened the door, he glanced back at Brit, who had sat down in her chair and picked up a book. "I'll be right back," he said.

Brit laughed. "I'd hope so. You really need your staff?"

Phillip looked at the staff clenched in his hand. "Oh, uh, not really, but you know how it is. I sort of feel naked without it."

"It's a bathroom. You're supposed to feel naked in there."

Phillip laughed a little bit too hard. "Good point! Yes! Good point indeed!"

He stepped into the bathroom, still carrying his staff, and closed the door behind him. He grumbled, "I'll come along, she says. Here I wanted to get this over with and instead I spend an hour and fifteen minutes wandering around aimlessly looking at things and buying lamb, which I remembered on my own, thank you very much! At least she won't want to come along when I come in here. Bloody undignified. Just have to pop back in a realistic amount of time."

He stood up straight, took a deep breath, and said, "*Transporto al aparta loko.*"

In an instant he was standing in an opulently—if not tastefully—decorated hallway. Sconces shaped like giant glowing seashells cast light on wallpaper featuring a tight repeating trellis pattern in reflective silver on a sea of glossy black. Below, there was wall-to-wall carpet featuring aqua blobs and lime-green slashes. Above, there was a dingy cream-colored acoustic ceiling.

Brit the Elder stood in the hallway, looking tired but alert. She wore yet another coordinated pant suit she'd stolen from Brit the Much Elder's closet, this one jet-black with slightly flared cuffs and collar, for a vague Jackie Brown sort of vibe, which was ruined by a pair of light blue foam-rubber clogs.

Brit the Elder looked down at her feet and shrugged. Phillip knew that any shoes she wore would start glitching out in a few hours and need to be destroyed. He could only assume that she'd decided that if she was going to ruin something, it might as well be something cheap and ugly.

Phillip started to speak, but Brit the Elder held a finger to her lips and pointed down the hallway. The hall was lined with numbered doors that clearly led to various condos. A half-dozen doors down, the hall turned left, and Phillip heard unseen people locked in a tense conversation around that corner.

A man who managed to growl while nearly shouting said, "Sadler is dangerous in ways you can't imagine. Going in there alone is—"

A quieter male voice interrupted, "Unwise. Ma'am."

The first speaker said, "I was going to say stupid."

The quieter voice repeated, "Unwise."

A woman's voice, which Phillip immediately recognized as Brit the Much Elder's, said, "I have a feeling, working with you, your partner has become an expert in the unwise, Agent Miller. I appreciate your concern, and the passion with which you've expressed your reservations has changed my mind."

"Good."

"Instead of waiting here by the elevator, Agent Miller, you and Agent Murphy will wait downstairs in your car. Is that clear?"

Miller made some strangling noises deep in his throat.

Murphy said, "Crystal clear, ma'am."

"Good. Maybe you can spend the time cleaning it, or spraying some Glade or something. That back seat reeks of bananas."

"Yes, ma'am."

"On your way, then. Off you pop."

Miller said, "We'll have to wait for the elevator, ma'am."

"Nonsense. You're two healthy men. The stairs are right there."

Murphy said, "Yes, ma'am." Miller made a noise that could have been either agreement or the growl of a large animal.

A door clicked shut.

Brit the Much Elder walked around the corner, wearing the exact same suit as Brit the Elder—but with stylish black shoes. She shook her head.

"Stubborn, aren't they?" Brit the Elder asked.

"Yes," Jimmy said, "but they aren't wrong. I am dangerous."

Brit the Elder and Phillip turned to see James Sadler, aka Jimmy, aka Merlin, standing in the open door to his condo wearing black pants and a slightly faded black polo shirt.

"Or at least I would be," he said, "if you weren't all three just as powerful as me, Madam Director. Brit. Heck, if anyone here's dangerous, it's Phillip, judging by the look on his face."

"You're supposed to be dead," Phillip said.

Jimmy winced slightly. "You thought I was dead. That doesn't mean I was supposed to be dead."

"I never really believed you'd died."

"Yes, and it's perfectly understandable that you'd be so angry to be proved right. If you'd all please come in, it would be better not to have this conversation in the hall."

They entered Jimmy's condo, an eclectic mix of interesting, attractive furniture and dark, glossy finishes his decorator had picked to convey a clear impression that Jimmy had exquisite taste in decorators. One whole wall was made up of glass, much like Brit the Younger's home. Instead of providing a portal into the deep sea, Jimmy's windows looked out into open space—low-slung suburban sprawl, and bare brown mountains in the distance, both of which, despite their size and substance, just made the space look emptier.

Jimmy offered his guests a seat and a drink. The Brits accepted both offers, sitting side by side on a black leather couch built with just enough irregular curves to be both uncomfortable and expensive to manufacture. Phillip sat in an equally uncomfortable chair, but only glared sullenly at Jimmy as he puttered around the kitchen. After a moment, Jimmy handed Brit the Elder and Brit the Much Elder two cups of tea, served in cube-shaped black mugs.

Jimmy settled himself into a squarish black leather chair with a chrome framework of brushed stainless-steel supports. He sipped his own coffee, then addressed his guests. "I'm dying to know what I can do for you."

Phillip let out a small, rueful laugh.

"But before you tell me," Jimmy continued, "I'm sure Phillip has questions."

"You faked your death."

"Yes. That's not a question, really. I know you meant it as one, but even then it wasn't very open-ended. This is why some of your conversations feel so uncomfortable, Phillip. If I just answer the question as asked, the conversation stops dead, and we're left with an awkward pause until you ask your next question."

They sat in silence for a moment: Jimmy smiling, Phillip scowling. Both of the Brits sat looking at their cups of tea with their mouths pressed shut.

Jimmy said, "Like that one, just now."

Phillip growled, "Why did you fake your own death?"

"Better. Much better."

"Just answer the question!"

Jimmy sighed. "Phillip, I did it because it's honestly what I thought was best for everybody."

"You thought it was best for yourself!"

"Well, yeah," Jimmy sputtered, "in that I am included in everybody. If I weren't, I'd have said everybody else."

Brit the Elder said, "You're just deliberately baiting him."

"Of course," Jimmy said. "He's sitting here openly wishing I was dead. He deserves some grief. Besides, treating him this way proves a point."

"What, that you're awful?" Phillip asked.

"Phillip. You're acting all wounded, but in reality I did you a favor. You didn't want me around. You didn't like having me around. Just looking at me irritates you. After what I did, none of you were ever going to really like me again, no matter what I did, and you certainly weren't going to trust me."

Phillip thrust a finger at Jimmy and shouted, "I agree with both of those statements!"

Jimmy raised his coffee mug to Phillip. "Cheers. But that was the problem. You didn't want me around because you didn't like me, but you couldn't let me out of your sight, because you didn't trust me. You had three options. You could keep me around, which you didn't want to do. You could send me away, which you didn't want to do. Or you could kill me, which you didn't want to do. I saw that having me around was making you all unhappy. If I had just escaped, you'd have just tracked me down. So, I had to make you think I was dead, or else you never would have relaxed until you'd found me, and there'd have been no point in leaving to begin with."

Phillip didn't so much smile as bare his teeth. "So you're saying that because we didn't trust you, you had to lie to us."

"Essentially, but that shouldn't imply blame, nor that I think there's wrongdoing on your part. After what I did, I don't blame you one bit for not wanting to have me around, or not wanting to let me out of your sight, and I think it speaks well of you that none of you wanted to kill me. Look, Phillip, I did awful things that I can never undo or make up for. All I can do is try to live the best life I can from now on, and do my best to prevent anyone from making the mistakes I made."

Phillip stared at Jimmy for a long moment, then looked away in disgust. "I'm going to have to think about this."

"I know the feeling," Jimmy said. "I think about it every day. So, now that we've got all that settled, what brings you here?"

Brit the Elder said, "We're going to be digging around in the deep code of a human being, like you did, and we want your help."

Jimmy blinked several times. "Brit, I don't know if you were listening, but I literally just said that I intend to prevent anyone from making the mistakes I made. Monkeying with other people's code was one of the biggest mistakes."

"We're going to do it for a totally different reason."

"Shooting yourself in the foot has the same effect whether you do it to get out of the army or to kill a mosquito on your shoe."

"We don't have a choice."

"Of course you have a choice."

"We don't. We have a serious problem, Jimmy, and if we don't get to the bottom of it, the results could be catastrophic."

"The results could be catastrophic?" Jimmy turned to Phillip. "They're talking to me about catastrophic results?"

Phillip shrugged.

Jimmy looked directly into Brit the Elder's eyes. "I killed a town. A town. Every man, woman, and child in an entire town, dead, because I was monkeying around in people's code and made a mistake. There's no way I'm ever going to do that again."

Brit the Much Elder said, "We're not going to ask you to make any changes to anyone's code. We're just going to explore the code to see if we can figure out exactly what's going on and hopefully find a safe way to fix it. We were hoping you could share with us anything you learned, to help guide us. And we're not going to be looking at the code of any large groups of people. Our explorations will be restricted to one person."

"Who?"

Brit the Elder said, "Me."

Jimmy looked at Brit the Elder, then at Brit the Much Elder, then at Phillip, who shook his head. Jimmy turned back to Brit the Elder. "You?"

"Yes."

"You are literally the only person I know of who isn't just one person. I've got two of you sitting here on my couch right now! Who knows how many more of you there are?"

"I know of at least one," Phillip said.

"But we won't be doing this to her," Brit the Elder said.

"Yet," Phillip muttered.

Brit the Elder kicked off one of her shoes, raised her leg up in front of Jimmy's face, and let him watch as her foot phased between its normal and low-polygon versions.

"See?" she asked. "See why we're willing to risk it? I've got an error, and it's getting worse. There's no way to know when it'll get so bad that my file gets permanently corrupted, or the whole program crashes. We need to get this fixed, for everybody's good, and you're the only person we know of who's ever dug that deep into a living person's code."

Jimmy leaned back in his chair and thought for several seconds.

Brit the Elder pulled her shoe back on. "Will you help us, or not?"

"You've put me in a tough spot. Whether or not I help you monkey with your file listing, it will probably end badly. What part do you want to explore?"

"The part of the file listing that deals with memory. Do you know anything about it?"

"I do."

"Good!"

"No, it's not. It's a minefield that's been planted inside your own brain. And now, if I refuse to help you and you make some tragic mistake, it's my fault for not sharing what I know. But if I do help you poke around in your own skull, and we make a mistake, which is almost inevitable, I'll be blamed for not knowing what I'm doing, and Phillip here will almost certainly claim I did it on purpose."

"That's true," Phillip agreed.

Brit the Much Elder said, "You missed a possible outcome. If you don't help us, and her glitch brings down the whole program, then you're just as dead as the rest of us."

Jimmy thought for another moment. "Yeah, I see your point. Okay, look, I'll show you everything I know, and I'll help you map out and explore the part of the file that deals with memories, but I won't be a party to making any changes to your, or anyone else's, brain. Hopefully you'll see how foolhardy and dangerous this all is and decide to come up with a better idea. Deal?"

"Deal," both Brits said.

Phillip groaned.

Jimmy sprung up from his chair. "Great. I gotta tell you, despite the awful reason for it happening, it feels good to have company and be working with people who know what's going on again. Say, how about before we get started, we all get dinner to celebrate? You could take in some local color. A genuine taste of Reno. No place on earth does mediocrity better. Down at the Nugget they've got a burger called the Awful-Awful!"

Phillip sighed. "Sounds appropriate."

18.

The midmorning light of a fresh new day in Leadchurch didn't so much cascade in through the windows of Phillip's rec room as it tumbled in reluctantly and hit the floor in a chilly, flat, gray heap. Outside, an unbroken ceiling of clouds drizzled chilled water. Inside, all the lamps were off, and the curtains were drawn just enough to let light in but send the message that the light was not welcome, and had better mind its manners.

The room's original entrance, and exit, was the staircase that led down to Phillip's séance room and storefront, but in the time since Phillip "remodeled," he had added two doors. One was a large wall panel that lowered like a drawbridge, designed to allow Phillip to drive his beloved Pontiac Fiero in and out, which he rarely did. The other was a simple wooden door set into the wall on the opposite end of the long, rectangular room. This door was linked magically to Brit the Younger's apartment in Atlantis.

It was the small door to Atlantis that creaked open, allowing in yet more light, a bleary-eyed Phillip, and the sound of a conversation that was already in progress.

"No," Phillip said, "I just didn't sleep well."

Nik's distant voice drifted in. "I could make you some tea."

"No thank you, Nik, I have it handled, thanks." He shut the door behind him, and instantly his body sagged. For a moment he stood there, breathing and listening to the silence.

This room was full of items Phillip had handpicked to make himself happy, but he took no notice of any of them, not even glancing at anything beyond the wet bar. He reached for a coffee mug and an empty diner-grade coffee carafe to which he'd applied one of his better macros. He tipped it over the rim of the mug and freshly brewed, steaming-hot coffee poured out into the mug.

Phillip stared down at the mug long enough to take two heaving breaths, blinked so slowly it almost counted as a nap, then muttered, "Why not." He reached for a bottle of Scotch and poured a shot into his coffee.

He spent about five minutes standing there behind the bar in his darkened rec room, eyes closed, drinking his spiked coffee in silence. When the mug was empty, he set it aside and, with Herculean effort, took the three steps back to the door to Brit's apartment. He gathered his energy, stood up straight, and opened the door.

"Okay, Brit," he said, cheerily, "I'm almost ready to go on that walk we discussed. I just need to visit the loo first."

Brit's voice was distant, but easily understandable. "Actually, dear, I've decided not to come along."

Phillip stepped into Brit the Younger's apartment and pushed the door closed behind him. "Oh, in that case, I suppose I'll just go get it over with. The sooner I start, the sooner I'll be back with you, after all."

As the door swung shut, Brit said, "But I thought you had to go to the bathroom?"

At the same time, Nik called out, "Oh, and while you're out, can you please get me—"

The door closed with a thud, and the room fell back into silence.

The haggard-looking Future Phillip leaned out from his hiding spot behind the GORF machine and scanned the room, making sure Present Phillip was truly gone. Convinced that this was the case, he turned to the large empty space where Phillip's Fiero usually sat.

"He didn't even notice," Future Phillip said. "All that trouble to steal my own car, and he didn't even notice! I figured he'd spend the rest of the day looking for it!"

Martin said, "He seemed pretty distracted."

Future Phillip jumped and spun around to see Martin's eyes and hat poking up from behind the bar.

"I wouldn't judge him too harshly. Neither of you noticed that I was hiding down here."

Future Phillip snarled, "What are you doing here?"

Martin held up one finger, asking for Phillip to wait a second. Martin turned and moved forward in small lurches, raising a few inches with each step, making it look as if he was walking up a staircase behind the bar. When he was standing fully upright, he said, "I love that gag."

"Yes," Phillip said, "hilarious. Now, what are you doing here?"

"Watching you. I've been watching you for a while now. I watched while you stalked Phillip, Current Phillip, when he was out for a walk with Brit, Current Brit, yesterday. I watched you lurk outside their home all night. I followed and watched as you snuck into Phillip's most private, personal space. I saw it all, and a disgusting sight it was!"

"You did all of those things, too!"

"Yes, but you did them to spy on Phillip and interfere with his life. I did them to protect Phillip and keep tabs on you."

"I am Phillip!"

"Sometimes a friend needs to be protected from themselves. And *I* didn't steal his car."

Phillip pointed out the window. "I was just trying to distract him. The Fiero's just outside, hidden under a haystack. I can have it back in here in less than a minute."

"Then I suggest you get to it."

Future Phillip sneered at Martin. "It didn't work anyway." He pointed his staff at the large drawbridge door set into the wall, but nothing happened. He tried again with the same result.

Martin snapped his fingers. "Oh, that's right. While I was waiting under the bar, I set up a zone around you where no magic can work."

Phillip's eyes grew wide, and he blurted, *"Transporto hejmo."*

Nothing happened. Martin smiled.

"Yeah, inside an eight-foot box, there in that corner of the room, you can't do magic."

"An eight-foot box?" Future Phillip asked.

"Yes."

"Right." Future Phillip took two determined-looking steps, then slammed headfirst into an invisible wall.

Martin came out from behind the bar and stepped closer to Phillip. "I also put up force fields to keep you from leaving the area where you can't do magic. Sorry, but I need to keep you from interfering with Phillip until I figure out what, exactly, is going on."

"You know what's going on! I told you what's going on!"

"And now I'll be able to verify it."

"You're just enjoying acting like a jerk, aren't you, Martin?"

"Look who's talking. You're the one who stole a man's car."

"It's my car! And I only did it to distract him! You know what, though, I can still get his attention. I'd hoped to avoid this, but you've forced my hand. All I have to do is yell loud enough, and they'll hear me in there." He pointed at the door to Brit the Younger's apartment. "Phillip will come running, and he'll see me, and that I'm him, and that you have him, i.e., me, trapped. That'll distract him."

"Phillip's gone for a walk."

"Then Brit and Nik will hear it, find us, call Phillip, and it'll be an even bigger distraction."

Martin shook his head. "You can't do that."

Phillip said, "Watch me," and opened his mouth to shout.

Martin touched the head of his staff to the force field that held Phillip in place and said, "Mute."

Phillip shouted, but no sound came out. He shouted again, louder, but with the same result: no sound at all. He extended his index finger, as if he intended to give Martin a piece of his mind, or poke him in the eye, or probably both. He took one step and ran into the invisible wall again. He let go of his staff and used both hands to explore the invisible wall by feel. It extended several feet on each side before bending at ninety degrees, completely enveloping him. Future Phillip bellowed at Martin with all of his might but couldn't make a sound.

"You like it?" Martin asked. "It's a macro I've been working on in my spare time. I call it the mime box. I was saving it for after Gary did something really over the line to one of us, which I figure is only a matter of time. I wanted to hold it for something special, because being trapped and forced to act like a mime is pretty much the worst noninjuring punishment I can think of."

Phillip pounded on the invisible wall and screamed, but no sound was audible.

Martin said, "I see you agree."

19.

"So, notice this number here," Jimmy said. He leaned forward and touched the computer monitor with his index finger. He was sitting in the office that Phillip and Brit the Elder had inhabited, at the workstation Phillip had used to sift through the Atlantis magic logs. Brit the Elder and Brit the Much Elder flanked Jimmy in rolling office chairs, watching over his shoulders in rapt attention as he walked them through Brit the Elder's own file entry.

Phillip stood at the opposite end of the room, peering out through the blinds in the window, trying not to listen to the sound of Jimmy explaining, or the Brits being nice to him.

"When I hit refresh, notice how that number goes up. Every time I hit refresh, it goes up some more."

"Is it counting refreshes somehow?" Brit the Much Elder asked.

"I wondered that, too, but if I wait a while between refreshes, it doesn't just go up one or two counts. Over time I figured out that this number progresses at a steady rate, whether I'm looking at it or not."

Brit the Elder said, "Like a clock."

"Exactly like a clock."

Phillip looked out at the parking lot. He could see a nondescript dark blue four door, with the figures of two men in the front seat, barely visible through the foggy windshield. "Seems like the nice thing to do would have been to give Miller and Murphy a few days off while Jimmy's in your custody."

Brit the Much Elder said, "Yeah, probably, but Miller's a real pain in the butt, and Murphy enables him. At least I let them take a flight out here. I could have made them drive out from Reno."

Brit the Elder cleared her throat. "You were saying, Jimmy?"

"Yes, of course. So, you've got this number that acts like a clock. Keep that in mind. Now, we're going to scroll down to another spot in your file entry."

Phillip continued peering out the window. He didn't find the parking lot of a federal building in Sacramento particularly interesting, but he found what was going on in the room interesting to the point of horrified fascination, in much the same way a condemned man finds the topic of capital punishment interesting. He was desperate to think about anything else, and the window was his only refuge.

Jimmy continued, "Now, here you'll see a callout. The code is sending some piece of information to another part of the program. That's nothing strange. A person's file is full of them. The file's nothing but a data store, after all, a silo that holds all the facts, figures, and describable parameters that make you you, and not someone else. But this callout is different. Do you see how?"

Brit the Elder said, "It's not calling out to the program. It's calling out to another part of the file."

Phillip said, "I just feel bad for them, Miller and Murphy, sitting in that car, watching the building, with nobody but each other for company. From what I've heard, they aren't very good company."

"Actually, they can be a lot of fun," Jimmy said. "And don't feel too bad. They're happier when they can keep an eye on me. Well, I don't think happier is the word, really."

"More comfortable," Brit the Much Elder offered.

"No, that's not it either. But they're definitely less happy and less comfortable when they're not watching me. It's like the unhappiness of watching me makes them happier. There isn't really a word for that."

"I bet the Germans have one."

"Yeah," Jimmy said, "And specific nightclubs where you can go to feel it."

Brit the Elder had taken little notice and no joy in the conversation, both quite deliberately. "Can we please get back to business?"

"Of course," Jimmy said. "If we go to the portion of the file it specifies, you'll see that it's in the middle of this weird sea of numbers, commas, and colons. We never really paid that much attention to it because nobody had any idea what it was, or how to find out. But, if you go to the exact point your file entry specified, you'll see it's made up of a long chain of three number sets. I figure the middle number in each set is the address of a location in some other file, one we haven't found, and frankly, I don't think we should look for it. The first and last numbers though, they match the formatting exactly of the number I just showed you."

"It's a time stamp," Brit the Elder said.

"I believe so. I believe that we're looking at the filing information for your long-term memories. The first and last numbers show the beginning and end points of the experience you'll remember, and the middle number is its name, or location, or some such."

Brit the Much Elder said, "A set of numbers was just added to the list."

Jimmy said, "Yup. Who knows? That could be you storing away the moment you realized how your long-term memory works. A fairly memorable experience, I'd say."

Phillip said, "This is just wrong."

"Hey, I'm with you, Phillip. I didn't even want to show you all this. I don't like that I know it myself, but all I'm doing is sharing the knowledge," Jimmy replied.

"What? No, not that. It's not right that we're treating Miller and Murphy this way. They're just doing their jobs. We should send them a pizza or something."

"No," Brit the Much Elder said. "They'd only take it as taunting. It'd just make them angry."

"Everything makes Miller angry," Jimmy muttered.

Brit the Much Elder laughed. "True enough. No, Phillip, you're sweet, but it's best just to leave them be. They're professionals, and they volunteered for this duty."

Jimmy smiled. "Besides, if they're hungry, they can just eat the banana that's in their tailpipe."

Brit the Much Elder looked aghast. "Still?"

"The macro follows them, not the car they had in Reno. Until I make it stop, every car Miller attempts to drive for the rest of his days will have a foggy windshield and a banana in its tailpipe, and the car will stall, even though the banana trick doesn't work."

Brit the Much Elder laughed again and hit Jimmy on the shoulder playfully. "You're so bad!"

Phillip and Brit the Elder both scowled at them, but for different reasons.

Phillip didn't know what he liked less, being called sweet, the sight of Brit, *any* Brit, laughing at Jimmy's jokes, or the prospect of Brit the Elder tinkering with her own long-term memories.

Brit the Elder was just impatient to get back to work. "So, what happens if you delete one of the entries?"

"I don't know," Jimmy said.

"What do you mean, you don't know?"

"I never tried, or at least if I did, I must have erased the memory of me trying."

Brit the Much Elder laughed. Phillip did not.

"Seriously," Jimmy said, "I wouldn't touch any of these numbers with a ten-foot pole. No way, no how. Too dangerous."

"I don't see where we have another option."

"And I don't see where this is an option to begin with. Brit, I only agreed to show this to you because I figured you'd see how vague and uncertain it is and you'd decide to try something else."

Brit the Elder shook her head. "There is nothing else to try. It's this, or do nothing."

Brit the Much Elder put a hand on Brit the Elder's shoulder, but she squirmed out from under it immediately. "Don't touch me."

Brit the Much Elder said, "I'm just trying to calm you down."

"Don't touch me, because you're me! I won't even be in the same room with Brit the Younger for fear of a world-ending glitch. I came to you without thinking, and I've kept you involved because it didn't seem to hurt anything, but we shouldn't press our luck. And in case you all need a reminder, that's what we're talking about, trying to prevent the entire known universe from blinking out and being replaced with a bong noise and a little drawing of an old-timey bomb."

Jimmy squinted and cocked his head to the side.

Phillip said, "She uses an original Mac."

Jimmy nodded.

"What do you suggest?" Brit the Much Elder asked. "That we just start erasing numbers willy-nilly to see how it affects you and, by extension, me?"

Brit the Elder rolled her eyes. "No, obviously not. We would carefully analyze the situation, handpick certain specific numbers of interest, then copy and delete them, in a sober, cautious manner, and see how it affects us."

Phillip shut his eyes so hard it almost hurt. "It's tempting to try it just to make you forget that Jimmy ever told you about this."

Brit the Elder said, "Listen, the problem started when my and Brit the Younger's memories diverged, right? Her memories seem to match reality. Mine don't. I think the most logical course of action, given what we've learned from Jimmy, is to find my memories that are different from hers, and swap them out."

Jimmy pushed back from the keyboard. "I'm sorry, everyone. Brit's problem's worse than we thought. In addition to her other memory issues, she seems to have forgotten what logic is. Look, Brit, I understand that you're under a lot of stress here, but we don't know nearly enough about any of this to even consider erasing any of these numbers. Even if we're right, and these are long-term memories, we don't know how they interact with the rest of your cognitive processes. Any number of vital subroutines could refer back to these memories on a regular basis. Anything you learn probably needs to refer back to this. Language use. Pattern recognition. Emotional responses to given situations or people. It's all tied into memory. So, no. I'm not going to be a party to changing any of this stuff unless we do a lot of careful testing first."

"Damn right," Phillip shouted.

Brit the Elder glared at Phillip. "You realize you're siding with Jimmy, your worst enemy, over me."

Jimmy said, "I'd rather you called me his greatest enemy, instead of his worst. Worst implies low quality. You could argue that Gary's his worst enemy."

Phillip said, "Gary's my friend."

"Which shows how bad at being an enemy he really is."

Brit the Much Elder said, "Jimmy, now's not the time. Phillip, there's no need to yell, and Brit, Phillip's not siding with Jimmy. Phillip and I are siding with Jimmy. Without careful testing, it's just way too dangerous to even consider changing any of those numbers."

"You're all being silly. Think about it." Brit the Elder pointed at Brit the Much Elder. "You're here. You're fine. And you're me in the future. The fact that you exist is all the testing we need. You prove that what I plan to do must work, or else you wouldn't be here."

Brit the Much Elder said, "No. That runs counter to the reasoning you used to get me involved in this mess to begin with. You're glitching out. You're part of the program. Thus, the program is glitching out, which means that me being here proves nothing and all bets are off. You're only trying to use me as proof because you want to mess with your code and you're looking for an excuse."

"Yeah," Phillip agreed. "Or, she's not you, just a kind of placeholder copy of you the program created for you to interact with, and your fate isn't tied to hers, just like I've said all along."

"No," Brit the Much Elder said, "That's even more stupid. I guess it could be argued that my existence might prove that at some point, somebody will do something to fix the glitch, and it will work. That doesn't mean that it's you, Brit, or that it's your idea, or involves Jimmy's idea at all."

"Hey," Jimmy said. "None of this was my idea. I want that clear. I had no idea."

Phillip said, "I'll vouch for that."

Brit the Elder thought for several seconds. When she finally broke her silence, she spoke slowly and quietly, giving the same sense of a barely contained catastrophe as a profoundly drunk person driving ten miles per hour under the speed limit, in a ruler-straight line. "Okay. You all said we'd need lots of careful testing before you'd feel comfortable proceeding. What, exactly, would this careful testing look like?"

Phillip said, "We could test on animals. I wouldn't feel great about it, but we get, I dunno, an elephant or something. Something well-known for its memory, and mess with its entry."

Jimmy pointed at Phillip with both hands. "Top man! I like it! Not only could we experiment with the animal's memory, but we could try to replicate the glitch to begin with. Not with the elephant, but like a rat or something. If we can replicate the problem, maybe we can come up with a better solution then memory replacement. Normally I'm not a fan of animal experimentation, but this is to save the entire world."

Phillip said, "Not a fan of animal experimentation? You experimented on the code of hundreds of people."

"Yeah, and I saw the consequence of my actions, and learned my lesson."

Brit the Elder stood up. "Wait a minute. How long do you think all of this experimenting will take?" She pointed at her thigh. "Need I remind you that our time is limited? I'd have already spent a few years fixing this myself then come back in time to give myself the antidote without bothering all of you if I didn't have a ticking time bomb working its way up my legs."

Brit the Much Elder said, "We could put you in slow time, like you did to Phillip to bring him here. That'd give us years to come up with a fix."

"While I stand there like a statue, waiting for you three to figure out a way to save me? No thanks."

Phillip said, "Look, we're all kinds of worked up. I think we should knock off for the day. We'll all go sleep on it, come back tomorrow, and hopefully one of us will have thought of something we can all agree to. Okay?"

Jimmy said, "Fine by me."

Brit the Much Elder nodded. "Brit?"

"Fine," Brit the Elder said, and disappeared.

Jimmy swiveled his desk chair to face Brit the Much Elder. "I assume that if she comes back tomorrow and still wants to run experiments on her own memory, we're going to put her in slow time against her will."

Brit the Much Elder said, "Absolutely."

Phillip wanted to argue against the idea, but the best reason not to do it he could come up with was, "She won't like that."

Brit the Much Elder shrugged. "No, but it's the right thing, and she'll see that in time. If the roles were reversed, she'd do the same to Brit the Younger in a heartbeat."

"Yes," Phillip agreed, "and Brit the Younger would be furious at her for it."

Brit the Much Elder said, "Yes, and they'd both be in the right."

20.

Martin materialized, standing straight and tall with a triumphant smile on his face, which faded quickly when he dropped two feet and landed in several inches of wet concrete. He bent at the knees and hunched over, swinging his free arm wildly to keep his balance while leaning heavily on his staff. He managed to keep from falling down into the gray mush, but his shoes and the hem of his already-tattered robe were covered.

Martin swiveled his head, taking in his surroundings. At first, he thought he had accidentally transported somewhere he'd never been, but soon he realized that this was the main room of Gary's living space at Skull Gullet Cave. It only looked different because all of the furniture had been removed, the entire kitchen area had been demolished, and the floor was awash in a uniform layer of wet concrete. In the center of the living room, directly under the spot Martin had teleported into, was some sort of broad, shallow pit that had been sectioned off with wooden forms, with a separate pool of wet concrete at the bottom of the lower section.

Martin pulled out one foot, looked at his ruined shoe, and shouted, "Gary!"

The door that led to the antechamber opened. Gary leaned through the door frame without stepping into the room. Behind Gary, Martin saw all of Gary's furniture arranged awkwardly around the stone pedestal. An episode of *This Old House* was playing soundlessly on the TV, green letters spelling MUTE superimposed over the top left corner.

"Hey, Martin. How's it going?"

Martin stomped his foot down, deliberately splashing it in the wet concrete. "You cleared the entire room, filled it with concrete, and lowered part of it just to get us to fall in?"

Gary glanced around the empty room. "Us? I only see one of you."

"The rest are coming."

"Excellent," Gary said, and leaned against the door frame, waiting for the show to begin.

Only a few seconds later, Gwen materialized in midair, where the floor level had been before, holding her wand in one hand, and a bundle of silver fabric in the other. She fell two feet, landing with a splash in the concrete. Martin rushed forward to hold her up, but stopped when it became obvious that she didn't need his help.

Gwen looked down at her feet, then up at Martin with a smile on her face. "He got us this time."

"Looks like it," Martin said.

Gwen turned to Gary and said "Well done," then turned back to Martin and said, "Hi."

"Hi."

Gwen smiled and Martin smiled back, uneasily.

When Gwen seemed happy to see him, it made Martin happy. When she seemed unhappy to see him, it made him unhappy. When she went from looking unhappy to see him to looking happy to see him with no explanation for the change, it made him profoundly uncomfortable.

Gwen held the bundle of silver fabric forward. "I made this for you. It's a new robe."

Martin took it. "Thanks! That's great! I'll put it on later, when I'm not standing in wet concrete."

Tyler appeared, far enough to the side that one of his feet was over the pit. His left foot touched down on the upper level while the right half of his body kept falling, finally stopping when his right foot hit the bottom of the pit. Normally, he'd have hopped to the side to regain his balance, but the wet concrete prevented this. Instead, he fell over sideways, twisting on the way down and landing flat on his back, as if he intended to make a concrete angel.

He seemed poised to unleash a torrent of profanities, but Gwen smiled down at him and greeted him with a cheerful, "Hi, Tyler. Looks like Gary saw us coming this time." She extended a hand to help him up.

"Yeah" Tyler said, taking her hand. "Looks like it, I guess. Gwen, good to see you. You seem . . . good."

"Yeah."

As he came to his feet, Tyler looked at Martin, who held up his new robe, still folded, for Tyler to see. "She made me a new robe."

"Oh. Nice. So you two have made up."

Martin smiled. "I guess?"

Gwen said, "We'll talk about it."

Martin's smile dimmed.

Roy and Jeff appeared at the same moment. Jeff materialized in the empty space over the sunken area and immediately fell in. Roy appeared on the higher portion of floor, and sunk into the concrete slowly, while cursing.

Martin said, "I hope you're satisfied, Gary."

"I am. I really, really am. It makes me wish I'd done this on purpose. I'm just having the floors redone. That hole you're all wallowing in is going to be my new conversation pit." Gary shouted, "Foreman!"

Banging, creaking, and sounds of human exertion became audible as one of the doors down at the end of the hall opened. Hubert leaned out of the door, wearing a hard hat and waders with his tuxedo coat. "Yes, Master?"

"I'm afraid my idiot friends have messed up the floors in here. You and the boys will have to come refloat it and the conversation pit."

"I see what you mean, Master. We're on the way."

The wizards all levitated into the air and gravitated to the outer edge of the room as thirteen dirty, undernourished young men in hard hats, rubber boots, and matching black T-shirts printed with an illustration of a tuxedo jacket, white shirt, and bow tie flooded out of the hallway and into the main room, their feet caked with wet concrete. They used flat boards and planks of wood to smooth out the tortured concrete while Gary stood in the doorway and shouted directions.

"That's it! Be careful, apprentices. The concrete flows like the currents of magic. It obeys its own laws, but with skill and patience you can guide it into the form you wish."

"Oh, Lord," Tyler moaned. "He's doing a Karate Kid."

"What's a Karate Kid?" Hubert asked, as he dragged a straight plank across the surface of the concrete.

Gary said, "It's an ancient and legendary teaching technique, invented by a great magician called Miyagi."

"Did he teach you, Master?"

"In a way he taught us all, Hubert. How's progress on the seductorium?"

"Work on your bedroom is going well, Master. We've completed the mirror-lined posing platform. We've moved on to pouring the floor."

"Very good. Apprentices, remember, as you swing your hammers, the motion is quite similar to the motion one uses when wielding a wand, so watch your form, and try not to bend the nails. It's wasteful, and looks amateurish. And I'd better not catch anyone writing their names in the floor in there."

Jeff muttered, "Concrete floors in the bedroom. Doesn't sound very seductive."

Gwen shook her head. "None of it does."

"The finished floors won't be concrete," Gary explained. "They're just laying down a nice flat slab. Later, they'll install the shag carpet."

Tyler absentmindedly stroked his chin. "I've always wondered, do they call it shag carpet because of how it looks, or because of what the owner hopes to do on it?"

Gary smiled. "Can't it be both?"

"It can," Gwen said. "Sadly."

The apprentices worked their way backward, down the hall, leaving a trail of perfectly flat concrete in their wake, until they finally disappeared back into the rooms in which they'd been working before.

The wizards floated through the door to Gary's ceremonial antechamber and lowered themselves to the floor.

Tyler rounded on Gary. "You put them to work remodeling your house?"

"Yeah," Gary said. "They wanted to do something, so I gave them something to do."

"They're expecting you to teach them magic."

"I'll let them all expend some energy, then I'll give them some sort of test to see if they have the gift, or something. They'll all fail, and I'll send them back out into the world."

"When?"

"When they've finished the remodel. And the yard work I'm planning."

Jeff asked, "There isn't a door to the outside from your bedroom, is there?"

"No."

"Then how are your apprentices going to get out without ruining the concrete themselves?"

Gary said, "I'll just levitate them out. It'll be a valuable lesson for them in the need to plan ahead."

"You just came up with that now, didn't you?" Roy asked.

"Yes. Which is a valuable lesson in the importance of being able to improvise."

"But why live in a home that was banged together by a bunch of amateurs when you can just make anything you want with magic?"

"The things we make with magic are just copies of things that were probably mass-produced to begin with. Sure, things that were made by hand have flaws, but they also have character. They have soul."

"These aren't craftsmen," Roy said. "They're untrained medieval peasants. The stuff they make will be nothing but flaws."

"So they'll have that much more soul."

Gwen stared at Gary in obvious disbelief. "Wait a second. Since when do you care about this kind of thing?"

"Since always," Gary said. "There's more to me than heavy metal and practical jokes."

"Yeah," Tyler said. "There's chasing women."

"Unsuccessfully," Martin added.

"And a love of handcrafted woodworking. You might have known if any of you had ever bothered to ask, or to even look around when you visit and think about what you see. Why did you think I had a book by George Nakashima on my shelf?"

Gwen said, "I never noticed, because the bookcase was made of cinder blocks and plywood."

Martin said, "Okay, we've gotten off track here. We can discuss Gary's remodel later, when it's done and looks like crap. I called you all here because an apology is in order."

Gwen crossed her arms. "Yes?"

"Yes," Martin said.

They all stood in silence for a moment.

Gwen said, "We're waiting."

"So am I, because you're the ones who owe me the apology. I told you that Phillip was being attacked, and you didn't believe me. You all acted like I was crazy. Well, I ask you, who's crazy now?"

Martin pulled out and flipped open the small silver box in which he carried his smartphone. He jabbed at the screen a few times, then pointed his staff at the far side of the stone ceremonial chamber.

The future version of Phillip appeared, standing with slumped shoulders, his staff barely hanging from his fingers.

Martin turned back to the group. "See!"

Tyler said, "It's Phillip. Hi, Phillip."

Future Phillip remained motionless, except for his right hand, which he slowly waved.

Martin said, "No, it isn't Phillip. I mean, well, obviously it is Phillip, but it isn't really. Not our Phillip. This is Phillip from the future. Look how beat down and wrung out he looks. Our Phillip would never leave the house looking that pitiful."

Future Phillip glared at Martin.

"I don't know," Roy said. "Maybe that's just from listening to your blather."

Martin said, "I caught him red-handed. If I didn't have him trapped, he'd escape right now. Show them how you're trapped."

Future Phillip breathed out, deflating noticeably, then pressed his free hand against the invisible wall of his prison. He asked Martin if that was good enough, but no sound came out of his mouth.

"Cool," Gary gasped. "Like a mime."

Martin said, "Right? I'm also working on a defensive weapon that forces people to walk into a heavy wind."

Gwen stared at Martin. "You've tried to convince us that you're not crazy by imprisoning your best friend."

"I can prove that this isn't our Phillip. He stole Phillip's Fiero and buried it under a haystack out behind Phillip's office."

"Is that really proof?" Gary asked.

Tyler mulled it over. "Well, I think we'd all agree that no sane man would steal a Fiero."

Future Phillip stopped glaring at Martin and started glaring at Tyler.

"The real question," Tyler continued, "is if Phillip's Fiero is under this haystack, did Phillip do it? There's no reason to believe you didn't do it yourself, Martin. You seem intent on tormenting Phillip."

"I'm the one trying to help Phillip!"

Tyler pointed at the captive Future Phillip, who threw up his hands as if to say, "I know, right?"

Martin said, "He's the one messing with Phillip, and he's the one who took the Fiero. Go look. If you go back in time to six o'clock this morning, you can watch him do it."

Roy and Jeff disappeared, were gone for a little less than five seconds, then reappeared.

"Martin's telling the truth," Jeff said. "We watched this Phillip steal the Fiero, drive it out, and bury it in hay."

All of the wizards turned and looked at Future Phillip.

Gwen asked, "Okay, what do you have to say for yourself?"

Future Phillip shrugged and leaned back on the wall of his invisible prison, reminding them that he couldn't speak if he wanted to.

Martin touched the end of his staff to the force field surrounding Future Phillip, and said, "Unmute."

Future Phillip said, "I expect you want me to thank you."

"We just want an explanation," Gwen said.

Future Phillip allowed himself to slide down the wall until he sagged in a seated position, like a wilted potted plant that hadn't received enough water. "It pains me to no end to say this, but Martin is right. Everything he's told you is more or less accurate, but what he's left out is that I've been trying, despite Martin's interference, to prevent a terrible catastrophe."

"What?" Jeff asked.

Future Phillip said, "I can't tell you."

"If you tell us we can help."

"No, you can't."

Martin said, "So, think about it. He says he's here to prevent a tragedy, but he won't tell us what it is and won't allow us to help. He seems to think it's something only he can fix, and for the life of me, I can't imagine what that would be or why he wouldn't tell us. Logically, I think either he's trying to prevent something that we wouldn't consider a tragedy, or the thing he has to do to prevent this mysterious tragedy is something we wouldn't approve of."

"Like what?" Gary asked.

"I don't know, and the Phillip of Tomorrow, today, here won't tell us, will he?"

Future Phillip shook his head.

Martin said, "It was a waste giving you back the ability to speak."

21.

Phillip materialized in the same alley in Atlantis from which he'd teleported, facing the same dead-end wall he'd faced when he left. Ten minutes had passed in Atlantis. For Phillip it had been hours, first spent listening to Jimmy lecture him and the two elder Brits about the file, then trying to talk Brit the Elder out of acting on what Jimmy had told them.

Okay, Phillip, remember. It's still morning here. I've been out for a brisk walk. I need to get Nik some salt, and then get home to spend the day with Brit the Younger. That'll be good. Besides, after the day I've had, a quiet afternoon with the woman I love sounds great.

Phillip spun around, took one step, then jumped straight up in the air and let out a frightened yelp. Brit the Younger stood, blocking the alley's exit. Her mouth slowly spread into a big, toothy smile. The back of Phillip's mind ruminated on the interesting fact that evolution has caused us to make an expression when we're happy that's similar to the face all mammals make when they're about to bite something. The look in Brit's eye left no doubt as to the intent behind this smile.

It would have been frightening enough had she been alone, but standing behind her, just to the side, peering over her shoulder, there was another her, a second Brit the Younger, wearing the same clothes, her hair styled identically. The only difference was that the Brit in back had a notebook, a pen, and a video camera on a tripod pointed directly at Phillip, its record light glowing red.

In a voice that sounded as if she already knew the answer and didn't like it, the Brit in front asked, "Where have you been, Phillip?"

"Why are there two of you?" Phillip asked.

"Never mind that," the Brit in front said. "It's part of an experiment. She's just here to observe."

The Brit in back scribbled down notes at a furious pace, with a furious look on her face.

"What experiment?" Phillip asked.

The front Brit said, "Don't change the subject. Where were you, Phillip?"

"I can't—"

"You can't tell me," the front Brit interrupted. "Why not? I already know, so really, you might as well tell me."

"You do? Then why ask?"

"She doesn't know yet." The front Brit pointed over her shoulder with her thumb at the Brit in the rear, who took a moment away from her frantic note taking to scowl at Phillip. Behind her, Phillip saw that the sound of tense voices had caused a bit of a crowd to start gathering behind the two Brits.

"I'd rather not—"

"Discuss it here?"

As the word here came out of her mouth, the front Brit started nodding slowly, her lips barely moving, as if she was counting to herself. Phillip started to step around her to his right, but she muttered "Five," and stepped to block him before he'd barely lifted his foot from the ground. Not that it mattered. The sound of voices engaged in relationship drama had started to draw the inevitable crowd. Even if he'd been able to get past the Brits, a thick gaggle of onlookers blocked his escape.

Phillip stepped back in shock. He saw that both Brits were now counting to themselves, but their rhythms were slightly off. The Brit in the rear noticed this, too, and looked at the back of front Brit's head.

Phillip tried to step around them to his left. As he shifted his weight, the Brit in the rear grunted "Eleven." The Brit in front's eyes grew wide, and she lurched to the side to block Phillip's exit.

The rear Brit said, "There's that timing issue you mentioned."

"I was at ten. Even when I knew to look for it, my count was slow."

"Yeah. That's definitely something we'll need to address."

The rear Brit made a note, then both of them turned to glare at Phillip as if even their timing problems were his fault.

Phillip said, "We're making—"

The front Brit said, "A spectacle of ourselves, and you'd rather discuss this in private. Yeah, fine. Whatever. We've got everything we need." She turned around, put a reassuring hand on the rear Brit's shoulder, then disappeared.

The rear and now only remaining Brit clicked her pen, tucked her notebook under her arm, and collapsed her tripod.

Phillip said, "I'll carry your tripod for you, if you like."

Brit said nothing. Every man in earshot cringed. Every woman who heard smirked knowingly.

Brit picked up her own tripod and stepped to the side, motioning for Phillip to lead the way. The citizens parted, creating a narrow passage for Phillip to walk through. Brit followed. All eyes stared at Phillip, but nobody said a word to him. Behind him, he heard women whisper encouragement to Brit the Younger as she passed.

He walked in silence to Brit's front door, which he held open for her. She didn't thank or even look at him as she entered. Phillip took one last glance across the street to verify that it was not his imagination—everybody was staring at him. He stepped into the apartment and closed the door behind him.

Brit stood in the middle of the room, her arms folded, glaring.

Nik leaned into the room. "Oh, good, you're both back. I see you caught up to him Br . . ." he trailed off as he saw Brit's body language, fell silent, and also glared at Phillip.

Phillip whined, "Oh, come on, Nik. You don't even know what this is about!"

Nik said nothing.

Brit asked, "What is this about, Phillip?"

"Nothing!"

Brit stared at him.

"Nothing bad."

Brit continued staring.

Phillip started talking, stopped himself, tried again, stopped again, thought for a moment, said, "Okay, look . . ." and then fell silent.

Brit said, "I asked you a question out there, and you said that you'd answer it if we weren't in public."

Phillip reran the conversation in his mind. He remembered Brit asking him where he had been, and he replied that they were making a spectacle of themselves, not that he would say in private. Phillip said, "Technically, I said—" but the look on Brit's face after he said *technically* stunned him back into silence.

"Please don't make me ask you again, Phillip."

Phillip sagged. "Brit, I hope you know how important you are to me, and that I always have your best interests at heart."

"I liked to think so."

Phillip tried his best to speak clearly while wincing. "Then I hope you'll understand when I tell you that, for your own good, I can't tell you where I went."

For a full ten seconds, the only sound in the apartment was the faint rustling noise caused by the scraping of Nik's tunic against his neck as he shook his head in disgust.

Brit said, "You won't tell me."

"I can't."

"Fine, I didn't want to have to do this, but I'll just go ask Brit the Elder. She'll remember what this was all about."

"No," Phillip blurted. "Don't go ask Brit the Elder! I mean, you shouldn't. Um, What I'm saying is, she won't be able, uh. Hmm."

"You were with Brit the Elder, weren't you?"

"You . . . would probably be unhappy about that, if it were the case, wouldn't you?" Phillip asked.

"Phillip, are you having an affair with Brit the Elder?"

"What?! No! I could never! The idea wouldn't even occur to me! Brit, how can you ask me that?"

"I should be enough for you, Phillip."

"You are."

"One of me."

"One is!"

"Which one?"

"Wha . . . Oh, come on! You are. You." He pointed at her. "This you. You you. The only you."

Brit the Younger remained motionless, studying Phillip. "It wouldn't even occur to you to have an affair with Brit the Elder?"

"No! Not in a million years!"

"Why not? Do you find her unattractive?"

Phillip gaped at Brit. He turned to Nik and saw no support, just genuine interest in Phillip's answer on his face. Phillip thought furiously for several seconds before finally saying, "There's no right answer to that question."

Brit the Younger said, "That was the wrong answer."

"Brit, you're asking me if I find a person who you believe is you attractive."

"Yes, Phillip, she is me, but she's also my worst enemy."

"I know the feeling."

"This isn't funny, Phillip! If I can't trust you then this relationship is over."

"Apparently not," Phillip said, "since you seem to believe I'm having some sort of relationship with you in your future, which, by the way, I'm not, so perhaps we are through after all, for, I might add, no reason!"

"So you admit she's me!"

"No! Never. Which is why it would be cheating if I got involved with her, and that's why I would never, ever, even consider it. That's all I'm saying. I would never cheat on you with anybody, even someone you think is you."

"I want to believe you, Phillip."

"I want you to believe me, too!"

"So where were you?"

"I want desperately to tell you, I really do, but I can't."

"Why not?"

Phillip looked at the floor. "Brit the Elder thinks it would be dangerous for you to know."

"Not as dangerous as it is to not tell me."

Phillip said, "Look, I want to tell you. Now that you know I've been sneaking away, I can go to Brit the Elder and make the case that it's impossible to keep this from you anymore. I'll go talk to her, and I'll figure out a safe way to tell you what's going on."

Brit said, "Fine, but the fact that you need help thinking of a way to tell me without endangering yourself doesn't give me confidence."

Phillip said, "Not safe for me. I'm afraid that ship has sailed. Safe for you, and her, and everybody else. Okay?"

Brit the Younger stared at Phillip for a moment and let out a disgusted grunt. "Fine. Go talk to Brit the Elder. I have to go look over my notes and memorize my lines so I can jump back in time and go confront you in the alley again."

She stormed off to her bedroom and slammed the door behind her.

Phillip turned to Nik, hoping to see or hear something, anything, that might make it better.

Nik asked, "Phillip, did you get me the salt I asked for?"

Phillip grimaced.

Nik shook his head and walked out without saying another word.

22.

Martin sat on the couch in the converted warehouse he called home, brooding on the confusing problem it seemed only he could solve. Across the room, an episode of the early 2000s reboot of Battlestar Galactica played on the TV. In this episode, Edward James Olmos, as Commander Adama, was brooding on a confusing problem that it seemed only he could solve. The show fit Martin's mood perfectly.

Sensing motion out of the corner of his eye, Martin turned his head and watched as Gwen materialized.

The two of them looked at each other for a moment, waiting for the other to speak so they could get an idea of the overall tone of the coming conversation. After several seconds of silent staring, they both had all too clear a picture of the tone, so Martin just went ahead and spoke up.

"Hey."

"Hey."

"Have a seat."

Gwen sat at the other end of the couch, as far away from Martin as she could possibly be while still sitting on the same piece of furniture. They both watched the TV long enough to see Colonel Tigh tell Commander Adama that they were in a terrible mess this time.

Gwen asked, "Okay, Martin, what's up with you?"

"What's up with me is that I've repeatedly asked you, and all of our friends, for help, and you all treated me like I was crazy, or stupid, or maybe both."

"I'm not talking about that. I'm talking about you and me. You haven't called me in days, Martin. Why not?"

"I have called you, repeatedly, to ask you for help. Remember? You treated me like I was crazy, or stupid, or both."

"No, you didn't call me, you called everybody. I want to know why you haven't called just me."

"Why, so you can mock me solo, without all the competition?"

"No, so we can talk about how we left things."

"Oh. That."

"Yeah. That. So, why haven't you contacted me?"

"Probably the same reason you haven't contacted me."

"That's . . ." Gwen paused a moment before continuing, relaxed, and in a softer voice, "a good point. You're right. I could have called you just as easily."

Martin nodded.

"Okay," Gwen said, "so, I'm calling you now, in person. Let's talk about it."

"I'm happy to, but I don't know that there's much more for me to say. I told you that I'm not proposing to you yet, but that I do expect to propose to you. You didn't say one way or the other how you felt about that, which sort of told me where you stand anyway."

"See that, Martin? There's part of the problem. You're making an assumption. You assume that me not saying anything means I don't want to marry you."

"Doesn't it?"

"No, it doesn't."

"It doesn't mean that you don't want to marry me?"

"No."

Martin squinted. "If I'm counting all the don'ts, doesn'ts, and nos correctly, you're saying that you do want to marry me, or at least you're not against marrying me, someday."

"That's right. Maybe. Someday."

"Thank you, Gwen. At some point in the future, you might make me the happiest man in the world."

"Martin. I like the idea of marrying you, but before we get serious about that, there's another conversation we need to have, and I'm not looking forward to it."

"Well, let's have it now, because if we don't, I'll live my life dreading that conversation, and I don't know what it is."

"Okay." Gwen pulled her feet up onto the couch, then turned to face Martin. "I want to have kids."

Martin smiled. "So do I! No more than three, though."

"Agreed, totally. I was thinking two."

"Cool. I'm fine with that. There, that wasn't so bad."

"That wasn't the conversation, Martin. That was just the lead-up to the conversation."

"Oh. Okay." Martin swallowed hard and asked, "What else?"

Gwen said, "I want us to be good parents."

"I'm not against that. So far so good."

"That means doing what's best for the kids even if it's not what I personally want."

"I understand."

"I've thought about it, and I don't want to raise our kids in Medieval England."

"Oh. Okay. I see why you were nervous about this. Asking someone to move is a big deal. But, Gwen, I think I could be happy living in Atlantis."

"I don't think we should raise them in Atlantis either. It's just . . . I want our kids to be normal, happy children. If we raise them in Leadchurch, Camelot, or Atlantis, they won't be normal. I don't want to raise all-powerful God children. Star Trek has shown us how that works out, and it isn't good."

"We wouldn't give them powers until they were old enough to handle it, Gwen."

"But we'd still have ours. Instead of being able to create anything they want for themselves, they can get their parents to give them anything they want. Reality TV has shown us how that works out, and, again, it isn't good either."

"What are you saying, Gwen?"

"I'm saying that I think the only way for us to raise well-adjusted children would be to move back to our original time, and not use our powers."

"You're asking me to choose either a package deal of magic, time travel, unlimited wealth, and immortality, or you?"

"Yes, but only for a while. We could limit ourselves while we're raising them, then tell them the deal when they turn twenty-one. Look, Martin, it's a big decision, and I don't want you to rush into it. You think about it for a while, and get back to me. Okay?"

Before Martin could respond, Gwen disappeared.

A thousand thoughts swirled in Martin's head at once, but he was certain of one thing: he needed to go to the bathroom. He stood up, stepped around the edge of the couch, stopped, shouted several very loud obscenities, then asked, "You heard all of that, didn't you?"

In the corner of the room, sitting in his invisible prison, Future Phillip smiled and nodded vigorously.

Phillip materialized in Brit the Elder's home. Brit the Elder had instructed him to teleport directly into the house for the time being to avoid suspicion, for all the good it had done them. Still, he felt self-conscious about barging into her domain in this manner, and made a point of appearing right by the entrance, as it felt to him like the closest thing to being outside he could manage while still, technically, being inside.

He called out, "Hello?"

He heard no answer, just a strange, distant, wavering, high-pitched whine he couldn't quite identify.

"Hello?"

Still no response. Normally, Phillip would have simply assumed that she was somewhere else, or didn't want to be disturbed, but something made him uneasy. It may well have been the weird noise. The more he heard it, the less he liked it. Focusing on the sound for even a second caused the hairs on the back of his neck to stand up.

Phillip walked slowly toward Brit's office. One could have described what he was doing as sneaking, if he hadn't continued shouting friendly-sounding greetings as he went.

"Hello? Brit? It's me, Phillip. Are you home?"

Through the partially open office door, Phillip could see that the office lights were off, but the room was illuminated in the bluish glow that in real life told one that a TV or computer monitor was on, and in films meant that something awful was about to happen.

Phillip gently pushed the door open. The high, keening noise got slightly louder. Brit the Elder's classic Macintosh sat on the desk, its monitor casting light on the empty space where her office chair usually sat. The volume of light and the direction of the shadows told Phillip that the Mac was not the only source of light in the room. He craned his neck to the right, and saw a second computer, a more modern desktop PC with a flat-panel monitor and cheap, factory-furnished keyboard and mouse set up on a small table in the corner. Brit the Elder sat at that keyboard in her office chair, staring into the monitor, motionless, her right hand resting on the mouse.

"Hello. There you are," Phillip said.

Brit the Elder didn't move. Now that he was in the room with the source of the high-pitched whine, Phillip could tell that it was coming from the general area of the computer.

Phillip took a step closer. "Um, hello?" Brit the Elder said nothing and remained perfectly still.

Half of Phillip wanted to grab Brit the Elder by the shoulders and force her to acknowledge him. The other half wanted to teleport out of there, move to some Island in the Caribbean, change his name, and never find out if what he suspected was true.

He took another step. In the back of his head he pictured a beach, a grass shack that didn't conform to standard building codes, and a closet full of Hawaiian shirts with laundry tags that read *John Smith*.

He said, "Brit!" His increasingly panicky-sounding inner voice said, *Maybe she's on to something and doesn't want to break her concentration to talk.* In his mind's eye, he saw the ignorant and happy Mr. Smith, hard at work at his new job teaching tourists how to operate snorkels. He was standing waist-deep in the cool blue ocean, saying "That's it, folks, the secret is to breathe only when the end of the tube is sticking up in the air."

Phillip reached out and gently grasped Brit the Elder's shoulder. She remained perfectly still. He saw that while it appeared that her right hand was hovering a fraction of an inch above the mouse, the only part of her hand making contact was the tip of her index finger touching the mouse's right button. Phillip exerted the slightest bit of force into Brit the Elder's shoulder. Her body was rigid, as if carved from stone.

On the screen, he noticed that next to the text window in which the file was displayed, there was a smaller window labeled "Untitled – Notepad." One of the three-number sequences Jimmy had spoken at length about earlier was copied into the Notepad window. Brit's left hand hung in space above the keyboard, her pinkie and index fingers resting on the control key and the letter *V*.

Brit the Elder had wanted to copy a section of Brit the Younger's memories over her own. Phillip thought they had talked her into taking a day to think it over. Clearly, they'd just given her time to do it anyway, without any interference.

As he watched, the computer flickered, its entire flat-screen monitor briefly turning into a smooth black rectangle with a blurry, large-print approximation of the display plastered onto its front like a sticker.

As the computer shifted back and forth between its normal and low-res states a few more times, Phillip noticed that the keyboard, mouse, desk beneath it, wall behind it, and Brit's entire body were flickering as well.

Phillip pulled on Brit's shoulder. As her entire body tilted back, her hands and feet all lifted without even the slightest muscle moving. Phillip spun the chair. Brit the Elder's left eye was three-quarters open. Her right eye was three-quarters shut. Her mouth hung open, her lips curled into an odd shape. She looked like she'd been frozen midword, making a face no human being would ever make deliberately for more than a fraction of a second. The computer and wall behind her shifted states again, and Brit did as well, briefly taking on the appearance of a character from a late-nineties video game.

As she regained her normal appearance, for just a moment, quick enough that Phillip wasn't sure he'd seen it, her facial expression changed, her features twisting into a picture of pure agony, then blinked back to look as she had before.

Phillip leaned in and turned his head away so that his ear was closer to Brit the Elder's mouth. The noise he'd been hearing was coming from her.

He cringed and recoiled in horror, flexing his right hand as if he'd caught a fast-moving baseball without a glove. Brit the Elder sat, motionless, randomly leaping between looking frozen, poorly rendered, and wracked with anguish and pain, all the while emitting a sound that could be a small fraction of a word, or the beginning of a shriek of agony.

Phillip rubbed his hands together and bit his lower lip. He didn't know what to do.

I have to do something, he thought. *I can't just stand here, rubbing my hands together.*

He looked down at his hands. His left felt normal, but the right felt odd. The palm was slightly numb, but also slightly itchy. At first both hands looked fine, but then, at the exact moment that the wall, the computer, and Brit the Elder all flickered, the palm of his right hand where he'd grasped Brit the Elder's shoulder also transformed, losing all texture and variation in its coloring before immediately changing back.

23.

Fifteen minutes later, Brit the Elder's main room was full of concerned wizards and a constant high-pitched tone coming from Brit the Elder in the next room.

Brit the Younger muttered, "How could she be so dumb?"

Phillip said, "It's not just her. We were both dumb."

Brit the Younger said, "Oh, I know. Believe me, I understand that. All I'm saying is that it's surprising for her to do something this stupid."

Phillip said, "I deserve that."

Brit the Younger said, "Again, I know."

They all lapsed back into silence, allowing the constant drone from Brit the Elder to reassert itself.

Brit the Younger said, "We could stuff a towel in her mouth."

"Brit!" Phillip scolded.

"Oh, shut up! It's not like she's breathing."

Louiza and Gwen emerged from the office. Louiza had been a doctor before she found the file and became a sorceress, so she acted as the de facto primary care physician of the entire magical community.

Martin asked, "How is she?"

Louiza shrugged. "What do you expect me to say? She's frozen. Stuck. I don't know what else to tell you. What's wrong with her isn't medical. No pulse. No circulation, no brain activity, and no respiration. I should declare her deceased, except that I know what dead looks like, and that isn't it."

"Why not?" Gary asked.

"Well, she's making noise, for one thing. Also, when a person dies, their tissues start deteriorating immediately. She's not. Her body's in perfect order, aside from the fact that it keeps phasing in and out, and doesn't seem to be functioning at all."

Brit the Younger turned to Phillip. "Let me make sure I've got this straight. She had a memory that didn't match what really happened, and her feet started looking weird."

Phillip held up his right hand, palm forward. All of the wrinkles, folds, and creases on the front of his palm and fingers briefly disappeared, replaced by smooth planes and sharp folds. "They did this. Her feet were doing this, just like the rest of her and her desk is doing in there."

"And the wall," Louiza said.

"Yes," Phillip agreed. "And a small part of the wall."

"No, not a small part." Louiza said. "Most of the wall behind the computer is jumping in and out like she is."

"I must not have seen how far it went. I was a bit distracted." Phillip turned his hand to look at his palm, made a fist, and lowered his hand to where he wouldn't have to look at it.

Brit the Younger said, "Whatever. So Brit the Elder has this terrible problem, and she tells you about it. But you chose not to inform me, even though you knew it would affect me in the future."

Phillip said, "Well now, I—"

"Do not," Brit interrupted, "tell me about free will. You know that I believe she's me in the future. So, you know that whatever happens to her, I believe will happen to me."

"I wanted to tell you. I was desperate to tell you. But they told me it wasn't safe—"

Brit the Younger shouted, "They?! You didn't tell me, but you did tell someone else?"

"No! Brit the Elder did before she told me! And it doesn't really count because . . . oh no! I'm so sorry. I need to check on someone. I'll be right back. *Transporto al la oficejo!*"

Phillip disappeared.

Brit the Younger let out a long, frustrated grunt.

Phillip reappeared with someone else in tow. "Everyone, this is Brit the Much Elder."

Brit the Much Elder nodded. "Good to see you all again. I don't like being called much elder, though. Please, just call me Brit."

Brit the Younger said, "No. Why haven't I met you before?!"

"We have. I mean, I've met you. You'll meet me again, someday, and that'll be the first time we meet, for me. I try to stay out of your life. You've got enough on your plate with Brit the Elder, who I hear has done something stupid. I'd like to see her."

Phillip started to get up. "She's in her office. I'll show you the—"

Brit the Much Elder put up a hand to stop Phillip. "You stay there. I remember where the office is. I used to live here."

Brit the Much Elder excused herself and disappeared down the hall.

Gary said, "Another Brit! Jeez, how many of you are there?"

Brit the Younger said, "I don't know. I've never met this one before. How did you meet her, Phillip?"

"Brit the Elder introduced me, I swear."

"You say that like you think it'll make this better somehow."

"Brit, I wanted to tell you what was going on, but I had two people who you believe are you, telling me that the two of you being in the same room might lead to a crash that would destroy the world."

"And the fact that there were two of them in the same room didn't do anything to disprove that idea for you?"

"No! I mean, yes, at first, but then they said that made telling you more dangerous, because then there'd be three of you. Look, it made sense when they explained it."

"I doubt that."

The constant high-pitched whine from the other room stopped abruptly. All conversation ended as every head turned to look at the office door. Brit the Much Elder came out.

"Did you fix her?" Phillip asked

Brit the Much Elder said, "I stuffed a towel in her mouth. It's not like she's breathing."

Brit the Younger allowed herself to smile for half a second before she went back to glowering at Phillip. "So all this time, you've been sneaking off to hang around with two other Brits and work on this problem."

"Not just us."

"Who else are we missing? Brit the Elder Still?"

"No, not another Brit."

"Who, then?"

Brit the Much Elder said, "You should tell them, Phillip. In fact, I'll go get him. He's more likely to know what to do than either of us."

Brit the Much Elder disappeared.

Phillip bit his lower lip. "Okay. I want everyone to be ready for a shock. Please know, I didn't want to involve him to begin with."

Brit the Much Elder reappeared with Jimmy, who was wearing his old green-and-gold wizard robes. Phillip put up his hands in a futile effort to quiet the howls of shock and protest he anticipated. The effort was futile, because the howls didn't come.

Phillip asked, "Why aren't you shocked? I don't think you understand. We didn't go back before Jimmy died to get him. This isn't Jimmy from the past. This is Jimmy after the whole slog with Todd. He faked his own death."

Tyler said, "We know, Phillip. You're the one who told all of us that you didn't believe he was dead."

"Well, here's proof!" Phillip motioned toward Jimmy. "Right here!"

Gwen said, "We didn't need proof. We were sure."

"No, you all thought he was dead."

Jeff said, "At first, but then Roy and I tracked him down. I check in on him every now and then, just to make sure he isn't causing any trouble."

Gary said, "Me, too."

Martin pointed to himself and Gwen. "We went together. Kind of made a long weekend of it. Reno can be a lot of fun, if you have the power to warp the laws of probability."

Tyler said, "And I haven't been checking up on him, per se. I've just gone to visit a few times."

Jimmy said, "And you're always welcome, Tyler."

Phillip didn't understand. "What?!"

Tyler shrugged. "Yeah, I mean, the first time I went, it was to make it clear to him that he hadn't fooled me, but then we got to talking, and it turns out we share a lot of interests."

"Like what?"

"Fantasy literature, for one thing."

"Well yes," Phillip said, "I suppose that checks out, since he killed everybody in a small town trying to turn them into hobbits, and made you disappear when you found him out."

"Yes, but he took his punishment, which lasted decades, from his point of view. When he came back, he proved that he'd changed his ways and put up with us still treating him like a monster, then he saved my life—yours, too, Phillip. Heck, he saved most of our lives. That doesn't erase anything he did, but, you know, you've got to let go of your anger eventually."

Phillip said, "So, you've all known that he's alive, and none of you told me or Brit?"

Brit the Younger said, "I suggest you think very carefully before you act mad at them for keeping something a secret from you, Phillip."

Phillip thought very carefully, then nodded. "Point taken."

Brit the Younger said, "Okay, so Phillip's been keeping his activities with the two elder Brits secret from me. We've all been keeping Jimmy secret from Phillip. Jimmy tried and failed to keep himself secret from all of us. Is there anything else anybody'd like to get off of their chests?"

Several heads turned to look at Martin, who shrugged. "Yeah, okay, I'll be right back." He disappeared, then rematerialized. Future Phillip appeared beside him, slouching and scowling. His face turned beet red, his oily hair whipped around, and spittle flew from his mouth as he unleashed a prolonged series of insults, obscenities, and threats, none of which could be heard since he was still trapped in Martin's mime box.

Phillip pointed at Future Phillip, but looked at Martin. "What? What is this?"

"It's you," Martin said, avoiding eye contact.

Phillip stepped closer, studying Future Phillip, who was now silently shouting directly back in his face. "Yes, I figured that part out. Why's he here, and why can't I hear him?"

"He's the Jawa. I said someone was messing with you. I was right." Martin pointed at Future Phillip. "He was messing with you. So I captured him."

Future Phillip ran out of breath and finally stopped his silent shouting. He put a hand out and leaned against the invisible wall of his prison, panting.

Martin smiled and touched the end of his staff to the force field. "Now that he's calmed down a bit, I'll let him talk. Unmute."

Future Phillip's loud panting became audible. He glared at Martin and in a hoarse growl, said, "You idiot! This is exactly what I was trying to prevent."

"What is?" Martin asked.

"This! This problem. This meeting. Brit the Elder being stuck midword in there. You all trying to figure out what to do about it." He pointed at Jimmy. "Him being here. Martin, if you had just stayed out of my way, I would have gotten in my own way, and we might have prevented all of this!"

"Well how was I to know?"

"I told you! Repeatedly!"

"You said you were trying to prevent a tragedy. You didn't say it was this."

"This isn't it. Not all of it. Just the beginning."

Phillip asked, "Okay, what else happens?"

"You'll find out," Future Phillip said. "It can't be prevented now, so we'll all just watch it together, and when it's done, we can all thank Martin."

Martin said, "That's not fair."

"None of this is fair, Martin. And, by the way, I knew about your stupid mime box. I've known about it ever since you told me about it, just now, all the way back when I was him." He pointed at Phillip.

"Then how'd I trap you in it?"

"You caught me by surprise. I didn't think you'd stoop so low as to trap me when—"

Martin blurted, "Mute." Future Phillip's voice went silent, despite his mouth's continued motion.

Martin grinned at Phillip. "I don't want to ruin the surprise."

Phillip asked his future self, "Can you please show me your right hand?"

Future Phillip held up his right hand.

Phillip asked, "The front of the hand and all of the fingers, please? Not just the middle one."

The older Phillip obliged, showing a perfectly normal hand with no sign of a glitch.

Brit the Younger said, "Well, this is all a fine mess."

Tyler said, "Or maybe it isn't! Maybe everything is fine. I think we're all looking at this the wrong way. I mean, Dirty Phillip says that there's going to be a tragedy, but Later Brit says otherwise, just by being here."

Phillip asked, "How so?"

Brit the Much Elder said, "What Tyler's thinking is that, since I'm a later version of Brit the Elder, and I seem to be okay, then everything must turn out fine. She has to either come out of it on her own, or one of us figures out how to fix her."

"Exactly," Tyler said.

"And he's wrong," Brit the Much Elder continued. "Brit the Elder was suffering a glitch. We can't know just how much of the timeline was affected. We can't assume that because I'm here, everything's fine."

"And Grungy Phillip's hand is okay."

"That doesn't mean there isn't a problem."

"No, but it is a good indication that everything works out. Look, I'm not saying that we shouldn't do anything. I think we have to do something. I'm just saying that whatever we do, it seems like it will work."

Jeff said, "This whole thing started because Brit the Elder had a problem with her memory, right? And now she's messed with her memory. She might have caused her own problem, retroactively. We could find the part of her code that applies to the memory that was out of sync. I'm betting it's the one she deleted anyway. Then we compare the code in her memory file to the code in both of you Brits' files, and make it match. In theory, that should restore her memories and fix the damage she did."

Roy stroked his chin. "It's certainly a simple solution."

Jeff said, "Thanks."

"And a damn sloppy one. Just rushing in and making changes is how she ended up the way she is. When you blunder your way into a problem, the solution's almost never to blunder your way back out of it."

Jimmy said, "I agree. We have to do something, but we have to be smart about it. We need to set up a simulator, or if we can't figure that out, test ideas out on rats or something. I wouldn't feel good about it, but it's Brit the Elder's life we're talking about."

Louiza said, "There are well-laid-out protocols for testing things on animals. I think, in this case, it could be done humanely. We'd be teaching them mazes and changing their code, not any painful medical procedures."

"How long would that take?" Brit the Younger asked.

Louiza and Jimmy looked at each other and shrugged. Jimmy said, "Weeks, if we're very lucky. Probably months. Maybe even years. There's no way to know. But we're time travelers. We can take as long as we need."

Brit the Younger shook her head. "You all keep saying we when you talk about someone doing all of this work, but let's be honest. We're talking about me. I'm the one who's going to have to do it."

"We'll all help you," Gwen said.

"Yes, you'll help me while I do it. It's not going to be as urgent to all of you as it is to me, because I'm the one it's going to happen to." She pointed at Brit the Much Elder. "It's not as important to her, because it already happened to her, and she's come out unscathed. We're talking about my problem."

Brit the Much Elder said, "You're right. She's right. It's her future we're talking about. She should decide what we do. So, what'll it be?"

Before Brit the Younger answered, Phillip put a hand on her shoulder and said, "There are only two options. Sure, one will take a tremendous amount of time, effort, and discipline, but it's the safest, wisest choice. The faster option Jeff suggested is just too risky, despite being far, far easier. Really, Brit, you have no choice."

Phillip smiled at Brit the Younger, who scrunched up her face in irritation without looking at him. He cast his eyes over the rest of the group, none of whom looked impressed. The only one making eye contact was Future Phillip, who stood in his invisible prison with a look of contempt and disgust.

Brit the Younger sat up straight. "Sorry. One second. I have a call. It's Nik. I should take it."

Roy said, "I didn't hear anything."

"It's set to vibrate."

Martin asked, "Nik can make calls?"

Brit the Younger glared at Phillip. "He might need me to pick up something for dinner. He knows he can count on me for that kind of thing."

She swiped her finger through several menu items only she could see and jabbed at the item she wanted. "Hello?"

Nik's voice, clearly under great stress, said, "Brit! Thank God! Brit the Elder isn't answering."

"Yeah, she's indisposed. What's up?"

"What do you mean, What's up? You don't know?"

"No. What's going on?"

"Get somewhere that you can see Brit the Elder's house! Half of it's acting weird. It's . . . I don't know how to describe it. All the edges are going all weird, and they're changing back and forth. Just go look. You'll see."

Brit the Younger said, "I'm *in* Brit the Elder's house." She and all of the others turned to look down the hallway, toward Brit the Elder's office. Martin, predictably, had risen to his feet and started toward the office, but stopped short when the entire hallway flickered into low-quality polygons and back.

Phillip said, "It's spreading."

Brit the Younger said, "We noticed."

The hall flickered again. This time part of the living room wall and floor flickered with it.

Phillip said, "And it's getting faster!" He looked at his hand and saw that the error had taken over the backs of all of his fingers.

Again, Brit the Younger said, "We noticed."

"I just wanted to make sure we're all up to speed."

Brit said, "We are. You aren't."

Phillip turned to look at her, and saw that everyone was headed for the exit but him and the future version of him, who was standing in his invisible prison, still looking at Phillip, shaking his head.

24.

Brit the Younger stood by Brit the Elder's front door, ushering everybody else out. At the back of the pack, Brit the Much Elder exited, levitating the frozen and error-riddled Brit the Elder out of the house she herself had damaged.

The only ones left in the house were Brit the Younger, Martin, and Future Phillip.

"Come on," Martin shouted. "We've gotta get out of here!"

Future Phillip knocked on the invisible wall of his cell.

Martin said, "I'll make it move with you. Come on!"

Future Phillip mimed a man walking with his fingers, then used the other hand to lift the little imaginary man he'd made and carry it.

"I'm not going to carry you," Martin said.

Future Phillip shrugged, crossed his arms, and held his ground.

"Fine!" Martin poked at his smartphone's screen, pointed his staff at Future Phillip's transparent prison, and swept the staff's head toward the door. As his cell moved, it shoved Phillip along, forcing him to stumble his way out of the house.

It was easy to see how the citizens of Atlantis had noticed the problem. Three-quarters of Brit the Elder's home was glitching out, the frequency and duration of the low-res periods both increasing, and with every transition, more of the house was affected. In the time it took the wizards to clear out of the building and hustle across the patio to the park beyond, the house was almost totally involved, as was a perfect circle of ground radiating from the rear of the structure and growing with every second.

The error started working its way across the stone patio. The two guards posted there did not move a muscle until Brit the Younger told them, "You're dismissed," at which point they took off, running at top speed.

Martin pried his attention away from the spectacle of Brit the Elder's house and looked up at the rest of Atlantis. Brit the Elder's home was located at the very bottom of the bowl. All of the terraces, all the way to the very rim, had unobstructed views of the house, and Martin could see that every one of them was lined with people looking down at the problem, watching to see what the wizards and sorceresses were going to do about it.

Martin turned to the others. "What are we going to do about this?"

Nobody spoke up. After a few seconds of furtive glances and noncommittal mumbling, all of their eyes converged on the two functioning Brits: Brit the Younger and Brit the Much Elder. One of them had built Atlantis long, long ago, and the other would build it herself someday, so they naturally had some jurisdiction over how to handle the problem that threatened the city.

Brit the Much Elder looked around, thought for a moment, then looked at Brit the Younger and said, "Uh, I got nothing. You?"

Brit the Younger shouted, "What?! No! I don't know what to do! It's not like I've ever dealt with this before! I mean, I have something I've been working on, but I don't think it's quite ready for this big a problem."

Gwen said, "What is it? I say we give it a try."

Brit the Younger said, "Another me comes back from the future and handles the problem while I take notes on what she does so I can come back and do it later."

Gary asked, "Would that work?"

Another copy of Brit the Younger appeared. "Yes, it will. I'm from an hour from now. It's all handled. Now, here's what we did . . . what you're going to do. Brit the Younger, you follow me and take careful notes of everything I do. Here's a pen and paper."

The new Brit held out a plain composition book and a cheap disposable pen. Brit the Younger took them, opened the notebook, and started writing.

The Brit from an hour into the future opened another composition book, identical to the first, except that it looked well used: the pages filled, the cover bent and creased, and several of the pages dog-eared. She opened the notebook and scanned the pages as she spoke.

"Brit the Much Elder, you take Brit the Elder and Hobo Phillip to Gary's. She'll be isolated out in the woods there and we can meet up after all of this and figure out our next move. As a bonus, the sight of her glitching out and Phillip's unwashed beard and hair might scare off some of Gary's unwanted apprentices. Is that all right with you, Gary?"

Gary said, "Yeah, sounds good. If you want any food or anything, Hubert will take care of you."

Brit the One Hour Elder said, "He'll offer, and you don't want anything. Now for the rest of us. First, I suggest we all levitate. The glitch is moving fast, and it's almost on us. We don't know what'll happen if we're standing on the ground when it starts going wiggy, and I don't want to find out."

All of the wizards lifted off of the ground except Gary, who stayed on the ground, smiling smugly. "Wait a second. If you don't know what happens if the error reaches us, that must mean that it won't get to any of us."

The new Brit said, "That's right, Gary, which also means that you must lift off before it gets to you, which it will in less than five seconds."

Gary looked down, saw that the error was only a few feet away and moving fast, and leapt into the air with an undignified yelp.

Brit the One Hour Elder said, "We need to evacuate the city. Martin, Phillip, you go up to the rim and commandeer as many boats as you can."

Tyler raised his hand. The new Brit pointed at him, but instead of asking what his question was, she glanced at her notebook. "Yes, Tyler, we could just use our powers to fly everybody out of here, but a major part of running a successful evacuation is keeping people calm. Boats calm people down. Flying through the sky completely under someone else's control does not."

Tyler lowered his hand. "Makes sense."

"Good. While Martin and Phillip get the transportation ready, the rest of us are going to start directing people up to the rim. We do everything we can to help them get up there, but we don't carry them. Understood? They need to get out under their own power. It'll seem less urgent that way, and keep them from panicking. Everybody got it? Good. Let's go."

Brit the Much Elder disappeared, taking the stricken Brit the Elder and the disheveled Future Phillip with her. The other wizards took off in every conceivable direction, leaving Brit the Younger scribbling furiously, Brit the One Hour Elder watching the wizards with deep satisfaction, and Gwen looking at the two of them skeptically.

"So, this is a system you've been working on?" Gwen asked.

Brit the One Hour Elder said, "Yes."

Gwen turned to Brit the Younger. "And you're taking notes of everything she does?"

Brit the One Hour Elder said, "You keep writing. I'll answer. Yes, she is."

"And you know what to do because you read her notes."

"That's right."

"So, if the notes come from watching what you do, and what you do comes from reading the notes, who came up with the actual plan in the first place?"

"Both of us. Neither of us. In general, the system's meant for emergencies, so it's sort of a given that we have more important things to worry about than who gets the credit. That said, I'm having to work harder than I should, since the notes are kinda sketchy."

Brit the Younger looked up from her notepad. "Well, what do you want? I'm under a lot of stress here!"

Brit the One Hour Elder said, "That's a really good note. Please write that down."

Brit the Younger went back to writing, but said, "When we tried this out on Phillip, we used the video camera. That was to watch how the experiment went, but I think it'd be good for just documenting the action."

"Yeah, and maybe instead of asking you to take notes while you're in the emergency, we should bring in another Brit to document everything after the fact."

Brit the Younger shook her head. "Another Brit. That's your answer for everything."

Martin and Phillip slowed to a hover as they rose just above sea level. Looking at the city from this angle always made Martin uncomfortable. When he saw Atlantis from a distance, all he could see was the wall-like rim and some building tops poking up above the surface of the ocean. It looked like an unusually well-built-up island. When he was down in the bowl, all he could see was the city around him and the sky above. Only when he hovered just above the rim, as he was doing now, could he sense the millions of tons of seawater pressing in, and the enormous hollow, a perfect hemispherical hole in the surface of the ocean, in which the city sat. The distance to the bottom of the city gave him vertigo, the motion of the waves made him queasy, and the precariousness of the entire arrangement made him nervous.

Looking down around the city's marina, he saw ships moored to docks that sprouted from the rim like a bird's plumage. Sailors and traders milled around, going about their business, unaware of the events at the bottom of the bowl.

Martin said, "*Ĉi tiu iras al la dek unu,*" triggering a macro that amplified his voice to a volume that would make the sound technician for a monster-truck rally suggest that he tone it down. He cleared his throat, frightening away every bird in the ships' riggings and drawing the attention of every living thing within the sound of his voice.

"Hello. Look, every person in Atlantis is in great danger. We're evacuating. It's imperative that everybody gets as far from the city as they can, as quickly as possible."

One of the sailors shouted, "Thanks for telling us!" He was barely audible over the sudden cacophony of all the ship's captains issuing orders to cast off immediately.

Phillip said, "Maybe you should've asked for their help, *then* warned them about the danger."

Martin shouted. "Wait! Don't cast off yet! We need your help! Come on! Stick around long enough for us to load some people onto your boats."

Someone shouted, "No thanks!"

Ropes thudded on decks and oars splashed as every vessel started pulling away.

"Hold on, guys," Martin shouted. "You're not in any danger. There's no need to rush off like this!"

"Good," a sailor shouted. "Then the people still in the city don't need to leave."

"Shut up!" Martin pointed at a particular sailor, the captain of a big flat barge meant for hauling supplies back and forth from the mainland. "Hey, you, hold up a second."

The captain and one of his three deckhands used long poles to shove off from the dock, then ran forward to unfurl the barge's square-rigged sail. As the captain fumbled with the ropes, he glanced up at Martin and said, "Sorry. Can't. I have a strict policy of obeying any order to evacuate."

Martin flew out to follow the barge. "Hey, you, how many people can this boat carry?"

"Four. Me and my crew. The rest of the space is set aside for paid cargo."

"Well how about you come back and let us load it up with people?"

"What does that kind of thing pay?"

"Couldn't you just do it for the joy of helping someone else?"

"Couldn't you just pay me for the same reason?"

For a moment, Martin seemed on the verge of losing his temper, but he stopped himself and hung in the air, not moving. Phillip flew up and watched his friend for a moment before quietly asking, "What are you doing, Martin?"

"I'm thinking. Before I do something rash, I'm taking a second to think about what the smart thing to do would be."

"And what have you come up with?"

"This." Martin flew forward, pulling the silver box that held his smartphone out of an interior pocket. He hovered above the barge, swiping through menus on his phone, then pointed his staff at the vessel, bathing it in an eerie green glow.

"Hey," the captain shouted. "What are you doing to my ship?"

The glow subsided, and Martin closed the box.

"Nothing now. I'm done." Martin turned to Phillip. "I'll be back in a second."

Martin disappeared.

Phillip shrugged at the captain.

Martin reappeared, nodded at Phillip, then turned to face Atlantis and raised his staff in the air.

The captain, standing at the stern of his ship as it pulled away, shouted, "What are you going to do?"

Martin looked back over his shoulder. "Oh, are you still here? Don't worry about it. You can go."

"Maybe I don't wanna."

"Oh, you wanna. It's about to get real crowded."

Martin quickly pulled his smartphone out of his pocket, and flipped open the silver box he used as a case. He pressed his thumb to the screen, turned his attention back to the city, and swept his staff through the air.

The sea between Martin and the rim of Atlantis filled with exact copies of the barge, occupying all the empty space, packed so close together that one could walk from the edge of the city to the far end of the flotilla without getting their feet wet. That was fortunate, since the instant the barges appeared, people started streaming over the rim, down the docks, and onto the ships.

The captain of the barge, his voice distant and faint, shouted, "Those are copies of my ship! They're rightfully mine!"

Phillip pointed his staff and created a force field that pushed the barge away at an unnaturally high speed. When the captain was no longer audible, just an angry, fist-shaking speck in the distance, Phillip said, "Well done, Martin!"

"Thanks.

"Who's going to man them?"

"They're self-driving. As each one fills up, they'll automatically break free from the pack and head for the mainland."

"Thinking before you act suits you, Martin."

"Yeah. The problem is, I usually don't think to do it."

Brit the Younger, Brit the One Hour Elder, and Gwen floated up through the center of the city, monitoring the progress of the error, which had engulfed Brit the Elder's house, the park that surrounded it, and the governmental buildings all clustered at the very bottom of the bowl. The glitch was still expanding, engulfing a roughly circular footprint that constantly grew, and accelerated at a steady rate.

Well above the ever-increasing error, the crowd of people fleeing from the glitch progressed at an even faster rate. The citizens of Atlantis made their way to the rim of the city, clogging the walkways and staircases, packed so tightly that one could crowd surf on them, if that person was under the mistaken impression that it was 1994.

Louiza, Tyler, Jeff, Roy, Gary, and all of the sorceresses of Atlantis flew around the interior of the bowl, shouting instructions and encouragement to the people, urging them to remain calm, but to leave as quickly as possible as they could.

Brit the Younger looked up from her notebook. "I'm surprised there hasn't been a stampede or a riot or something. Nobody's panicking."

Gwen said, "They're leaving because we're telling them to, but we've coddled these people so much, they think nothing really bad can happen to them as long as we're all here to save them."

Brit the One Hour Elder said, "It's kinda the opposite of the problem we had in Leadchurch, with the dragons. There they thought they'd all be killed by our mistakes. Here, they think our mistakes can't hurt them."

"I can't help noticing that the common denominator is us making mistakes."

"On that note . . ." Brit the One Hour Elder held up a finger to pause the conversation, snapped her copy of the notebook shut, and projected a glowing blue force field that shot toward a small boy who had slipped off of a walkway and was now falling to the next path, four stories below. The force field rocketed forward and intersected with the boy's trajectory right after he had passed.

Tyler streaked into view and caught the boy by the arm. As he flew the child back to his grateful parents, Tyler took a second to glance at Brit the One Hour Elder, his expression clearly asking, *What's your problem?*

Brit the One Hour Elder said, "That's exactly how it went down before. It just underscores the need for a way to time our response to events down to the split second if this system's going to work."

Gwen asked, "How are you going to do that?"

Brit the Younger, still writing notes at a furious pace, said, "We have an idea. It'd probably work, but it's kinda . . . I dunno, dorky."

"Yeah," Brit the One Hour Elder said. "But I haven't come up with a better idea in the last hour."

The three of them gained altitude, rising above the rim of the city and drifting out over the marina. Gwen pointed into the distance. "What's the story there?"

Martin and Phillip hovered motionless above the waves, arguing with a man standing on a barge that was identical to all of the others, except that it only had a few people on it and it was anchored in place.

Brit the One Hour Elder smiled and placed a call to Phillip, who answered instantly.

"Yes? Brit? I'm so glad you called!"

Brit the One Hour Elder said, "Be quiet a second. We want to hear what's going on over there."

In the background, Gwen and the two Brits heard Martin say, "I made them. I own them. I can do what I want with them."

The man on the barge said, "But you made them by copying my ship. They're copies of my property, therefore, they are my property."

"Are you arguing that I copied your ownership when I copied the ships?"

"Yes."

Brit the One Hour Elder ended the call without saying a word to Phillip.

Gwen and Brit the One Hour Elder busied themselves assisting the other wizards and sorceresses, directing people onto the barges, breaking up fights, and assuring people that they didn't need to struggle to keep their families on the same barge, as all of them were going to the same beach on the mainland.

Twenty minutes after beginning the evacuation, the wizards watched as the last of the citizens stepped down from the dock onto one of Martin's automated barges. Most of the wizards followed the flotilla, flying a few yards above the ocean. Even Gwen moved on, putting distance between herself and the magic-made city that now seemingly had been destroyed in a magic-made disaster.

Only the two present Brits, Brit the Younger and Brit the One Hour Elder, remained behind, looking down into the bowl. They watched the entire city, the city they had imagined and would one day build, randomly flicker between looking perfectly normal and resembling a poorly rendered mock-up of itself.

Brit the Younger said, "At least the water seems to slow it down."

As the glitch spread down the docks to the very farthest points from Brit the Elder's home at the city's rim, the water lapping at the affected surfaces did change, flickering in unison with the rest of the city, but the spread of the error slowed to a crawl once it hit the water.

"Maybe it's because the water's in motion," Brit the Younger said. "Or because the molecules aren't bonded to one another."

"Doesn't matter," Brit the One Hour Elder said. "I'm not cheered up by the idea that the inevitable destruction of all things has been slowed down. If we don't think of a way to fix this, it'll spread to all of the world's water, and all of the land that touches it, like some kind of digital ice-nine."

"In a way, I think Vonnegut would be pleased."

"We have to think of a way to fix this."

"Maybe we do," Brit the Younger said. "Or maybe, any second now, another me will turn up and fix everything."

They floated there in silence for a moment, then Brit the Younger started to write something in her notebook.

"You don't have to make a note of the fact that nobody showed up," Brit the One Hour Elder said. "I'll remember. Look, my job's done here. I'll be on my way. I'd say that I'll see you later, but you'll be me an hour from now."

With that, Brit the One Hour Elder disappeared.

Brit the Younger placed an invisible spherical force field around the entire city, more to keep people from wandering into the error than to prevent it from spreading. After that, she flew out toward the flotilla, past Martin, Phillip, and the captain of the original barge.

Phillip said, "The barges aren't going to be of any use to you. We're just going to make them disappear when the people have unloaded."

The captain shouted, "Are you threatening to destroy my property?!"

25.

Three hours later, most of the wizards sat around in Gary's newly remodeled home in Medieval England.

Shortly after they all reconvened, Louiza and Jimmy left to put their heads together on a solution to the glitch without distractions. Brit the Younger excused herself to go be Brit the One Hour Elder and guide the evacuation of Atlantis. She returned in a matter of seconds, and the two functioning Brits got to work.

Brit the Younger and Brit the Much Elder had made it clear that the only way the others could really assist them would be to stop trying. Since then, the others had merely sat on the two built-in sofas that lined the sides of Gary's brand-new conversation pit, feeling utterly superfluous yet too emotionally invested in the proceedings to leave. Besides, the Brits could declare that they were ready to try their fix at any moment, and everyone wanted to be there, either to watch it happen or try to stop them. The others wouldn't be sure which until the time came. They sat as far from the Brits as they could, lest the grim silence grow too distracting for them.

The Brits worked on two identical high-powered computers, set up on the dining table with two monitors each. Every monitor had the same sets of windows, open in the same pattern. Martin found the whole scene weirdly fractal, but he looked at the faces of his friends and chose not to mention it.

Brit the Elder hung, suspended in midair, frozen in the exact position she'd sat in back at her home. Her left arm was extended in front of her as if it rested on her desk. Her right hand hovered in space, the index finger extending downward to press the button of a mouse that was nowhere to be found. A dry washcloth protruded from her mouth, deadening the constant squeal she produced. The washcloth had long since started glitching at random intervals, just like Brit the Elder herself.

Clear down at the far end of the room, Future Phillip sat, leaning against the wall, sulking in his silent prison. He'd been told that he could go free if he'd just tell them how to fix the mess they were in, but he said nothing and stayed in his transparent box.

Across from Martin were Tyler, Gary, and Roy, looking around in a bored, uncomfortable manner, each exuding that unique attitude that most men are capable of but only use in theaters and airplanes: that they don't want to seem uncomfortable sitting next to each other, but are still going to great pains to make sure that there is no physical contact whatsoever.

Martin glanced at Gwen, who sat beside him on the couch, drumming her fingers. They were all in a terrible, stressful situation, but he and Gwen had made up, and Martin refused to feel guilty for being happy about it. Beyond her, Phillip sat, ramrod straight, with his eyes closed in thought.

All in all, the wizards had little to do but stand by, look concerned, and examine Gary's redecorated home.

The quality of the décor was all too predictable. Gary had created a stylish bachelor pad as envisioned by a man with little or no style. Dim lights almost illuminated walnut paneling and an assortment of darkly colored furnishings, as if Gary had figured that if people couldn't really see his home, they would simply assume it was cool.

"Where are all of your apprentices?" Jeff asked.

Gary said, "Out in the clearing in front of the cave, doing some landscaping. I'm thinking of putting in a swimming pool. I'd disguise it to look like a pit full of blood or lava or something, but it'll be a normal pool full of water, with a diving board and a spa."

"Inground or above ground?" Tyler asked.

Gary grimaced at him. "Inground! Who's ever heard of an above-ground pit of blood? That'd just look cheap."

Martin said, "You should have had them make you a shoe rack. If you're going to make us take off our shoes before we come in, you should give us somewhere nice to put them, instead of just making us leave them in a heap outside the door."

"I've got a brand-new carpet to protect, and I like the shoe heap," Gary said. "If any locals see it, they'll assume the shoes belonged to my victims."

Martin ran his foot across the cream-colored shag, noting that his toes almost got lost in the strands. "It is quite a carpet. I didn't know they made them this . . . thick."

"I had to special order it. It's the deepest pile they can make."

Gwen said, "The pile is deep, I'll give you that."

Roy examined the joinery of one of the dining chairs. "I'll admit, the workmanship's really good for a bunch of untrained medieval peasants."

Gary laughed. "No, this isn't the stuff they made. I went to the future, bought what I wanted, then had the guys try to make something similar. When they were pretty much done, I swapped what they made with the good stuff in a cloud of smoke and a light show, and told them the tools I gave them were enchanted."

"Why go to the trouble?" Tyler asked.

"I wanna build up their confidence, make them feel like they're capable of accomplishing things."

"So you lied to them?"

"Yeah. I didn't know any other way to do it, in their case."

Martin looked at Phillip. He had been through an awful lot, and Martin was concerned for his friend. "How's your hand?"

Phillip flexed the fingers of his right hand. He had put on a black glove, and pulled his robe sleeve down to cover his wrist. "It feels okay. I think it's almost up to the elbow, but I kinda don't have the nerve to look. I saw Brit the Elder's problem spread to her shoes, but I just didn't think about it spreading to other people. What's done is done. I've got more important things to worry about. You know, I considered going with a sequined glove, as sort of a tribute to Michael Jackson."

Martin said, "Eh, I'd suggest a metal gauntlet, like in Army of Darkness. It's a bit less dated of a reference."

Gwen muttered, "Just a bit."

Phillip looked up toward Brit the Younger, who was pouring all of her concentration into the computer monitor. Martin saw a strange certainty in Phillip's eyes, as if he had made some momentous decision and now intended to act on it.

Martin said, "No."

"What?" Phillip asked.

"Don't do it."

"Don't do what?"

"Whatever you're about to do."

"You have no idea what I intend to do."

"True, but I know it's something, and anything you could do, other than sit there looking unhappy, would be a mistake."

"I'm just going to tell Brit—"

Martin put up a hand. "I'll stop you there. Making contact, any contact with Brit, any Brit, is a terrible move. One of them can't talk to anybody, and the other two don't want to talk to you."

Phillip said, "I know, and that's why I need to talk to them."

Gwen shook her head. "You see? You see what women have to put up with?"

All of the male wizards who weren't Phillip nodded.

Roy said, "Phil, when your engine overheats, do you let it cool off or do you step on the gas? Give them time to cool down."

"I need to make it clear that I'm sorry, and that I want to help."

Tyler nodded. "Understandable."

"Thank you."

"And you intend to do so by doing something you know they don't want."

"I rescind my thank-you."

"You shouldn't," Gwen said. "You should double down on it. The guys are giving you good relationship advice. I'm as surprised as anyone. If you're smart, you'll listen, and do nothing until some Brit gives you a signal that she wants to talk to you."

Phillip said, "You're probably right. I should wait for them to make a move."

"Yes, you should."

"Unless . . ."

"No!" Gwen pointed at him. "No unless!"

"Unless by not talking to me, they're leaving me an opening. They could be waiting for me to make the first move. Why, if you look at it that way, I'd be a fool not to go talk to them."

"Yes," Martin said. "If you look at it that way, that way being incorrectly."

Phillip stood up, straightened out his robe, and asked Gwen, "How do I look?"

"Like a man about to make a terrible mistake."

Phillip ignored her and walked to the edge of the conversation pit, near the table where Brit the Younger and Brit the Much Elder were hard at work, conferring in hushed tones over some line of code or other.

Phillip smiled sheepishly, looked up, as he was standing in a pit beneath the Brits, and cleared his throat.

Brit the Younger said, "No."

Phillip walked up the two steps out of the pit. "I just wanted to—"

Brit the Much Elder looked at him, not entirely unsympathetically. "You heard her."

Phillip didn't slow his pace as he hooked around in a tight U-turn, stepped back down into the pit, walked back to his seat, and sat down. As he settled into his seat, he noted the looks of sadness mixed with amusement on the faces of his friends. Out of the corner of his eye, he saw Future Phillip, sitting, disconsolate, in his invisible prison, making an obscene gesture at him.

"That went exactly as well as I expected," Gwen said.

A high-pitched warbling sound rang out. Gary held up his left hand. A flat image of Jimmy giving a thumbs-up in front of the famous *Reno: The Biggest Little City in the World* arch floated in the empty space above his upturned palm.

"You gave him a custom ring image?" Phillip grumbled.

Gary answered the call. "What's up, Jimmy?"

"Louiza and I have been talking, and we have a suggestion to make. Is everyone still at your place?"

"Yeah."

"Mind if we come over?"

"Sure. See you soon."

Gary hung up.

Phillip asked, "Are you really comfortable having Jimmy in your home?"

Gary said, "He called before he came over. That's more than any of you does anymore."

Jimmy and Louiza appeared.

Jimmy said, "Hey, everyone. Louiza and I have been looking at things."

Gary said, "Shoes."

"What?"

"My carpet. It's brand-new. Please take off your shoes."

Jimmy and Louiza both hastily slipped off their shoes. Louiza bent at the knees, scooping her shoes up off of the ground in a single fluid movement. She looked around for a moment, then asked, "Where should we put them?"

Gary said, "There's a big pile of them just outside the door."

"Clearly, you think how we treat your carpet is more important than how we treat our shoes."

Gary shrugged. "To me, yes. It's my carpet, and they aren't my shoes."

Once they'd deposited their shoes on the top of the pile of footwear just outside the door, Jimmy said, "So, as I was saying, Louiza and I have been looking at things. Combining what she knows about medical research and what I know about altering people's file entries, we've worked out a schedule for how to safely research Brit the Elder's problem and, in time, come up with a solution."

Everyone faced Jimmy and Louiza except Brit the Younger, who kept her eyes on her monitor.

Brit the Much Elder said, "Hey, Brit, they say—"

"I heard what they said."

"Well, don't you think you should listen to—"

"I am listening to them. I can listen and work at the same time. That's how I heard him in the first place."

Brit the Much Elder shrugged and turned her attention back to Jimmy and Louiza.

Louiza said, "Everyone agrees that we need to figure out what's gone wrong with Brit the Elder, and by extension Atlantis and Phillip's hand. Jimmy and I have laid out some protocols for how to ethically experiment with the code in a way that will slowly build until, eventually, you'll be able to make certain specific changes to Brit the Elder's code with a reasonable certainty of safety."

Gwen asked, "Could you please define what you mean by a reasonable certainty of safety?"

"Don't bother," Brit the Younger said, still focusing on her monitor. "Tell me about eventually. How long is that?"

Louiza shook her head. "It's impossible to say for sure."

"Take a guess."

"You can't rush these things."

"So, how long will I be wishing I could rush it?"

Jimmy bit his lip. "Phase one should take around . . . I'd say six months."

Brit the Younger took her eyes off of her monitor and spun her chair to the side so she faced Jimmy and Louiza. "It should take around six months? Should, about. There's a lot of wiggle room in those words. How long would it take, exactly?"

Jimmy said, "Probably somewhat longer."

"Probably, somewhat?"

Louiza said, "We can't tell you exactly, because we don't know, but we believe it would take at least six months."

"For phase one?"

"Yes."

"And how many phases are there?"

Jimmy said, "Something like five."

"*Something like?*"

"Depending on how successful it is. If any of the phases fail, we'll need to repeat it until it works."

Brit the Younger said, "No, thank you."

"But then we can come back in time with the solution, and Brit the Elder, Atlantis, and Phillip's hand would all be fixed immediately."

"That's not the problem. Look, Brit the Much Elder and I have found the chunk of memory we think got corrupted. It'll take us maybe another twenty minutes to make sure we have all of it, then we can replace it with the uncorrupted section from our memory, and we should have this all handled within the hour."

"It's risky."

"Maybe. There's a chance that something could go wrong, or that it won't work. The same thing's true of your plan. It's dangerous too, and it has a one hundred percent chance of taking years of work to execute. If my choices are fast and dangerous versus slow and dangerous, I'll take fast and dangerous every time."

Jimmy said, "Yes, but remember, we're time travelers. We wouldn't experience it in real time."

"The rest of you wouldn't but I would," Brit the Younger nearly shouted. "For all of you, a future version of me would pop up any second now, present the fix she worked on for years, and then you all will say *Problem solved, then*, and get on with your lives. I'm the one who'll be stuck doing the years of work."

Phillip said, "You wouldn't have to do it alone. We'd all help."

Brit the Younger shook her head. "But it's not all of your future, or all of your brains, we're talking about. It's mine. Your hand, and Atlantis would get fixed as a byproduct of dangerous experiments on my head. I would need to supervise everything, and in the end, I would end up doing most, if not all of the real work myself. We're talking about me making the saving of Brit the Elder my life's work while the rest of you help out on an occasional basis. I can see where this is an attractive plan for the rest of you, but I'm not buying it."

"Okay," Gary said. "You're against it. Does that mean it's off the table, really? Something this important, shouldn't we put it to a vote?"

"A vote?" Brit the Younger asked. "We're discussing my time and effort, put into performing a dangerous procedure that I've already said that I'm against, on me, and you think we should put it to a vote?"

"It just seems like the most democratic way," Gary said, his voice growing quieter with each word.

"It would be, but I don't remember ever making my personal life choices a democracy."

Roy said, "Look, you're right that this affects you more immediately than it does the rest of us, but we are all involved. If her glitch continues unchecked, it could crash the whole program, and then we're all done."

Brit the Younger said, "All the more reason to get this fixed fast."

No," Roy said. "All the more reason to get it fixed right."

"Okay," Brit the Younger said. "Think about this. The idea is that we, and by we, I mean me, we spend however many years fixing this mess Brit the Elder made, then, what, we, and again, I mean me, come back and fix her here, in our present, her—future me's—past? If that's what we end up doing, then where's the future whoever with the solution they spent years on? Where are they? I mean, if it were me, you'd think they'd turn up right now, just to prove the point, wouldn't you? So let's wait a second and see if any more of me turn up."

They all stood in silence for a moment, more out of awkwardness than any real expectation that visitors from the future would materialize. Nobody appeared.

Brit the Younger nodded. "Right. So, I guess that settles—"

She stopped abruptly as another iteration of Brit appeared, raised her hands in the air, and held that pose as a wave of energy emanated out from her, filling the room.

When the light had dissipated, all eyes turned to Brit the Elder, who still floated, frozen and unresponsive, flickering at random intervals. Phillip pulled the black glove off his hand. The entire front was still affected, with only a small patch on the back of his hand left unchanged.

Brit the Much Elder said, "It didn't work. I hope you didn't spend too much time on that."

The Brit who had just appeared said, "I didn't. I'm only from a couple of minutes in the future, and all I did was put everyone who isn't a Brit into one of Martin's mime boxes so they can't keep us from handling this the way we want." She disappeared as suddenly as she'd appeared.

The wizards all pressed their hands against the unseen barrier that held them in. They shouted magic spells meant to transport them out of their invisible prisons. When that failed, they shouted various things, first at the Brits, then at the mime box itself before they settled into shouting at Martin. He tried to tell them that he couldn't hear them, but they couldn't hear him and kept shouting.

26.

Brit the Much Elder shut her eyes and pinched the bridge of her nose. "Why did you do that?"

Brit the Younger smiled. "I didn't, but I'm going to."

She sat down at one of the computers and started moving and clicking the mouse with great purpose. "Let's see. If the mime box is a macro, it should be available in the Leadchurch shell program."

Brit the Much Elder looked at the other wizards, all of whom attempted fruitlessly to talk to her. She shrugged at them and turned back to Brit the Younger. "Why? Why are you doing this? Why are you trapping your friends? They're just trying to help you."

"How can you possibly ask me why I'm doing anything? You, of all people, know why I'm doing this, why I do everything! Because one of you future versions of me already did it, so now I have to. For once, one of you has done something I'm excited about, and I'm not letting you mess it up for me."

"Just hold on a second and think."

"No. Thinking'll just make me angrier. I've spent years stuck in Brit the Elder's freaky time wake. No matter what I do, it's what she decided I'd do years before. Then, finally, a situation comes along where we're in uncharted territory, and the very first thing she decides is that I can't know. So she tells my boyfriend and convinces him to keep it from me. A future version of him remembers what a mistake that was, though he seems to have forgotten about bathing in the process, and instead of coming and telling me, he just starts messing with his former self. Martin sees that happening, and he tells literally everybody else but me. They discuss it several times, and the only thing they agree on is not letting me in on the secret. And now, when my future health and the next several years of my life are on the line, they all want to tell me what to do."

Brit the Much Elder said, "I remember how much I resented . . . *you* resent Brit the Elder. And I don't blame you at all for being mad at your friends."

"Then you won't get in my way."

Brit the Much Elder shook her head. "I'm afraid I have to."

Brit the Younger said, "And I'm afraid you can't."

Brit the Much Elder opened her mouth to speak, but no sound came out.

Brit the Younger looked at her watch. "Note to self: set a timer to put Brit the Much Elder in a mime box eight seconds ago."

Brit the Much Elder pressed her hands against the invisible barrier.

Brit the Younger turned to Martin. "That's the first thing everybody does. Funny, isn't it?"

Martin didn't laugh.

Brit turned back to the computer and hunted and pecked a bit. "Okay, found it and copied it over the Atlantis interface. Be right back." She swiped her index finger through a few menus only she could see floating in the air in front of her, then disappeared.

Everyone silently glared at Martin.

Martin held up his hands in an exaggerated shrug, then pointed at Brit the Elder, then Phillip, then Brit the Much Elder. Phillip looked angry, and Brit the Much Elder shook her head, but everyone else just sort of shrugged or nodded, as if to say, Yeah, you have a point.

Brit the Younger reappeared, looking pleased with herself. She sat down at one of the computers and started working without a word.

The wizards shouted and pounded on their invisible prison walls but made no sound. After a moment, Brit looked up and saw all of her friends freaking out.

"Look, calm down. I'm going to release you all in just a minute."

The wizards relaxed a bit.

"Right after I've taken this piece of memory from my file and copied it over the chunk that's slightly different in Brit the Elder's."

The wizards freaked out with renewed vigor.

"It's going to work." Brit the Younger pointed at Brit the Much Elder. "She's the proof. I know, I know, possible glitch that negates all of that. Uncharted territory. Blah blah blah. I don't buy it. All of this is preordained. It's all happened before, and it'll all happen again, like a reboot of Battlestar Galactica. The glitch was an excuse Brit the Elder used to keep anyone from involving me."

Phillip threw a silent fit in his cell.

"I know. You disagree. And nobody wishes I was wrong more than I do. But I'm not. I'm going to fix her, and I'm going to do it in the next few minutes, with a simple cut-and-paste operation. Then we'll move on to your hand and Atlantis. Just watch."

Brit went back to working on the computer. The wizards gave up stopping her and just watched, experiencing a strange mix of being angry at Brit the Younger and horrified at what she was doing, but also hoping desperately that she was right.

"Okay," Brit the Younger said. "Here we go. I'm going to make a change to the code in a later version of my file, which is my right, nobody else's. Brit the Elder is going to spring right back to her old obnoxious, controlling self. Is everybody ready?"

Brit the Younger looked up and saw all of the wizards except for the Phillip from the future leaning against the fronts of their invisible prisons, watching with rapt attention. Future Phillip was sitting, looking at her, his face bland and unreadable, as if he were watching a movie he'd seen before and didn't enjoy.

Brit the Younger moved the mouse around and clicked a few times. "Copied and pasted. All I have to do now is execute it, and she should be back to normal pretty much instantly."

Brit the Younger hit the enter key.

Brit the Elder began moving, as Brit the Younger predicted, pretty much instantly. Brit the Elder's entire body strobed between her normal self and a crude approximation of her shape made up of large triangles and solid colors. The two versions flickered back and forth for a few seconds. The pace of the transitions slowed and became irregular. Brit the Elder remained either her recognizable self or the low-polygon version for longer intervals, but switched unpredictably. Every time she regained her normal appearance, her arms and legs changed, moving instantly to new positions that made no sense with each other. Her face also contorted, changing instantly with no intermediate steps through various extreme expressions, none of which conveyed happiness.

Brit the Younger furiously worked the mouse and the keyboard, her eyes darting between the monitor and Brit the Elder's body flailing and bucking in midair. The violence of her movements expelled the washcloth from her mouth. The single sustained tone she had been making was gone, replaced with a new sound, like a badly scratched CD of people screaming, skipping as the car in which it was playing drove over a bumpy road.

Brit the Younger pounded at the keyboard in a panic, ending with hitting the enter key much harder than was necessary and pushing back from the computer, standing to look over the table at Brit the Elder.

Brit the Elder hung in the air, motionless, her arms frozen mid-flail. Her body from the waist up was frozen in low-polygon form. Her hands looked like flesh-colored mittens. Her arms were each made up of two tapered cylinders with a rough joint at the elbow. Her torso looked like two pyramids glued to a trapezoid, the bodice of her dress just a pattern painted on the surface.

The most disturbing part was her face: a rough nose made of three triangles protruded from the front of an almost rectangular flesh-colored head. The rest of her features—hair, eyes, eyebrows, and mouth—looked printed on. Although there was no opening to her lungs or larynx, if she even had them at this point, a steady sound came out, similar to the high-pitched tone before but rougher, like it was made up of several notes that didn't quite harmonize. Below her neck, some portions of her remained flesh and bone, covered with clothing, while others were simple primary shapes and colors. Her shoulder, for example, led to a flesh-toned cylinder, then a human elbow and forearm, ending in what looked like a small oven mitt.

Brit the Younger leaned forward, her elbows on the table, and rested her head in her hands. After several deep breaths, she used one hand to swipe through a floating menu to release her friends from their respective mime boxes.

Nobody said a word. Brit the Much Elder, looking shell-shocked, went to sit in front of her own computer and looked at the monitors. Phillip pulled up his sleeve. His wrist was perfectly rectangular. He slid the sleeve back down.

Tyler and Roy approached Brit the Elder. They looked at each other for a moment, then at the frozen face emitting its high-pitched whine. After a moment of thought, Roy said, "Can you hand me that washcloth? Maybe I can tie it on or something."

Tyler bent down to the floor. "Yeah. One second."

Phillip pulled up a chair on Brit the Younger's other side. He put out a hand to touch her on the shoulder, but withdrew his hand before making contact.

Phillip glanced over at Brit the Elder as he heard the sound of duct tape ripping from the roll. In a moment the noise stopped, muffled by the washcloth now taped over what passed for her mouth. He turned back to Brit the Younger. "We all wanted it to work."

Brit the Younger said, "And I want you to go away."

Phillip stood up. As he turned to walk away, his eyes swept across the room. Everyone avoided eye contact with him except Future Phillip, who looked on the verge of tears.

Phillip walked over and looked down at him. "Hey, Martin."

"Yeah?"

"Give him the ability to talk. I have some questions for me."

Martin walked up beside Phillip, muttering, "*Li parolu*," as he did.

Future Phillip remained seated on the floor, looking up at them, and said nothing.

Phillip said, "You're from the future?"

Future Phillip laughed. "That's your question? I think it's already been pretty well established that I'm from the future. Furthermore, you could have simply asked Martin that. Or you could have asked me and had me nod. It's a yes or no question, after all."

Phillip turned to Martin. "Am I always this annoying?"

"Not always."

Phillip looked back down at his bedraggled later self. "If you're from the future, you know how this mess gets fixed."

Future Phillip looked over at Brit the Younger, still sitting at the computer with her head in her hands. Gwen and Brit the Much Elder sat on either side, consoling her. "I wouldn't say fixed. Resolved is closer. I know how it all works out."

"Okay. So what do I do?"

Future Phillip smiled up at him. "What do you do? Well, first, you completely lose your faith in free will, from the looks of it, and start trying to use future events as a road map, just like everyone you've been arguing with."

Martin said, "I take it back, Phillip. You're never this annoying."

"Yes, he is," Future Phillip snapped. "You want to know what you do after that? After you give up your primary core belief in hopes of somehow undoing the damage that's been done? Is that what you want to know?"

"You know it is."

"Yes, I do. And the answer, Phillip, is nothing. You do nothing. This situation resolves itself, to the extent that it does, without any meaningful input from you."

"But things will get back to normal?"

"No! Things are never the same!"

"There's got to be some way to fix things."

"Some things, yes, but not everything, and what does get fixed, you won't be the one doing the fixing."

"There's got to be something I can do."

Future Phillip leaned forward. "I do have one idea."

"Yes?"

"Yes. You go back in time and try to distract yourself so that you won't get mixed up in all of this in the first place."

Phillip furrowed his brow at Future Phillip. "But that won't stop Brit the Elder from having her glitch."

Future Phillip laughed. "Oh yeah, that's right. You still think Brit the Elder's glitch is the terrible thing I'm trying to prevent."

Martin and Phillip looked at each other, confused.

Future Phillip looked across the room at Brit the Younger, and said, "That's it. I'm done talking to you two idiots."

Phillip walked down into the conversation pit and plopped into one of the built-in sofas.

Martin sat opposite him. "He knows how to set this right. We'll get it out of him."

Phillip shook his head. "Are you suggesting to me that we torture me, to get me to talk?"

"What?! No! Never! I was thinking we'd bribe him . . . you, with something you want."

"Oh," Phillip said. "Yeah. I don't mind that plan. Won't work though."

"We have to try something."

"I don't know. Trying things hasn't worked out well for me."

"Oh, don't be that way, Phillip. I know, it all looks bad, but things could always be worse."

Phillip said, "The woman I love is furious with me, the woman I tried to help is worse off than when we started, and even I won't help me. I really don't see how it could get much worse."

From across the room, Future Phillip said, "Just wait."

Phillip had just enough time to register what Future Phillip had said, then a great many people and objects materialized.

27.

The cameras were the first to appear. Multiple identical video cameras set up on tripods in all four corners of the room.

The next thing Phillip saw materialize was Brit. Not Brit the Younger, or Brit the Much Elder, but another Brit. A new Brit. He made eye contact with her, noted the look on her face, and immediately christened her Angry Brit. She appeared in the corner, her skin pale from lack of sun, with deep bags under her eyes. She stood next to one of the cameras with a notebook and a pencil in hand. A large boom box sat at her feet.

Phillip had just enough time to moan before Martin—a second, presumably later Martin—appeared, standing in the conversation pit directly in front of where the current Martin sat. Across the way, later iterations of Tyler, Jeff, and Roy materialized, standing in front of, and looming menacingly over, their current copies. Up near the kitchen, a second Gary appeared directly behind the current Gary. The new Gary tapped the pre-existing Gary on the right shoulder. As Current Gary turned to see who it was, the new Gary ducked and sidestepped to the left, leaving the current Gary looking at an empty space with a confused look on his face.

Over at the table, a new Gwen arrived, sitting calmly across the table from the current Gwen. The new Gwen said, "Hello."

"Hi," Gwen replied.

Brit the Younger and Brit the Much Elder noted all of the new arrivals, looked over at the third copy of themselves with the notebook, cameras, and boom box, and leaned back, as if preparing to watch a show.

Martin tried to stand up, but the new Martin poked him in the forehead, throwing off his balance and causing him to fall back into the couch.

"Hey, what the hell, man?!"

"You just stay put, junior," the new Martin said.

Martin asked, "What do you—"

"Want?" the second Martin asked, finishing his thought for him. "You want to know what we want, Martin? Phillip. We want Phillip."

Martin glanced at Phillip, who was still seated on the sofa next to him.

"Our Phillip! We want you to let go of the Phillip who's let himself go!"

From the far corner of the room, Future Phillip shouted, "Thanks for that."

Gary looked at the floor and whined, "Shoes, guys, you know shoes aren't allowed in my new place."

The other Gary said, "It's cool. I told them I was rescinding that rule."

"You could have talked to me about it first!"

"That's what I'm doing right now."

Gary shook his head. "Wait, what?"

"I know, it's confusing. Brit had to explain it to me, you see—"

Future Martin shouted, "Garys! Cool it for a second, okay?"

Both Garys fell silent.

Future Martin looked down at Martin and continued. "We want our Phillip back. He's our friend. You kidnapped him. We're here to rescue him."

Future Tyler added, "By force if necessary."

Future Roy said, "And it will be."

Martin sputtered, "But, why, if . . . Look, I only took him becau—"

"I know why you took him," Future Martin said. "I was there. I was you!"

"I just thought—"

"No, you didn't! You never did! It's one of the things I dislike most about you."

"But, I'm—"

"Yes, you're me. That doesn't mean I can't dislike you."

Future Phillip said, "Quite the opposite."

Martin said, "I just want him to tell us—"

Future Martin said, "How to fix things. I know, and he's not going to."

Martin growled, "Will you please stop—"

"Interrupting you? No. I won't. Now release our Phillip, or things will turn ugly."

Martin rolled his eyes. "Look, I'd be happy to! Just tell us—"

"How to fix things? No. We gave you a chance to do this the easy way. Ugliness it shall be!" Future Martin nodded at the Brit with the cameras, who reached down and pressed the play button on the boom box. The future iterations of Martin, Tyler, Jeff, Roy, and Gary all leapt into the air. They floated unnaturally out of the conversation pit, landing back-to-back in a tight cluster, brandishing their staffs and wands, ready to fight. The boom box emitted a sound like a warped recording of a roller-rink organ repeating on a loop. Over that, a female voice with a difficult-to-place accent repeated, "We're going to dance," three times before concluding, "and have some fun."

Martin scrunched his face at the Brit with the boom box. "I think I know that song. Is that 'Groove Is in the Heart'?" She said nothing, scribbling furiously in her notebook.

The music gave way to a bass guitar and bongo drums.

Martin nodded. "Yeah. Totally. 'Groove Is in the Heart.'"

The five wizards from the future all tapped their feet or nodded slightly in time with the music. Future Tyler's staff transformed into a fencing rapier. Future Gary saw this, said, "Oh yeah," and his own staff became a samurai sword.

Future Tyler muttered, "No originality."

Future Martin shouted, "One, two, three, four." Everyone ran forward to attack their earlier iteration.

The current wizards stood, dumbstruck for a moment, then all reacted to the aggression by fleeing. For a moment, Gary's great room played host to a chaotic scene of people running in every direction, shouting either threats or alarmed cries, over the throbbing bass line and bongo drums being laid down by Deee-Lite.

Martin ran two full laps of the conversation pit, Future Martin hot on his heels.

"We don't have to fight," Martin shouted back over his shoulder.

"Yes, we do," Future Martin said.

"Why?!"

"Because we already did! When we were you, they, you know, them, the other us, leapt straight into fighting and wouldn't back down no matter what we said. So, now that we're them, it's your turn to be us! And brother, it's gonna suck!"

Martin stopped running laps of the pit, straightened his trajectory, and charted a course along the length of the room. He had to sidestep around Future Tyler, who was standing facing Current Tyler, both holding fencing rapiers. As he juked around behind Future Tyler, Martin heard him saying, "Three. Four. One. Two."

Martin got into the open, feinted to the left, then lunged right and swung his staff low, hoping to catch his future self in the shins.

Future Martin leapt as gracefully as a hurdler, without the slightest hint of hesitation or surprise, muttering, "Jump. Two. Three."

Future Martin landed on his feet, performed a well-practiced dive roll, and came up facing Martin. He pointed his staff forward and said, "Mummenschanz alpha," loudly, following under his breath with, "Two. Three. Four."

Martin felt a wind stronger than any he'd ever experienced. He leaned far forward, momentarily touching his hands to the floor in front of him. His feet got precious little traction on Gary's shag carpeting. Martin slid back several feet, struggling to maintain his balance and gain some sort of purchase. He shielded his face with his forearms and managed a couple of steps forward. He looked to the side and saw the two Tylers stepping lightly forward and back with no effort. As Future Tyler deftly brushed off an attack, Martin heard him say, "Parry. Spin. Jump." The momentum of his sword hand carried him through a quick pirouette on his left foot, then he hopped up onto the end of the table.

"Don't try it," he said, looking down at Tyler. "I have the high ground!"

Tyler swung his rapier at Future Tyler's ankles, but Future Tyler leapt over the blade as casually as a child skipping rope, muttering, "Jump, and three, and four, and one."

The distraction of watching the Tylers not struggle with the wind caused Martin to lose focus and get blown back several feet. He put his hands down again to stop his slide and looked up, the wind stinging his eyes, at the other Martin, who stood at the far end of the room bobbing his head to the music, looking pleased with himself.

"I decided to build on the mime theme," the new Martin said, "since you were so happy with your invisible box. I hope you're enjoying walking into your own private wind. And yes, I know how weird that sounded."

Grabbing the leg of the oversized table to anchor himself, Martin managed to work his way back up to his feet. Future Tyler leapt off of the tabletop and out of Martin's field of vision. Martin let go of his staff to free up both of his hands. The staff blew back behind him, then lost all speed before it had traveled a foot, and fell straight down to the floor, where it lay motionless next to the spot where Martin continued struggling with the wind.

He pulled himself, hand over hand, along the side of the table. As he reached the computers, he noted that Gwen was still seated, her hands resting on the table in front of her, talking to Future Gwen.

Gwen asked, "Why aren't we—"

Predictably, Future Gwen finished her sentence. "Fighting? Because we didn't fight to begin with. There's really no point. In general, I find that women need a reason to fight. Men need a reason not to."

Martin hunkered down, back on all fours, and made an effort to push himself away from the table into the open to cast some sort of counterspell.

Future Martin said, "Mummenschanz bravo!"

The wind pushing against Martin suddenly stopped. He fell forward, landing primarily on his face, as some unseen force pulled his hands back behind him, preventing them from helping him catch his fall. Because he was tilted forward at such an acute angle, and his hands were drawn behind him, their most natural path was to extend behind and beneath him, passing back between his own legs. The right hand felt drawn to the far wall of the room, away from Future Martin. The left felt less of a pull, but was utterly incapable of straying further than a foot from the right. Whatever was pulling on Martin, it yanked him across the floor like a dog dragging its rear on the carpet, only his position was reversed, with his face scraping against the floor and his rear end sticking up in the air, leading the way.

The pull on Martin's hands continued, but his feet gained just enough traction to stop moving. Of course, with his hands moving and his feet remaining still, the result was a few seconds spent in an uncomfortable, undignified position. Then his lower body flipped up over his center of gravity and Martin essentially body-slammed himself. He slid on his back, hands first, across the carpet and to the far wall.

Martin lay there for a moment, seeing the room and all of the chaos it held with the sort of clarity a person only experiences when he or she is deeply confused.

He saw Phillip, standing and looking down at Future Phillip. Future Phillip was shaking his head no. It was possible that Phillip had asked him a question, or it was just meant as a general commentary on how things were going.

"Groove Is in the Heart" continued. Lady Miss Kier sang something about her succotash wish, which made as much sense to Martin as anything else that was happening at the moment.

Jeff stood at the far end of the conversation pit. Future Jeff stood nearer, with his back to Martin. Both of them shot powerful-looking beams of light from one of their hands, which met in the middle in a point as bright as a welder's torch. Future Jeff's left foot was tapping in time to the music, and he was saying: "Three. Four. Right, two. Three. Four." As he said *right*, he extended his right hand and shot some sort of beam, perfectly anticipating and blocking a magical attack from Jeff. The earlier spells dissipated as the new spells gained intensity and created a new bright spot in the space above the conversation pit.

Future Jeff said, "Two. Three. Right," and shot another beam, which again completely blocked an attempted sneak attack from Jeff.

Martin pressed his feet against the wall and hauled back on his hands with all of his strength. He managed to gain a few feet of clearance between his right hand and the wall. His feet again slipped in the thick carpet, sending him back to the floor. Future Martin remained standing at the far end of the room, smiling like a jackass.

Martin struggled upright and managed to take several labored, backward steps away from the wall, his hands held at waist height, pulling against the invisible force drawing them to the wall.

Out of the corner of his eye, Martin caught sight of Brit the Younger and Brit the Much Elder, both of whom had made their way over to where the Brit with the notebook and boom box sat. Good, he thought. Go get her, ladies. She's clearly in charge. Cut off the head and the body will die.

Brit the Younger said, "You ended up going with background music, eh?"

The Brit with the notebook said, "Yeah. For a big complex thing like this with multiple people, it's just the easiest way to keep track of the timing. We tried a click track, but the guys kept losing their place."

Brit the Much Elder said, "Why didn't you go with a song that's . . . I don't know, *fightier* than 'Groove Is in the Heart'?"

"I thought about 'Ballroom Blitz,' but you need something with a good dance beat, and during rehearsal you hear the song like a thousand times. You need it to be something fun. Also, this song's the right length."

Martin labored his way backward across the room, dragging his heavy load of nothing behind him. He looked over his shoulder at Future Martin just in time to watch him spread his arms wide and shout, "Mummenschanz charlie."

All of the resistance released from Martin's hands, sending him to the ground with great force. His butt hit the carpet and he rolled onto his back. He would have simply sprawled out on the floor like a rag doll, but his head and neck struck an invisible barrier. Momentum carried his legs back, and for a moment he lay there on the floor, head and legs raised in an undignified crunch, until his legs finally came back down to the ground.

Martin performed another crunch while attempting to lift himself from the ground, rolled to one side, then sprung to his feet. He felt the invisible barrier with his hands. It seemed flat and featureless until his left hand felt a doorknob. Martin smiled, turned the invisible knob, and pushed.

Nothing happened.

Future Martin said, "Try pulling."

Martin pulled the invisible door open easily. He went through the door, took two steps, and ran into a second door. He found the knob, pulled, and nothing happened.

Future Martin said, "This one you push. Oh, relax, Martin. Someday you'll find this funny. This day. The one I'm experiencing right now."

Martin lifted his hands to cast a spell at Future Martin, but stopped short as Gary sprinted between them, an oversized broadsword in his hands. He slowed slightly and raised his sword just in time to block a powerful overhand blow from Future Gary, who had the same sword. As the two blades met, a deafening clang sounded, drowning out the song right as Lady Miss Kier suggested that DJ Soul was both de-lovely and delicious.

Sparks shot from between the blades as they struck. Future Gary continued pressing forward with his blade. Gary held it back with his own, sliding backward under the force of Future Gary's attack.

"Hard to get traction," Future Gary said, "with only socks on."

Gary took two halting steps backward until he ran into the side of the table. They stood there, pressing their swords against each other with all their might. Future Gary mumbled, "Two. Three. Four. Grind. Two. Three."

Future Gary maintained the forward pressure as he slid his blade along the edge of Gary's. A shower of sparks cascaded down from the point where the blades met, bouncing off of the table and burning small holes in the carpet.

As soon as their blades were unencumbered, Gary let out a great, inarticulate shout of aggression and took a long, slow, powerful swing at Future Gary's side.

Future Gary's sword was there to block almost before Gary started the swing. As the blades struck and a fresh shower of sparks fell, Future Gary let out his own consonant-free shout of rage. He lifted his sword sideways over his head and took three steps back, again passing between the two Martins as Gary shouted and rained down multiple crushing blows with his sword, none of which connected with anything but his enemy's sword, nor produced anything but noise and sparks.

As another blow came down, Future Gary stepped to the side. Gary's sword swung through empty space and hit the floor, cutting a large hole in the carpet. He lurched forward, trying to keep his balance. His shout changed from angry to confused, mid-bellow. He spun to defend against any coming attacks from his enemy.

Tyler stepped into view, moving backward, bouncing on the balls of his feet, his fencing rapier a blur, pouring all of his concentration into fighting off Future Tyler's attacks, and ran into Gary's back. Future Tyler pursued Tyler, muttering, "Left. Another. Uppercut. Feint right. Lunge."

Future Gary opened his mouth, allowing an assortment of vowel sounds mixed with flecks of spittle to come out, and swung his sword as hard as he could at Gary, who barely managed to block it in time.

Tyler cringed at the sparks bouncing off of his head and neck. "Gary, trust you to rob swordplay of all its style."

"What do you mean?" Gary asked between blocking blows. "This has tons of style."

"It's brutish."

"Brutishness is a style. It's better than tap dancing around, tapping your swords together like fancy lads."

"That's not what we're doing."

Future Tyler stepped back, stood up straight, swished his sword through the air several times in a figure-eight pattern, and shouted, "*En garde!*"

Gary said, "Whatever. I just hope you've studied your Agrippa."

Martin turned to Future Martin, and instead of casting a spell, he simply said, "This is—"

"Pointless?" Future Martin interrupted. "Not entirely. Yes, the fight is completely futile and meaningless, but it does keep you all busy while that happens." Future Martin pointed toward the computers.

At first, Martin thought he was pointing out Roy, who had worked his way into the back corner behind the table, attempting to punch his future doppelganger in the face, a pair of magical glowing brass knuckles on his hand. None of his punches landed, as Future Roy kept deftly stepping out of the way in an overly graceful, dance-like step, sarcastically counting to four in time with the music.

Martin got so carried away watching the Roys that he nearly didn't notice yet another Brit materialize in front of the computers. He looked over by the boom box, and saw Brit the Younger and Brit the Much Elder both still asking the note-taking future Brit questions. Brit the Elder remained floating in the air, immobile, and disturbingly glitched out.

The new Brit looked profoundly tired. She glanced around the room, shook her head in dismissive disgust, and sat down at one of the computers. Both Gwens watched as she plugged a flash drive into the computer's front and started manipulating the mouse.

Martin asked, "Is she—"

Future Martin said, "Fixing Brit the Elder? Yes."

Martin said, "So this is—"

"All over? Not until after . . ." Future Martin cocked an ear, listening to the song. He waited three or four seconds, one finger sticking up in the air. As the rap break featuring Q-Tip started, Future Martin said, ". . . this."

As if on cue, the front door burst open.

28.

Just beyond the door, Hubert stood in his grass-stained tuxedo, wide-eyed with horror. Behind him and flanking him on every side, bedraggled young men all smeared with dirt and plant clippings jockeyed for position and craned their necks, trying to see into Gary's home.

One of the young men, a stout but malnourished-looking fellow wearing a hard hat with a large crack in it, shouted, "The master and his friends are under attack!"

"By the master and his friends," Hubert added.

"We must defend them," the young man in the cracked hard hat said.

"How?" Hubert asked. "And who, from who?"

They watched the fight for a few more seconds, then the man with the cracked hard hat said, "We'll attack them all. In the end, the strongest wizard will be left, and we'll pledge our fealty to them!"

Hubert shook his head. "I don't think—"

"We'll use our tools! Our magical tools! They were given to us by our master, now we must use them to defend our master!"

"You're planning on attacking the master!"

"Either way! Come on, fellows!"

Hubert stammered as the rest of the apprentices flooded past him through the door, brandishing their hammers, chisels, and other assorted woodworking implements. The last in line ran by wielding a hand-powered wood drill, its gears grinding as he cranked it at top speed.

The untrained-workmen-turned-untrained-warriors flooded into Gary's home, and chaos ensued. Martin put up a force field just in time to save himself a blow on the head from a claw hammer held by the man in the cracked hard hat.

He made a beeline for me, Martin thought. *They always come straight for me. Whatever awful thing happens to us, it usually happens to me first. I wonder if it's the shiny sequined robe.*

Martin extended the force field, using it to scoop his attacker into the air and hold him there, harmless. He looked over at Future Martin to see how he'd fared.

Future Martin feigned an unconvincing look of horror as the apprentice wielding the hand drill ran straight into him, leading with the drill, cranking furiously.

The drill sank into Future Martin's sternum like a hot wire cutting into a block of wax, if the block of wax was full of many gallons of highly pressurized blood.

The blood shot out as if from a fire hose. It blew the drill out of the hole and hit the apprentice who had used the drill square in the chest, knocking him off balance and causing him to fall. Future Martin stood his ground, bending slightly at the waist so that the stream of blood remained aimed at the man who had inflicted his wound.

Martin spun around. He saw the Tylers fighting two more apprentices. Current Tyler used his rapier to parry away multiple attacks from an apprentice swinging wildly at him with a handsaw. Every time the saw blade struck the rapier, it made a high twanging sound that both hurt Martin's ears and made him want to laugh.

Future Tyler used his own sword to keep a young man armed with a pair of pliers at bay. The stalemate held for several seconds, but then

Tyler bumped into Future Tyler, who jostled in anticipation of the hit, turned to look at Tyler, lowered his sword, and said, "Watch where you're going." He looked back up in time to see the apprentice, now right on top of him, clamping the pliers on his nose.

The apprentice twisted, and Future Tyler's nose twisted with them, but his face remained stationary. The twisting action propagated through Future Tyler's face, and spread to his body, strengthening and exaggerating as it went, until Future Tyler resembled a bath towel being wrung out. As the twist grew tighter, Tyler's mass seemed to dissipate, and soon his entire body twisted itself out of existence, and vanished completely.

Fake, Martin thought. *They're letting the apprentices win. They have it all choreographed out, complete with macros to make their deaths look good.*

Beyond the man with the pliers, Jeff and an apprentice were pressing against each other with all their strength, each holding on to what looked like a large level.

"Seriously," Jeff grunted. "What do you think you're going to do with this? Make sure I'm plumb?"

The apprentice said, "Hit you with it. It's heavy."

Jeff said, "Oh, fair enough. *Transporto hejmo.*" Jeff disappeared. The apprentice fell face-first to the floor, still clutching his spirit level. Jeff reappeared next to him and sat down on the man's back, rendering him helpless.

Future Jeff, meanwhile, was lying prone, shielding his head with his right arm while an apprentice worked at his wrist with a coping saw. Future Jeff cried out in pain as his hand fell off bloodlessly and hit the ground with a dull thump. As the severed hand lay lifeless on the ground, Martin caught a glimpse of the flat edge where the saw had cut it off. Instead of blood and bone, it was a featureless flesh-tone stub, as if Future Jeff were a living statue sculpted from bologna.

Future Jeff stared at it, shrieking, as the apprentice started sawing at his shoulder.

Martin turned and saw Roy, standing straight and tall. An apprentice stood behind him, attempting to strangle him with a tape measure, but with so little success that Roy couldn't be bothered to try to stop him. Instead Roy seemed transfixed, staring at the spot where Future Roy had been standing, now inhabited by an apprentice holding a wood plane, standing ankle deep in a pile of Roy shavings.

Gary stood motionless while one of his former followers repeatedly placed a chisel up to his chest, but every time the apprentice hauled back with his hammer to strike the chisel, Gary moved.

Hubert stood beside Gary, groveling. "I am so sorry, Master. We heard such awful sounds and I chose to investigate. The others followed me. I did try to talk them out of this."

Gary said, "Yeah, I saw," as he again stepped aside just as the apprentice meant to strike the chisel.

"Hold still," the apprentice shouted.

Gary shook his head. "Why would I?"

Another of the apprentices rushed Future Gary, brandishing what appeared to be a sanding block. He and Future Gary circled each other warily, knees bent, each ready to either attack or defend. Martin noticed that Future Gary's head was bobbing slightly in time to the music, and his lips were moving, counting out the beat.

The apprentice pounced. At the exact same moment, Future Gary executed a well-rehearsed dodge to the left that looked great, but failed to take him out of harm's way. The two men's bodies twirled around for a moment, and the apprentice found, to his obvious surprise, that he had Future Gary in a headlock. He pressed the block to Future Gary's head and sanded him furiously. Future Gary cried out in pain for a moment, then collapsed into a pile of sawdust that hit the ground with a dull *whoomp,* then swirled back into the air, coating everything nearby, particularly the confused man with the enchanted sanding block.

As all of the iterations of Brit, Gwen, and Phillip present were standing aside, watching, working, or making light conversation, the only action left in the room was Future Martin, hand drill still protruding from his rib cage, continuing to douse his attacker, and a large portion of Gary's shag carpet, with torrents of fake blood.

When he was sure he had the room's undivided attention, Future Martin spun, stopping momentarily to writhe in fake agony at the exact points where the torrent of blood from his chest hit the various apprentices, drenching them. He swept back and forth like a macabre lawn sprinkler, not stopping until the stream of gore weakened to a limp arc, and most of the room, along with most of the wizards in the room, were doused in fake blood.

Everyone stood, winded from exertion and stunned into silence by the stimulus overload of the previous few minutes. They panted and stared around, wide-eyed, as the bass line of "Groove Is in the Heart" slowed to halt, and Bootsy Collins laughed and said, "Y'all are crazy, man!"

The note-taking Brit reached down and pressed the stop button. The boom box responded with a loud kachunk.

The room was a shambles. The two Gwens and four Brits present were in a small cluster behind Future Martin and had avoided the blood spray. But the rest of the room, all of the apprentices, the remaining wizards including both Phillips, and the piles of Gary dust, Roy shavings, and large Jeff chunks were coated with blood like attendees of a *Carrie*-themed prom.

A weak stream of blood still poured out of the hole in Future Martin's chest like water from the end of a garden hose, hitting the ground with an audible splash. He turned to Gary, redirecting the gout of blood to a slightly drier spot on the floor. "Sorry about the mess,

Gar. I know you'd just redone the place, but let's be honest, you were going to have to redo it again anyway."

Gary said, "True enough."

"Why?" Tyler asked. "Why did this happen? Why did we . . . attack . . . us?"

Future Martin said, "You'll get an explanation, but it's all kinda high-end wizard stuff."

Martin realized immediately what Future Martin was getting at. Getting hosed down with blood had taken the fight out of the apprentices, but they were still present, looking at the aftermath of what they had done, some studying the tools in their hands as if they were radioactive waste.

Gary said, "Guys, uh, good job, I guess. Thanks for helping us kill . . . us. Why don't you go out front and clean up. I'll come out and we'll talk about it in a bit."

Hubert, who had witnessed everything but had not taken part in the carnage, held the door open as the bedraggled and blood-soaked young men filed out.

"Okay," Tyler said. "We're alone now. Why did you do this?"

The tired-looking iteration of Brit sitting at the computers said, "Because that's what happened. It was pointless and destructive, and it gave a few of us nightmares for years to come, but it happened, so it had to happen, and before any of you try to complain about it, I suggest you remember who you're talking to. Anyone have anything to say?"

Nobody said a word.

"Good. Okay. Everyone on the assault team might as well take off. I'll talk the rest of them through what just happened." She pointed at Future Phillip, still sulking in his invisible prison. "They're going to be taking their Phillip with them, so if any of you have anything to say to him, now's the time."

Phillip said, "Their Phillip? You're not from the same time frame as them?"

She tilted her head toward the note-taking Brit with the boom box and the cameras. "No. She is. She choreographed this whole fight according to her notes and videos, then came here to take the notes and the videos." She turned to Brit the Younger. "She'll leave the notes and videos for you so you can get to work on the fight straight away."

Brit the Younger said, "What if I don't want to get to work straight away?"

"We both know that you don't, and we both know that you will. You know I don't like it any more than you do, seeing as I'm you."

Brit the Younger sighed so heavily she seemed to deflate. "How long will it take me?"

"Planning and executing the fight? Just two months."

Brit the Younger said, "Only two months?"

Phillip said, "Wait? If she, and all of the . . . us . . . everyone that was just here fighting are from just two months in the future, that means he—" He pointed at Future Phillip.

The Brit behind the computer said, "He's you in two months, Phillip."

Phillip looked down at the disheveled, haggard figure and muttered, "What? That can't be."

Future Phillip sneered up at him. "Oh, like you look spring fresh! It's been a tough two months!"

The Brit at the computer said, "Men often let themselves go for a bit after the woman they love dumps them, and they know it's their own fault. In your case, seeing what becomes of you magnifies the effect. It sort of tightens the shame spiral."

Future Phillip growled, "Can we please get out of here? I can't stand to look at him anymore."

Future Phillip, the Brit with the notebook, Future Gwen, and Future Martin all disappeared. One last gout of fake blood from his chest splashed on the saturated carpet in the second after he'd gone.

The Brit at the computer closed her eyes and ran her fingers through her hair. "All right. Look, there are about a thousand better ways I can think of to do what we needed to do, but the big fight and the blood Super Soaker was the way it was done to begin with, so that's what we were stuck with. I apologize for all the stress, but believe me, someday, you'll do the same thing. I could give you the exact date, if you want."

"But what were you trying to do?" Phillip asked.

"Keep all of you out of my way so I could do this." She hit the enter key on the keyboard in front of her. Brit the Elder, still floating in midair, flickered in and out of the high-polygon and low-polygon versions of herself before locking into the normal high-resolution version. She drifted over the table, then lowered until she lay on the table, unconscious.

"You might want to take off the washcloth you taped over her mouth. Now that she's fixed we don't want her to suffocate, though I can tell you for a fact that she doesn't."

29.

Phillip almost ran across the room, sliding on the congealing fake blood, to remove the washcloth.

"Why's she asleep?" Martin asked.

"She'll wake up in a few minutes," the Brit at the computer said. "The macro that installed the fix has a few timed events that are still coming up. I couldn't let her hear any of the conversation we're about to have. I know you all have questions. I'll start with Brit the Younger's. Eight years. I've been working on researching the problem and designing this fix for over eight years."

Martin placed a hand on Phillip's shoulder. "Hey, Phillip. Your hand?"

Phillip looked at Martin, shook his head as if to ask what Martin was talking about, then looked startled and removed his glove to reveal a perfectly ordinary-looking hand. "Okay," Phillip said. "Good. Thanks for asking, Martin, but I have more important things on my mind."

The Brit at the computer said, "More important than me fixing your hand for you, and maybe saving your life?"

Phillip said, "But, I'm sure I helped. I'm sure we all helped."

"Not you. I didn't let you. Some of the others did. Jeff, Jimmy, and Louiza were useful. Gwen did quite a bit, but still, it was just a day or two, every now and then. For me, it was a full-time job for eight years."

"Why wouldn't you let me help?" Phillip asked.

She rolled her eyes. "Sorry, everyone. Apparently I can't explain how I fixed the problem that messed up Atlantis and threatened the rest of the world, because Phillip wants to talk about himself. I didn't let you help me, Phillip, because you helping me is part of what got me into this mess to begin with. You tried to help me by lying to me, keeping secrets from me, and sneaking out to spend time with my worst enemy."

"But you believe that the person you're calling your worst enemy is you!"

The Brit at the computer shrugged. "That's true for most people. It's just a little more obvious in my case. And what I believe isn't as important as what you believe in this case. I've had eight years to think about it, and while you'd like me to see this as you keeping a secret from me to help a later me save every me, that's not the way you claim to see it. You've always insisted that Brit the Younger and Brit the Elder aren't the same person, and that the fate of one isn't tied to the actions of the other. Haven't you?"

"We all know I have, which means that you didn't have to toss me aside just because some other Brit did."

"True, but you believing that is also the very thing that makes me want to. I believe that the person you were sneaking off with was me, but you don't. In your mind, you were sneaking off, lying to me, and keeping secrets from me to help some other person, who I can't stand."

"Can't you try to look at this from my point of view?" Phillip asked.

"That's exactly what I just did."

"You're not being fair."

"Well, you know the old saying. Hell hath no fairness like a woman scorned. Anyway, in a minute or so, the fix will fully kick in. Brit the Elder will wake up. Atlantis is back to normal, too. You're welcome." She turned to Brit the Younger and Brit the Much Elder. "Also, I've planted some code in your head as well."

Brit the Younger said, "You can't just mess with my memories without my permission!"

Phillip said, "Yeah! That's completely—"

Both the Brit at the computer and Brit the Younger said, "Oh, shut up, Phillip!"

Tired Brit nodded. "I know, Brit, and you're right. I'm sorry. If you think about it, and you will for eight years, you'll see that I have no choice. I made it so that Brit the Elder won't remember any of this. I gave her some false memories to fill the gap. Because of how the timeline falls, those memories will cascade to Brit the Much Elder as well."

Jeff asked, "How'd you do that?"

"I can't be bothered to explain right now. Ask her in eight years. Anyway, Brit, her false memories will tell her that you caught Phillip cheating on you."

"What?" Phillip cried.

"When she wakes up, she's going to believe that Brit the Younger caught you in a lie and discovered you'd been sneaking off to have an affair. She chose to confront you here, at Gary's, in front of everyone, and Brit the Elder came because she remembered what an awful experience it was and wanted to offer moral support."

Brit the Much Elder laughed. "Huh! I remember that! It didn't happen, eh?"

"No," Phillip said. "It didn't. I didn't cheat on Brit. I'd never cheat on Brit."

The Brit at the computer pointed at the unconscious Brit the Elder. "Yeah, well, try telling her that. She won't know who you cheated with. You denied it, of course, but she caught you repeatedly sneaking away to be with whoever it was, claiming you were just going for a walk. I find the most believable lies are the ones that are pretty much the truth. Brit, while you're fixing Brit the Elder, and Atlantis, and Phillip's hand, and Brit the Elder's memory, you'll also have to come up with eight years' worth of plausible memories for Brit the Elder. Not what she had for lunch, or how often she blinked, just the highlights. That's still a lot of work, believe me. As a cover, to explain all the work you'll be doing, you'll make Brit the Elder believe you're working on a different project: trying to find the purpose of the program and, if possible, who wrote it, since it's the first question everybody always asks. She'll remember the project as a total failure and a complete waste of time. She's a real pain about it, by the way. Constantly picks at you. Ugh! Anyway, then you'll have to encode all of these fake memories into her brain, and put them in your journal so that the whole thing won't get spoiled when Brit the Elder reads it."

"Wait, what?!" Brit the Younger sputtered. "You read my journal?"

"No," the Brit at the computer said, pointing at Brit the Elder and Brit the Much Elder. "I edited my journals, just like you will. They read our journals."

Brit the Much Elder said, "Wait a minute. They're our journals, too. And I don't read them. Not anymore. Brit the Elder does. I did, but that was a long time ago, when I was her. And apparently you two were using them to lie to me anyway. Phillip never really cheated on me, is that right?"

"That's right."

She smiled at Phillip. "Huh. That's good to know. I mean, in time I stopped being angry at you for it. Never fully trusted you again, but now I see the whole thing differently."

The Brit at the computer said, "Yes, you do, but you won't for long. When the fix kicks in you'll forget this conversation and believe he cheated on you again."

"But why mess with my memories?" Brit the Much Elder asked.

"For the same reason I'm doing all of this in the first place. It's what happened before, so now I have to make sure it happens this time. Furthermore, all of us Brits are the same person. All I'm doing here is messing with your memories! It's galling that I have to explain all of this to you, but then again, I wouldn't have to if I hadn't already messed with your memories. You'd remember why you did it, back when you were me. You're gonna forget this whole fiasco, and that you were ever here as Brit the Much Elder. It may seem unnecessary to you, but it doesn't to me, because I don't want to remember anything about any of this, even way off in the future, when I'm you."

Martin spread his hands out, drawing attention to his surroundings. "But what about the mess? Brit the Elder's going to wake up and find the place trashed and all of us standing ankle deep in a blood-soaked carpet."

"Yeah, that was difficult. I had to make her false memory of the confrontation pretty traumatic to explain this mess. But it's plausible. All I can say is, if you're dating a sorceress, don't be unfaithful."

Brit the Much Elder closed her eyes and concentrated on her memories. "Yeah, heh, things did get out of hand. I was piiiiissed!"

"Yeah. It didn't help that Phillip lost his cool and said a lot of things he couldn't take back. Brit the Elder got so upset by it all that she fainted."

"But she didn't! That didn't happen! None of that ever happened!"

"No, but when she wakes up, Brit the Elder will remember it, and eventually all the rest of us Brits will too."

Phillip grimaced, sank down, and sat on the floor, making an unpleasant squishing noise and taking on the exact posture Future Phillip had.

The Brit at the computer said, "The code in Brit the Younger's head, my head eventually, will lie dormant for now, but in the future when we're Brit the Elder, just before the whole dragon thing starts, it'll kick in and change our memories so that we'll think Kludge turned down the offer. After we and our Brit the Younger discuss it, our legs will start glitching out and the whole mess will kick off."

"So, you caused Brit the Elder's memory problem?" Gwen asked.

"No. I didn't cause any of this. I'm just fulfilling my part in it."

"And your part is to write the program that starts it all?"

"Yes, this time." She pointed at Brit the Much Elder and Brit the Younger. "But *she* did already, and *she* will again."

"So there never really was an error?"

The tired, angry Brit said, "Yes, there was. It just wasn't in the layer of the program we thought it was. We thought it was a problem with the code, but the code was sound. The error was a logic issue caused by the way we interacted with each other. Who or whatever wrote the program, whatever it's for, didn't design it with time travel in mind, didn't think we'd start interacting with earlier iterations of ourselves, and certainly didn't expect us to lie to our former selves through our boyfriends. We all always knew we might cause some sort of terrible paradox someday that could screw everything up. Well, this was it."

Tyler asked, "But there isn't any flaw in the program?"

"Yes, there is. A logic error, as I said. The fact that it appears to have been created by my efforts to solve it is what makes it a logic error!" said angry Brit. "Our having access to the file and enough intelligence to use it is a flaw in the program. This problem was a symptom. We, all of us in this room, *we* are the glitch. We're not supposed to be here! We're assets from other parts of the program all clustered together in a place and time where we shouldn't be, doing things that make sense to us, because they're in keeping with the rules the program set out for us, but that any objective viewer would have to say are completely bizarre."

Phillip looked at his surroundings: his friends from various walks of life, geographical areas, and decades, all standing in a demolished, blood-soaked bachelor pad built inside a cave that resembled a skull, in Medieval England. "It's hard to argue with what you say."

"And yet you're trying to," the Brit at the computer said.

Phillip asked, "So, why did you make the error spread to my hand?"

"I'll tell you what, just for fun, let's see if anybody has managed to follow the situation better than you have, Phillip. Anyone want to tell him why I had to make his hand glitch?"

Pretty much everyone but Phillip mumbled words to the effect of *she had to, because that's what happened before.*

"That's right," Tired Brit said. "All I've done is what I saw me do. That said, I've spent eight years hard at work, going over and over all of this, and getting madder and madder at you, so giving you the ick was one chore I did sort of enjoy. And speaking of things I'll enjoy, I'm going to leave. The changes are about to take effect, and I don't want to be here when they do."

"Because you don't want to have to explain to Brit the Elder why you're here," Gwen said.

"Correct. And I don't want you to have to explain to me why I'm here. I'm wiping my memory of all of this as well. I passed the technical information I acquired to Jeff, but in a minute or two, I'm not going to remember any of this. I'll have a ton of false memories, mostly about being mad at Phillip for cheating on me."

Martin shook his head. "I understand why you're angry with Phillip. I just don't see why you're this angry."

"Because if Phillip had been right about free will, and had committed to it, he could have prevented all of this. But he didn't have the courage of his convictions, and he was wrong to begin with, so he's spent our entire relationship giving me false hope and telling me that what I know to be true was a lie. Either way, I've had over eight years working full-time on a subject I don't find interesting, doing things I don't like, mentally going over and over his failure in my mind. I'm bitter and angry, and I don't like who I've become, which just makes me more bitter and angry. So I'm going somewhere nice and forgetting all about this mess. Brit the Much Elder, you have to scram, too. Thanks for all the help you're going to give me, everybody. The first dance-fight rehearsal is in one week."

She teleported away, leaving an empty seat in front of the computers. Brit the Much Elder shrugged and teleported out as well.

For a moment, nobody said a word.

Gary said, "I just had this place redone."

"Yes," Gwen said. "And now you have the chance to do it better."

Tyler said, "Yeah, and this time I suggest not having a conversation pit. It, uh, really collected a lot of the blood. It's like a wading pool in here."

Phillip said, "Brit, I—"

"Don't," Brit the Younger said quietly.

"I just want to say—"

"And I don't want you to say it."

Phillip nodded. "Okay. I understand. Just know that—"

Martin said, "Phillip, drop it."

Roy agreed. "Yeah, Phillip. Think about the fact that Martin is telling you not to do something."

They sat, bathed in fake blood and awkward silence for a few more moments, then Brit the Elder started to stir. Everyone rushed forward, a cacophony of wet squishing noises coming from the carpet.

Brit the Elder's eyelids fluttered, her head jerked up, and she was awake. She looked around at the small mob of wizards surrounding her.

Brit the Younger asked, "Are you okay?"

Brit the Elder swallowed hard, blinked several times, and said, "Yeah. I'm fine. I guess I just passed out. I guess I must have gotten too upset, remembering what Phillip did."

30.

Later that night, after all of the wizards and the Brits had gone home, Gary sat on his ruined couch in the conversation pit of his blood-drenched living room, thinking about what he would do differently when he remodeled. He lifted his left leg, a prosthetic from the knee down made to look like a skeleton leg and foot. He noted that the entire sole of his foot, or the mass of tiny bones that made up the sole of his foot, was coated in blood. He watched it drip in thick drops from the heel bone, and thought about setting up a macro so that the prosthetic foot would leave bloody footprints wherever he stepped.

He heard the door to the vestibule open. He looked up and saw Hubert peeking around the door.

"Master? The lads and I would like to have a word. Is this a good time?"

"Sure, come on in. Have a seat."

Hubert said, "No, Master, I think we'd prefer to stand." The apprentices all filed in. Gary noticed that Hubert, who had been spared the direct blast from the fake-blood hose, was still wearing his tuxedo. The rest of them had changed out of their work clothes and had put back on the filthy burlap rags they had worn when they first arrived on his doorstep. The apprentices stood at the opposite edge of the conversation pit, looking down at Gary who remained seated in his bloodstained robe, on his bloodstained couch, sitting in a bloodstained hole.

"What's up?" Gary asked.

"Master," Hubert said, "the lads and I have been talking. Today was the first time any of them fought anyone with magical weapons, or, most of 'em, fought anyone at all."

Gary nodded. "Yeah, not surprised. What did you think of it?"

"It was all quite a bit more . . . hands-on than they expected, Master. They had always pictured fights between wizards being more at a distance, using spells and charms and such to do the dirty work."

Gary nodded. "Yeah, that's the hope. It usually starts that way, but it doesn't last. It's like when two guys fight. It starts out as a cool-looking boxing match where they both stand up straight and dance around each other, but as soon as someone starts losing, they'll grab the other guy around the waist, pull them down to the floor, and start punching them in the crotch."

Hubert said, "That's what we suspected, Master. The thing is, fighting people in a rough, brutish manner is a career option that was already open to us. We wanted to learn wizarding to avoid all of that."

"I see."

"So, we thank you for the opportunity, but we're going to stop the training. Is that all right?"

Gary smiled. "Yeah. That means I'll have to remodel this place on my own, but I'll manage."

One of the apprentices, a small, thin young man with a stooped posture and dried fake blood behind his ears, asked, "Can we borrow the magical tools from time to time, if we need them?"

Gary said, "Um, you know what? I don't think that'd be a good idea. It was okay here because you were under my supervision, and we're miles from anybody who might be bothered by the screaming if things go wrong, but the tools are too powerful to just let you borrow. But if any of you ever need anything, or just feel like coming by to say hello, feel free."

"We will, Master. And I have a request."

"Sure, Hubert. What is it?"

"I was hoping that I could perhaps stay on as your buttster."

"Butler. It's called a butler. You'd want to do that without the magic training? You mean, just, like, a job?"

"Instead of going back to sifting dung, yes, Master."

"Well, of course, Hubert. I'd love to keep you on."

"Splendid, Master!"

"And, Hubert, you don't have to call me master anymore."

"No?"

"Of course not. Calling me sir will be fine."

Martin knocked on the front door to Phillip's shop and waited.

He knocked again, and waited some more.

It became clear to Martin that Phillip either wasn't there, or was not going to answer the door.

Makes sense, Martin thought. *He probably wants to be alone.*

Martin teleported past the door into Phillip's shop. He ducked his head through the beaded curtain that led to the séance room and found it empty. He walked around the table to the door that led upstairs.

He knocked, waited a tasteful amount of time, then teleported to the other side.

The first thing Martin noticed was the sound of a quiet piano and an anguished voice promising someone that if they ever changed their mind, he'd be there.

Martin walked up the steps to Phillip's rec room. When his head rose over the level of the banister, he paused to look around. He saw Phillip sitting on his white leather sofa, staring at the wall, motionless. Martin knocked on the wall.

Phillip didn't move.

Martin knocked again.

Phillip remained still.

Martin said, "Okay, I know you're concentrating on your moping, but you're going to want to acknowledge me, because the next logical move is to knock on your forehead."

Phillip shook his head. "If I wanted company, I'd have answered the door."

"I know. There's a difference between what you want and what you need."

Martin picked up Phillip's iPod and scrolled through the active playlist. "'One More Night,' 'Throwing It All Away,' 'Against All Odds,' 'Misunderstanding,' 'Separate Lives'? Geez, did Phil Collins ever have a successful relationship? I wonder if it ever occurred to him that maybe he was the problem. Phillip, it isn't healthy for you to be listening to this stuff right now." He ended up setting the iPod to play "In the Air Tonight," because it was at least a different kind of morose.

Martin looked at the bare patch of wall that had, until recently, held the enchanted door that led to Brit the Younger's home in Atlantis.

"I guess that's one bright side," Martin said. "All you had to do to move out of the place you shared with Brit was remove the doors. No cardboard boxes or piles of stuff thrown out on the lawn. Nice and clean."

Phillip said, "I wish it had been that easy. No, I had a bunch of stuff strewn around Brit's place. I had to gather it all up. Nik followed me around the whole time. He said he knew I was prone to forgetting things."

"Not fun."

"No. Not fun at all."

"Phillip, I know you want to be alone, but I told everyone I'd check up on you."

"Everyone?"

"Yeah."

"Even Brit?"

"Yes. I mean, don't get the wrong idea. She didn't want me to check on you, or ask me about you at all. She was just present when I said I was going to check in on you."

"And what did she say?"

"Nothing. She was busy. All she wants to talk about lately is how she's too busy to talk."

Phillip shrugged.

Martin slowly approached the couch. "So that's what I'm doing. Checking up."

Phillip shrugged again.

"So, how are you?"

Phillip didn't look at Martin but took a deep breath and said, "I've been thinking about this whole mess."

Martin sat down in a chair opposite the couch. "Yes?"

"And I've come to a conclusion."

"Yes?"

"There has to be some way I can go back in time and put things right."

Martin nodded, reached into his robe, and pulled out an envelope. "I wrote down my prediction of what you were going to say and sealed it to avoid tampering. Would you like to read it?"

"No."

"Because it says you think you can go back in time and fix this."

"I'm sure it does."

"You can't go back and fix this. You'll try and fail. You understand that, right?"

"You don't know that, Martin! You only predicted that because you talked to the future version of me who went back in time to try to fix things."

"Yeah," Martin said. "That doesn't mean I'm wrong. In fact, I got the idea for the prediction sealed in the envelope from him. He told me I did it, and now I have."

"But, this time—"

"This time will be the same as last time, Phillip, because this time is last time, or will be last time, and was the next time. Phillip, you're going to try. All of us know that. You're going to do it alone. Again, all of us know that. And, in the end, you're going to fail. Almost all of us know that. But you aren't going to try for another two months."

"Yes," Phillip said. "I've got two months to plan. You know, you could help. If you told me everything about the times you fought with me . . . the other me, future me . . . I could avoid the same mistakes he . . . I . . . made."

Martin shook his head. "I'm not going to tell you any of that. I want you to make those mistakes. They're how I caught you."

"If you're not going to help me, why'd you even bother to come here?"

"I am going to help you, just not in the way you think. Phillip, I'm going to give you the thing you need more than anything else in the world."

"A more helpful best friend?"

"A project. Something to get your mind off of all of this. I'm cooking up something really cool, and I think it'll be right up your alley."

31.

Miller sat in the driver's seat, leaned way to the side, his head turned so that his nose and mouth pointed more toward the open window than the steering wheel.

Murphy sat in the exact same posture, only mirrored, so that he got most of his air from the open passenger-side window. "I hoped the smell would go away when we emptied the back seat. I didn't know some of the bananas at the bottom of the pile had gone rotten and started oozing—"

"I know," Miller snapped. "I was there. I'll never forget it as long as I live."

"The task force is never going to get the damage deposit back on this car," Murphy said.

"Not our problem."

"The chief'll probably be pissed."

"That *is* our problem, but let her be pissed. She's the one making us maintain the stakeout even after she brought Sadler in to consult. What's the point in having us keep him under surveillance now that he knows we're here?"

"He knew we were here be—" He stopped short when he saw the look on Miller's face.

Murphy sat silent for a moment. When he did speak again, it was in a quieter voice. "Maybe him knowing is the point. Maybe the chief wants him to know that we're watching him."

"Murph, I'm pretty close to giving up on figuring out what she's thinking."

"What who's thinking, agent?" Brit the Much Elder asked.

Miller turned, saw her standing next to the car, and let out a frightened yelp in spite of himself.

Murphy bent down and craned his neck to see who had spoken to Miller, then fumbled with the door handle and hit his head on the headliner as he bolted out of the car. "Ma'am. Hello! What, uh, what brings you to Reno?"

"I'm here to talk to you two."

"Yes, ma'am?"

"But I'd rather not do it out here on the street. It's a bit cold for my blood."

"If you'd like to get in the car, we could turn up the heater."

"No. The smell of rotten banana is overwhelming already. Let's go inside."

Miller and Murphy followed as Brit the Much Elder led them across the street and into the lobby of the Luxurious Rothschild Building, the agents growing more uncomfortable with every step. Once inside, she tipped the doorman to stand outside for a moment. When they had the lobby to themselves, she invited the agents to take a seat in a pair of overstuffed, threadbare chairs flanking a large black vase holding several dead branches.

"Agents," she said, "you've been working under difficult and uncomfortable conditions, and I want you to know that it hasn't gone unnoticed or unappreciated."

Murphy said, "That's certainly good to hear, ma'am."

Miller nodded wearily. "Uh-huh."

"So, as a reward, I'm reassigning you to a detail I think you'll find much more comfortable, and more interesting."

Murphy said, "Really?"

"Yes," Brit said.

Again, Miller said, "Uh-huh."

The three of them sat in awkward silence for a moment, Brit the Much Elder and Murphy smiling at each other, with Miller suspiciously eyeing the both of them. Finally, Murphy broke the deadlock.

"You didn't have to come all the way out here, ma'am. If you're reassigning us, you could have just recalled us to Sacramento."

"No, you both have been through so much torment already, I thought I'd save you the coach flight back to home base. Besides, it was more efficient for me to come out here."

Murphy said, "Oh."

Miller asked, "And why is that?"

Brit smiled and ignored the question. "You will be part of the personal detail of a very important civilian contractor. A valuable partner who is in a position to be tremendously beneficial to the task force."

Murphy said, "Oh."

Miller moaned, "No."

Brit said, "You will work hand in hand with him, travel with him, assist him in his work, and in the process, keep tabs on him. What better way to keep track of what someone's doing than to help them do it?"

Murphy said, "I see."

Miller said, "No. No. No, no, no. Nuh-uh."

Brit smiled at Miller, which silenced him more quickly than a harsh word would have.

Murphy looked at his partner, then at his boss. He thought for a moment. "Madam Director, who are we going to be working with?"

The door to the emergency stairwell opened. Jimmy stepped out, a maddeningly genuine smile on his face. "Agents, I can't tell you how happy I am that we're going to be working together again."

Miller leapt to his feet. "No! No-ho, no!"

Brit the Much Elder stood up and stepped directly in front of Agent Miller. "Yes."

The two stood motionless. The only sound in the room was Murphy moaning quietly, because either he and his partner were being assigned to assist their worst enemy, or his partner was about to get them both fired. He didn't like either option but wasn't sure which he liked less.

Though she was substantially shorter than Miller, Brit stared him down. Miller's attitude shifted to angry defiance, then to angry resignation.

"Ma'am, this man can do things you wouldn't understand."

Jimmy laughed.

Brit nearly laughed but managed to contain it with a smirk. "And now he'll be doing those things on our behalf."

"He's dangerous, ma'am."

"That's why I want you two working with him, to keep him in line."

"Ma'am, please, this man can't be trusted."

"And I don't trust him. That's why I have the two of you looking out for the task force's interests. Agents, in a moment, I'm going to ask you if you're in. If you answer in the negative, you'll be unemployed, on your own; you'll know that Mr. Sadler is out there doing something, and you'll be powerless to do anything about it, or even find out what it is."

Murphy asked, "You ever heard the phrase, *If you can't beat 'em, join 'em*?"

Miller scowled. "That's the worst thing I've ever heard a law enforcement officer say."

Brit the Much Elder asked, "Agent Miller, are you in?"

Miller stared into Brit the Much Elder's eyes, then turned to look at his partner. Murphy sighed, stood up, stepped behind Brit, nearer to Jimmy, and shrugged.

Miller looked at Jimmy, who spread his hands welcomingly, and favored Miller with a smile and a wink.

Miller said, "Yeah, I'm in. I'm in it up to my neck."

Jimmy rushed forward. "Great! That's great! Agents, I'm so excited to be working with you both again. The old team's back together, just like old times. You know what, we should hop a boxcar. Just for old time's sake. Or we could get an old car to drive around in!"

Miller grunted, "Don't push it, Sadler."

Brit said, "Agent Miller, you are assigned to assist Mr. Sadler. From here on out, if he chooses to push it, your job is to roll up your sleeves and push it with him."

Jimmy said, "Look, we have a lot of exciting things to talk about. Why are we doing it in the lobby? Let's go upstairs. I have so much to show you!"

Miller reluctantly followed the others into the elevator. Jimmy pressed the button for the top floor, and they all stood in silence until the doors closed.

"Okay," Miller said. "What exactly are we going to be doing?"

Brit the Much Elder said, "Pretty much the same thing Professor Xavier and Magneto did in the *X-Men* movies."

"What, fight constantly?"

Jimmy said, "We'll probably do our share of that, but between the fights, they worked together to find young mutants."

Brit said, "You are going to assist Mr. Sadler as he seeks out and finds people who have found the same computer file he did, intercept them before they can do too much damage, and document them in the process."

"So we're going to prevent people from getting the kind of powers Sadler has?" Murphy asked.

"Yes," Jimmy said. "That would be terrible. Unimaginable. I shudder to think if other people had the same kind of abilities I have—"

Brit said, "You hush. We don't want people with weird powers just running amok. We aren't planning to intervene in any preventative way unless we're forced to. In general, you're there to provide guidance and gather data."

The elevator doors opened. Jimmy stepped out, turned to the left, and proceeded down the hallway. Brit the Much Elder followed. Miller and Murphy stepped out into the hallway but stopped, confused.

Miller pointed down the hall, the opposite direction from where Jimmy had led. "Sadler, your penthouse is this way."

Jimmy and Brit stopped. "Yes. My penthouse is. Yours is this way. Gentlemen, you're working with me now, so I got you a comfortable place to stay."

He dug into his pocket for keys as he walked toward a large door at the end of the hall. "Last time we worked together, my resources were limited, and we had to rely on the generosity of the Treasury department. Now I'm in a position to return the favor. The top floor's taken up by two penthouses, mine and this one. I own the building, so when the second penthouse went vacant I kept it empty. I'd planned to knock down the walls and take the whole floor for myself, but I don't really need the space. I think it's better used by you two."

Jimmy unlocked and opened the door, revealing a large open space with floor-to-ceiling windows and a view of downtown Reno in the distance. They all entered, and as their eyes adjusted to the light coming in the window, they got a good look at the penthouse.

The first thing that jumped out at Miller was the furniture. It was clearly a matched set, made to look as if it had been assembled from assorted parts from several Conestoga wagons. Every piece of wood was turned on a lathe or burned at the edges to give the impression of age. The cushions were a dark red chintz that matched parts of the red-and-brown mottled carpet and the background of the Victorian patterned wallpaper. The foreground pattern was in a dull gold color that matched the fringes and tassels that adorned the edges and corners of every lampshade, pillow, and curtain.

Miller opened his mouth to mock the décor, but instead let out a powerful sneeze that blasted its way out of his nasal passages with almost no warning.

Jimmy said, "*Gesundheit*. The former owner used to be a cattleman—not a very successful one, from what I understand. Then he sold a big chunk of land right in the middle of his ranch to a casino. That made him some money, but most of his fortune came from leasing the land around the casino to people who wanted to build pawnshops, liquor stores, and smaller casinos. Anyway, he loved all of this cowboy stuff. We can remodel the place."

"But why would we?" Murphy said, running across the room to examine a bronze sculpture of a wiry man on a galloping horse who was turned around and aiming a rifle at whomever or whatever was chasing him. "It's so homey. It makes me feel like I'm nine years old again! It's perfect as it is!"

Miller rubbed his eyes. "Murph grew up in Wyoming. This place smells like the last owner was a mangy German shepherd who smoked cigars! That is the yellowest ceiling I've ever seen."

Jimmy nodded. "Yeah, he died of emphysema. His grandson took the dogs."

"Dogs?" Miller used one finger to poke at the cushion on the back of a chair. "How many dogs? Everything's coated with dog hair."

Jimmy said, "Four malamutes. Beautiful animals, but they shed so much you could see a trail of hair floating in the air behind it when they ran."

Miller clapped to try to remove the dog hair sticking to his fingertip, sniffing the entire time. "I'm allergic to dogs."

Murphy said, "We'll get some Febreze and lint rollers. This place is perfect! It reminds me of my grandpa's house! I'm gonna go check out the kitchen!"

The bat-wing saloon doors squeaked as Murphy passed through them, and they continued squeaking as they flapped back and forth before finally grinding to a halt.

"Hey, there's a flame broiler in here! And a salamander, and a cast-iron griddle!"

"Yeah, he cooked a lot of steaks. He ate pretty much nothing but red meat and Tex-Mex. The bathrooms . . ." Jimmy looked Miller in the eye. "Agent Miller, I'm going to have a team of cleaners go over this place with a fine-tooth comb before you two move in. I promise, anything that can't be made clean will be replaced. We're working together now. The days of me actively tormenting you are over."

"Actively."

"I can't promise not to passively torment you, Miller. Nobody can. You've got the whole world on your nerves."

32.

The grand hall of the golden castle of Camelot echoed with hushed conversation and the rustling of bodies. One would have had to listen closely to hear the telltale signs that the sound was recorded, piped in on a loop as part of a simulation. Looking at the crowd, their artificial nature was more obvious. Their heights and genders varied, but all wore identical skintight black body suits, and everyone had black hair and unnaturally blue eyes. People filled the entirety of the main floor, save for an aisle down the middle of the hall and a raised stage at the end where a small group of people stood in two diagonal lines, flanking a large set of double doors.

The imitation crowd stood at attention. None flinched when, without warning, the piped-in crowd sounds were replaced with the Brian Eno–composed theme from the 1984 David Lynch movie *Dune*, a ponderous cluster of four power chords played with tremendous drama.

Martin walked out onto the stage wearing a replica Fremen stillsuit from the film: a bumpy black bodysuit just like those the artificial witnesses wore. In the movie and the book, the suits recycled a person's bodily fluids, but in reality just made the wearer look more muscular than they actually were, which was enough. Martin nodded to his friends, all of whom were either standing on the stage or sitting in the front row. He then turned and looked to the doors at the far end of the hall.

The doors opened, and Gwen stepped through, wearing an elaborate gown with a large, exaggerated collar intricately decorated with gold embroidery. As she walked down the aisle, fake Fremen turned to watch her pass. Power chords echoed through the rafters. She reached the raised platform at the end of the hall and ascended the golden stairs until she stood beside Martin.

Gwen cast her eyes over their friends, smiling. "I feel weird not wearing a stillsuit. That's what Sean Young wore in the movie."

Martin shook his head. "No, if you read the books, this is more accurate to Frank Herbert's original vision. Besides, you wouldn't have gotten to wear that dress."

Gwen looked down at her gown. "Yeah, and I did have a lot of fun making it."

The music changed from the theme from Dune to an ominous-sounding orchestral sting. A panel on the wall at the back of the stage slid to the side, and what appeared to be a gigantic aquarium slid out into the room. Large clear panels of glass edged with ornately carved black edges revealed an interior filled with sickly looking yellow smoke. Deep inside the smoke, something seemed to stir. The vapors swirled and streamed past the glass, then parted as a giant fleshy mass revealed itself. Its bulbous, misshapen head held two tiny eyes on the sides of the cranium and a small, twisted mouth that spewed more of the foul-looking orange gas each time it opened.

Making a noise that wasn't so much a voice as an articulate rumble, the creature said, "People of Arrakis, members of the Padishah Emperor's royal court, honored Fremen warriors. We are gathered here together to join this man and this woman in matrimony. But first, a few words on the subject of love. True love. That blessed arrangement. That dream within—"

Gwen whispered, "Poor Phillip. He looks so sad."

Martin looked, and had to agree. Phillip stood in the traditional best man's position next to Martin, wearing a gray military uniform, oversized fake eyebrows, and a painted-on purple stain around his lips. He saw that Martin was looking at him and smiled gamely, but his heart wasn't in it.

"Yeah," Martin said. "He's still taking everything awfully hard. At least Brit's bad mood plays into her costume."

Brit the Younger stood by Gwen's side, wearing a robe that covered her completely from the flat-topped hat she wore on her head all the way to the floor, exposing only her face and the blue contact lenses in her eyes.

The fleshy blob in the tank continued, "Do you, Martin, heir of Duke Leto Atreides and leader of the Fremen, Kwisatz Haderach, take this woman to be your wife, for political purposes?"

Martin said, "I do."

"And do you, Gwen, daughter of the Padishah Emperor Shaddam the Fourth, take this man to be your husband, for political purposes?"

Gwen said, "I do."

Phillip stepped forward and opened a polished wooden box. Inside, on a velvet cushion, there were two simple wedding bands.

Phillip muttered, "I was surprised that they don't look like the Duke's signet ring."

Gwen said, "I told him if they did, I'd put them both on and punch him with them."

The blob in the smoke tank said, "By the power vested in me as a third-stage guild navigator, I now pronounce you husband and wife. This never happened. I was never here."

The tank receded into the wall, and the panel slid back into place. Martin kissed Gwen as the theme from *Dune* again blasted through the hall. All of the simulated Fremen warriors stood at attention and held their crysknives aloft in salute.

Martin turned to Gwen and whispered, "You've made me the happiest man in the world."

"By marrying you, or by marrying you like this?"

A single tear rolled down Martin's cheek. "Both."

Martin and Gwen's friends who weren't already on the stage ran up to congratulate the happy couple. Jeff, Roy, and Tyler wore identical stiff-necked, dark blue military uniforms. Roy had a fake scar on his cheek, while Jeff had a small diamond painted on his forehead. They vigorously shook Martin's hand, and just as vigorously hugged Gwen.

Phillip arched an oversized eyebrow at Gary, who kept his distance, standing alone at the corner of the stage. "Come on over, Gary. It's not like you to be shy."

Gary looked down at his flesh-toned muscle suit and blue Speedo adorned with art deco wings. "I don't know. This outfit, it's kinda making me want to not get too close to other people. It feels . . . rude somehow."

Phillip nodded. "I can understand that."

Gary laughed. "Oh well. It seemed like a good idea at the time."

"No," Phillip said. "Not really."

Brit the Younger hugged Gwen, completely enveloping her in fabric, and hitting her in the forehead with her big flat hat. She shook Martin's hand. "I can't wait to take off this ridiculous outfit. The blue contacts I kinda like, though."

Martin said, "They suit you."

Phillip said, "Yes. Very becoming."

Brit the Younger's smile curdled. She curtly congratulated Martin, then walked away.

Martin said. "It'll take time, Phillip."

Brit the Elder said, "Yes, it will."

Martin and Phillip both spun around to look behind them, where Brit the Elder stood in a black-and-gold dress, a bald cap, and a black headdress clamped to the sides and back of her head.

Brit the Elder said, "It will take quite a while, but in time Brit will forgive you, and even think of you as a friend."

Phillip said, "A friend."

"Yes." Brit the Elder put a hand on Phillip's shoulder. "I said she'd forgive, but she won't forget, and she'll never truly trust you again. And really, since you cheated, can you blame her?"

Phillip said, "But I never—"

Brit the Elder held up a hand and gave him a disappointed look. "Don't, Phillip. Just don't bother."

Phillip and Martin watched as she walked away, shaking her head.

Gary finally overcame his shyness and shook Gwen's hand. "Congratulations. I gotta say, I'm surprised you agreed to this."

Gwen said, "Yeah, well, we'd talked a little bit about getting married someday. Then the whole thing with the Brits and Phillip showed us that a lot can happen we don't expect, and that by putting off marriage, we were kind of giving fate more of an opportunity to screw it up for us."

Gary said, "Yeah, I see what you mean, but I wasn't talking about that. I always figured you two would get married. I'm surprised you agreed to the whole *Dune* thing. Most women seem to want a more traditional ceremony."

"Oh, we're going to have one of those, too. We're going to take a quick trip to Alaska and use Brit the Elder's trick to get Martin up to my time, lay some plausible groundwork for appearances' sake, then have a big wedding for our families."

"Oh." Gary said. "I can see that. And it makes sense why none of us are invited to that one."

Brit the Younger, Jeff, and Phillip looked at their shoes or the ceiling. Tyler said, "Yeah. None of us."

Gwen changed the subject. "So, I guess now it's time to go back to Martin's place for the reception!"

Martin said, "Not yet. There're a couple more things to do here before we go. I know entertainment and refreshments are usually done at the reception, but I know we're all going to change back into normal clothes, and I wanted to do this while we're in costume."

Martin opened the wooden box he kept his smartphone in and jabbed at the phone a few times. All of the fake Fremen disappeared.

Martin smiled. "Gwen, get ready to cut the cake."

A table appeared on the floor in front of the stage. On the table was a punchbowl full of clear fluid with a fake baby sandworm floating in it, and a large themed cake: a fondant and gum-paste sculpture of a sandworm cresting a sand dune, its three-flapped mouth open, displaying thousands of white-painted candy-corn teeth as it towered over tiny little modeling-chocolate men. Finally, floating in the air about ten feet above the floor, there appeared a piñata shaped like Baron Harkonnen.

In the upper gallery, Gilbert, Sid, and their two teenage assistants looked down as Gwen, blindfolded, swung Martin's staff at the Harkonnen piñata. She hit it on the leg, sending it spinning and showering candy over all their friends. A cheer went up from the group, and they all scurried to gather as much off the floor as they could.

The dark-haired girl said, "What a bunch of dorks."

Sid said, "Quite."

The boy said, "I don't know. They aren't hurting anyone, but it's all kind of self-indulgent, isn't it?"

The girl said, "It is their wedding day."

The boy said, "I understand that it's their wedding. I just didn't expect it to be a big, extravagant party like this that's just meant to impress their friends."

The girl laughed. "You didn't expect that? Are you sure you understand what a wedding is?"

The boy scowled. "I just didn't think they'd be so . . . I don't know, frivolous."

Gilbert patted the boy on the back. "Don't judge 'em too harshly. They were young."

The girl said, "I'm just surprised that they invited an enemy to their wedding."

"Just because they might be enemies now doesn't mean they always were, does it?" Sid said. "And anyway, we promised to show you how Martin and Gwen were when they were younger. We didn't promise that you'd like them, or that what you saw would make sense."

Gilbert nodded. "You need to have a real understanding of who your parents are if you're going to have a chance at saving them."

ALSO BY SCOTT MEYER

Basic Instructions Collections:
Help Is on the Way
Made with 90% Recycled Art
The Curse of the Masking Tape Mummy
Dignified Hedonism

Magic 2.0:
Off to Be the Wizard
Spell or High Water
An Unwelcome Quest
Fight and Flight

Master of Formalities

The Authorities

Run Program

ACKNOWLEDGEMENTS

And now, the part of the book where I express gratitude to various people. This time around I want to thank Eddie Schneider and Joshua Bilmes for being great agents and for helping me make this book better than it would have been without their input. And I'd like to thank Steve Feldberg for being a terrific and supportive editor, and for also helping me make this book better than it would have been without his input.

I'd like to thank Matt Sugarman, for helping me in ways that go beyond his professional responsibilities, and at times when he had little to gain beyond feeling good for assisting a clueless writer.

I'm also grateful to Luke Daniels, because he makes my books sound great; Eric Constantino, because he makes the covers look great; and Scott [last name redacted]. I redacted his last name because he copy-edited the book, and while he did a tremendous job, my kung fu is so strong that a few typos and errant commas almost certainly slipped past. I don't want him to take the blame for not catching a few of my far-too-numerous mistakes. He is only human, whereas I am an unstoppable typo machine.

I'd like to thank my two primary test readers: Rodney Sherwood, the world's most positive man; and Missy, my wife, who improves not just my work, but every other aspect of my life.

Finally, I'd like to thank the people who read my work. It's your attention and support that have made the continuation of this series possible. I hope you understand just how grateful I am.

Oh, and don't worry. Phillip will be fine.

ABOUT THE AUTHOR

After an unsuccessful career as a radio DJ, and a so-so career as a stand-up comic, Scott Meyer found himself middle-aged, working as a ride operator at Walt Disney World, and in his spare time producing the web comic *Basic Instructions*. He slowly built a following, which allowed him to self-publish his first novel, *Off to Be the Wizard*. The book's success brought him a publishing deal.

Scott lives in Arizona with his wife, their cats, and his most important possession: a functioning air conditioner.

Made in the USA
Columbia, SC
04 February 2024

31419265R00178